A DRAGON IN A PET SHOP . . .

"It's cute," said the woman. "For a lizard."

"Something really special. And no trouble at all to keep," said the pale-faced clerk.

"What is it? Some kind of iguana?"

The clerk peered myopically at the cage. "I have to be frank with you . . . I have no idea. . . ."

A KNIGHT APPEARS IN SPANISH HARLEM

The great white stallion snorted, its nostrils showing like two red crescents. A crowd had gathered. There was silence. Then a woman leaned one foot on an up-turned trash can and stared. "Shee-it," she remarked.

IN THE READING ROOM OF THE NEW YORK PUBLIC LIBRARY . . .

"So that's the dragon," whispered Sanchi. "Wow. Is that about how big they get? Or do they come bigger?"

Sandra shrugged. Where did it say she was majoring in dragons . . . ?

NEW YORK
BY KNIGHT

NEW YORK
BY KNIGHT

Esther Friesner

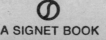

A SIGNET BOOK

NEW AMERICAN LIBRARY

NAL BOOKS ARE AVAILABLE AT QUANTITY DISCOUNTS WHEN
USED TO PROMOTE PRODUCTS OR SERVICES. FOR INFORMA-
TION PLEASE WRITE TO PREMIUM MARKETING DIVISION, NEW
AMERICAN LIBRARY, 1633 BROADWAY, NEW YORK, NEW YORK
10019.

SIGNET TRADEMARK REG. U.S. PAT. OFF. AND FOREIGN COUNTRIES
REGISTERED TRADEMARK—MARCA REGISTRADA
HECHO EN CHICAGO, U.S.A.

SIGNET, SIGNET CLASSIC, MENTOR, ONYX, PLUME, MERIDIAN
AND NAL BOOKS are published by New American Library,
1633 Broadway, New York, New York 10019

First Printing, September, 1986

1 2 3 4 5 6 7 8 9

PRINTED IN THE UNITED STATES OF AMERICA

For my daughter, Anne Elizabeth,
secure in the knowledge that she is more than
a match for any dragon around

Chapter I

THE KNIGHT

Even in the dark he could tell he had made a miscalculation. His steed whickered nervously, shying away from the litter of broken glass underfoot, tossing its snowy head at the harsh smells, going into a sideways gait whenever they passed an open tavern door and the sounds of strange language and stranger music spilled out into the night air. It was not like the white stallion to turn skittish over trifles. Together they had taken a road through desolation and dreams, and never once had the beast acted so afraid. He believed he could have ridden his mount to the gates of death. But his stallion knew death. Here was a world past knowing.

The knight shifted his grip on the battle lance and glanced from left to right through the slits in his visor. Runes in scarlet and blue and green hung suspended in the air to either side. Men sprawled in the gutters. Couples strolled arm in arm. Women in gaudy dresses and tight breeches ambled along, their hips rolling like ships on heavy seas. He recognized them for what they were and they did not alarm him. Later, when his search was ended, if he still lived, he would come back here and take one of them to forget. If he still lived.

The great white stallion snorted, its nostrils show-ing like two red crescents. The knight touched its side lightly with his gilded spurs, urging it into a trot, but the beast refused. It was getting hard to see in the dark, in spite of the blue-white light of the lanterns suspended high in the black arches of the sky. Strange things slipped past the knight and his horse, long and sleek and brightly colored, with twin lanterns that could have been eyes. The knight considered whether or not he should couch his lance and be on guard for battle, then thought better of it. They were starting to notice him, the people here. They were going to be afraid. If they had their first full sight of him as a warrior ready to attack, they would panic. He didn't need their fear. He needed information.

The horse reared and stamped its forefeet, com-ing to a dead halt. A battered container full of refuse blocked their path. Two bold rats with snap-ping eyes flashed their teeth scornfully at knight and steed, then went back to burrowing in the garbage. A tall, skinny man faced them across the barricade.

"Hey, man," he said. "What *is* this? Some kinda advertising stunt, man?"

The knight waited for the words to translate. He had come too far, across too many bridges, for the first awkward moments on this new battlefield to frighten him. The change came slowly, impercep-tibly, but certainly. Always there were these few initial moments of emptiness when he emerged fully into the new world and did not yet under-stand the language.

"Oh, wow, you getta loada this, baby? I mean, you see where this freaky dude, he comin' from?" asked one of the women. She had sauntered up to take her place beside the man, the pink satin of her dress reflecting in a rosy blur on the surface of the knight's shield. Three others who had been with her crept up slowly, timidly. When the horse reared again, they ran back to crouch against a storefront.

There were more people coming. The knight let them approach, holding his steed on a tight rein and murmuring words of calm encouragement under his breath. The horse seemed to understand. It took the beast somewhat longer than its master to realize who was friend and who was foe on a new battleground.

They gathered around in a ring, gaping. Small boys, no older than novice pages, clustered together and dared each other to run up and touch the horse. One of them took the dare, zipped up and slapped the great stallion on the left flank. The horse clattered backward, lifting ironshod hooves. The boy dashed to safety.

"You people," said the knight. It was awkward, but it was a free translation of the formal address that every knight must use when summoning the shire's aid in the pursuit of a quarry. He closed his eyes as he said it. It was foolish of him to cling to the old forms, but it was all he had left. Behind closed lids that blazed crimson, he saw them pass in phantom array as he had seen them do each time he gave the call. Time had not taken the pain from his memories of battlegrounds reached too late. Ruins were ruins, and the dullness of leaden skies would haunt him forever, but still he could not shake the ghosts that followed him each time he gave the cry for aid.

"You people," said the knight, fighting phantoms in his head, "aid me now. I call upon you as true-born citizens to aid me. I am on quest and seek a quarry. If you have hearts, aid me now. Tell me what you know."

He had given the call on many worlds. Once he had given it to a crowd of beings that had not yet discovered how to form words of their own, so he gave it in his own tongue while they moaned and grunted and prostrated themselves at his feet. Once he had given it to a race that dwelt in cities built on clouds, who snatched the call from his mind while he was still forming it on his lips. Once he had given it to a world of trees.

There was silence. Then the woman leaned one foot on the upturned trash can and stared. "Shee-it," she remarked.

"Say it, Mama," answered a fat man behind her. Beyond that, the knight got no reply.

Perhaps it was necessary for them to see his face, he thought. His lance was secure in its socket, his sword sheathed, his battle mace strapped tightly to his saddle, but with his helmet on he must still present a warlike appearance. He didn't want to scare them. He felt that they were afraid, in spite of the fact that they had come so close, gathering courage from numbers. He removed his helmet and gave the call again, for they must acknowledge his call before he could tell them the nature of his quest. That was the code.

It was ill-timed. The trail he had followed was true, his calculations off by only a small distance, the foe he sought was nearby, but the time he had chosen for taking off his helmet was the worst possible moment. It was exactly the time when the kid who had touched the stallion found a brick.

The knight did not look like them. The knight looked human, but he did not look like anything or anybody they had ever seen before. On the last world he had changed his features slightly, because it was the law of that land that warriors must make their faces into masks of terror before battle. The change back was not yet complete. If he had thought it over, if he hadn't been in such a hurry to find his foe, he might have remembered to wait until his face had gone back to what it normally was.

"A mistake, however small," said the dead wizard, "can be more deadly than a sword."

The woman screamed.

The boy threw the brick.

His friends found more bricks. The woman in pink satin grabbed an empty bottle from the trash. Someone got hold of a broken chunk of cement. They weren't afraid of him anymore. The first brick had drawn blood; he was vulnerable. The flung bottle scared his horse so that it bolted, taking him by surprise. He lost his saddle and tumbled down. They closed in slowly, still cautious even if no longer afraid. Blows fell with hollow sounds, denting his armor, but the brick had hit him in the head and stunned him. He wavered to his feet, too dazed to raise his mailed hands and shield his face, too bewildered to draw his sword.

"A dragon—" he gasped, and fell with a clash of steel on the shadowed pavement.

"Have mercy," breathed the woman. "He dead." She dropped the bottle. Smashing glass on the sidewalk scared the rats. From far away came the thin wailing of sirens. The woman sidled away into a darker street. The others took the hint.

"Honey," said a boy to his girl friend, "when the rats goes and the whores goes, we better."

"Say it, brother," remarked the fat man, waddling quickly around the corner. "Just say it."

Riley slouched down in the prowl car, hating what he saw. His partner was older, used to this neighborhood. It wasn't so bad, as he constantly reminded Riley. It wasn't even uptown enough to be called the real heart of Harlem. It was what they liked to call a marginal neighborhood.

Riley didn't see where they drew their imaginary margins. All he saw was heartbreaking poverty and burned-out lives. He saw kids playing at what they thought were grown-up games, ending their lives before they could get a good start at living. He saw grown-ups give up hope and sink down as far as they could go until the depths killed them. He saw babies born to girls who weren't old enough to know what they'd done to deserve it, and he saw the way those girls tried to get enough money to live on. Riley was sick of everything he saw, and sicker when he realized that no matter how much misery he witnessed it was hopeless. So he slumped down in his seat and tried not to see.

Suddenly Riley sat bolt upright and tipped his cap off the back of his head, staring. "Hey, Sam, I saw a horse," he said.

"Where, man, a butcher shop?" chuckled his partner.

"No, really, I tell you I saw me a horse. A big white horse with a fancy saddle on his back. He went down that street back there. When he took the corner, this big thing sticking up out of the saddle went flying off and rolled in the gutter. Turn around, Sam. We can go back and see what it is."

"No way," said Sam. "No way you're gonna get

me to stop this car to look for a—prob'ly stickball bat. Only time I stop us is on official business, and you know it."

"But I swear I saw—oh, my God!"

"What? What?" shouted Sam, making the prowl car do a skid to the curb.

"I saw a kid in armor!" yelled Riley, leaning out of the window and craning his neck. "Swear to God! It was way too big for the little bastard, but there he went, done up like something outa *Monty Python and the Holy Grail*."

Sam caught his breath and started the car again. "Never saw it. And neither did you. Look, I got nothing against cooping, but chase your dreams on your own time."

"I tell you, I *saw—*"

"Right," said Sam. "You saw." A week later Riley was transferred to the Fifth Avenue beat. He hadn't earned it. Most of the cops on Fifth Avenue sported enough distinguished-service ribbons to deck a parade float. Not Riley, and he knew it, but he also knew better than to question his good luck.

"Shoulda said I saw white horses in Harlem long ago," he muttered, slipping a sugar cube to one of the nags drawing hansom cabs in front of the Plaza Hotel. The horse glared at him and nipped his fingers. "Son of a—" Riley began, then studied the dingy horse carefully for a time before shaking his head. "Nah," said Riley. "No way. Musta been someone else."

He raised his hand to stroke the beast's muzzle, then thought better of it. He walked away with a carefree gait, whistling.

Chapter II

THE DRAGON

Necessity. He lived by necessity. Because of knowing what was practical, what was reasonable, what was to his best advantage, he had managed to survive from the gates of time past telling. And he would continue to survive, to live forever, because he always did what was sane, what was needful.

For the moment he was humiliated. Death had come too close to him on the last world. He had relaxed his guard for a moment, and when he turned around he found himself facing his enemy in open battle. He disliked open battle. Long ago he had lost count of the number of men he had slain, but only a fistful had died facing him. He was large, he was powerful, he was hideously wise, and yet he did not like to fight when he had no advantage beyond his size, strength, and cunning.

See where his carelessness had brought him! He wrinkled his scaly nostrils at the stench coming from the next cage. He was surrounded on four sides by cages, and in them there twisted and squirmed and tumbled a quartet of furry, yapping little abominations. He folded his earslits against the noise, dropped his cloudy eyelids to shut out the sight of them, and still the smell assaulted him.

He shuddered, raising the rainbow crest high above his armored back, flexing his talons. In his present size they were small and pearly ineffectual things, but soon . . . soon. . . .

How soon? Conditions were not right. He was strong, but the patterns that bound him were stronger. Older. He had lived so long because he had conformed to the patterns. It was the secret of his success. But now another eye had opened the midnight book and seen the ancient inscriptions and understood all that was written there. One whom he had trusted, in an earlier moment of carelessness. One who would try to kill him.

He dragged his silvery belly across the litter of gravel and shavings in the bottom of his prison. Water dripped from the cold metal spout of a bottle suspended upside down from the top of the cage. There was still a smell of furry things clinging to the mesh, strongest around a sagging wire wheel in one corner. He avoided it. It was intolerable. There was a dish of food beside the water bottle, filled with wilted greens and bits of ground meat. He tried to close his senses against the disgusting sight. He drew himself into himself and waited for a memory.

Gold. Dreams of gold.

Gold enveloped him. He was writhing in piles of gold. He cut fabulous capers on glittering mountains and rolled to the bottom of jeweled slopes. He burrowed deep into the heart of diamond hills, slipping kingly crowns onto the tips of his claws to admire the effect. He was very, very young.

They came with their swords and torches and took him. They wanted to kill him, but the wizard prevented it. Always he would remember that lined face, hard and seamy as a withered apple, and the long gray beard that flowed on forever, a beard that trailed away like the steam from his own nostrils.

The bearded one raised a black staff and spoke words of command. The others put down their swords and went away. He was left alone with the wizard.

He startled awake, shuddering with the indignity of rough hands lifting him out of his cage and slapping him down on a counter as if he were a slab of beef for the carving. Two people were in earnest conversation over his head. He shook himself fully conscious, poised for action, watching.

"It's cute," said the woman. "For a lizard."

"Something really special. Look at those colors! And no trouble at all to keep," said the pale-faced man who had hoisted him out of the shavings.

"What is it? Some kind of iguana?"

The man thought awhile, peering myopically at the cage. "I have to be frank with you, Miss Barnet. The label's come off the cage and I wasn't the buyer. It does look somewhat like an iguana, but smaller and more delicate."

"Oh, delicate? I don't know. I mean, I don't have time to have a pet that needs a lot of special care."

"Its *health* isn't delicate. I mean the way it's made. See these?" He grabbed the dragon's toes and spread them so that the pale-blue and sea-green webbing showed. The iridescent claws gleamed in the light.

The woman absently fluffed her long blond hair and looked thoughtful. "Well . . ."

"I tell you what," said the man hastily. "You came in here with a complaint, right? No luck with that gerbil. Now, I'm not saying we sold you a sick animal—"

"Oh, of course you're not," returned the woman sarcastically.

"But," the man went on, ignoring the gibe, "to make it up to you, I'm willing to take full responsibility for the health of this animal. The health and manageability. If you're not satisfied, I'll waive our ordinary no-returns policy and give you a full refund."

"And if he dies?"

"Bring him back here, dead or alive, and you'll get your money back."

"Um . . . I still don't know if I—"

He squirmed under the thin hand that held him on the counter and looked up at the woman. He found her eyes and waited. His own eyes shone, opaline, flickering with hidden promises. They beckoned. He drew her to him slowly, lovingly, subtle in his arts. The woman caught her breath.

The new cage smelled better, but it didn't matter. He would soon be free of it. He surveyed his new domain and was pleased. The walls of this room were hung with creamy silk the color of doves. From the next room he could hear her speaking to someone else. She was using the telephone. Yes, that was the word. He had seen instruments like it and instruments that were the germ of it, and instruments that were fantastic children of the humble plastic cradle she held in her hand.

He sighed and scratched the multicolored pebbles on the bottom of the cage until he had made a bald spot. Unthinkable to demean himself by sleeping on this rubble; he would rather sleep on the bare, cold steely floor. But it would change. Soon it would all change.

She was telling someone to come to a party. She'd been giving the same message to a lot of people ever since she'd brought him to this place in that soggy cardboard carrier. No doubt she wanted to show him off to her friends. So be it. He would give them a fine show, making her proud to own him. When they felt pride, they grew heedless. Heedlessness was one of the first things he needed.

Gritty light shone into the room through gauzy curtains, warming him. Since he could do no more than wait, sleep was allowed. He slept, seeking other times in dreams.

With his eyes closed he saw the book, the sweetest of all possible memories. He was very young and very stupid. The silver bridle that he wore galled him, and in trying to rub it off he had used the edge of the wizard's desk, much as a bear will use a fallen branch for a back-scratcher. He rubbed and rubbed, but silver forged in high enchantment is strong. He toppled the desk, and the book fell on his head.

It lay sprawled open, a drunken butterfly shape on the flagstone floor, and he stared at it, not yet realizing what he saw. The dragon chuckled at his own past ignorance and shifted onto his side, the better to enjoy the triumph of the dream.

But a hand reached out and seized the book. A boy who was almost a man snatched it away from him and read it, his eyes growing brighter with each page he turned, his breath growing shorter, as if possessed by love. He saw the stern face, the beautiful green eyes, the skin that had grown pale over the many years of service in the dragon's lair. The boy finished the book. He slammed the ponderous covers closed with a deadly ringing sound.

"You know!" gasped the dying wizard. "How—? I thought you were too ignorant to know what you read. By the gods, I've unleashed death on half a host of worlds by my stupidity. With my own consent I've made my death. But the day—" The dream became a wash of blood.

And now I have done the same, thought the dragon. Made my own death, perhaps. Only perhaps. For I had the strength to kill a wizard and the wisdom to live on as I have lived so long. But the one who comes after me has only got a sword.

I will run no more.

On this world I will stand.

I will fight.

I will kill him.

And when he is dead, I can live as I used to, without fear or foe. Gold for my bed again, fearful ones to serve me, and life to feed my life, power to feed my power. I will make a throne of this world. I feel it must be a rich world. Yes, I will have it all when he is dead, he and any who would dare to follow him.

"Diane! Where did you get such an *adorable* pet?"

"Oh, just at that pet shop near Bloomies. You know, the one on Lex."

"Adorable? Ugh! How can anyone call a slimy creature like that adorable—"

"It's not slimy, Jon. Lizards aren't—"

"It's still ugly."

"Oh, shut up and get me a drink, bitch."

"Well, excu-u-u-se *me!* Get your own drink, smartass. Or get the lizard to do it for you, if you're so hot for it."

"Can we take it out of the cage, Di?"

"Well—"

"Oh, come on. Look, it's letting me touch it. I think it wants out. Can we feed it?"

"Jesus, don't let Chris feed it. He'll slip the poor bastard some 'ludes."

"I never did!"

"The time you fed my tropical fish some flaked hash? Nearly drowned."

"He's cute, Diane. For a lizard."

"I think," said Diane, "he's an iguana."

"They eat iguanas in Mexico," said Richard, stroking the jeweled scales. The dragon raised its rainbow crest and permitted them to touch him however they wanted. He was testing them, reading their eyes. Eyes to eyes he entered them, feeling his way slowly into the webs that held them together until he could find the central cord and jerk it this way, that way, any way he chose.

They drank and ate and passed the dragon around the little circles of people. The dragon saw the things they drank and smoked and swallowed, calculating the weight of the gold ornaments they wore, judging the cost of their clothing. Their conversation was vacant and superficial, centering on what each of them had done, how important they thought themselves, and how very privileged and bored they all were.

Because of the shape of his mouth, what he wanted to do was impossible. But under the perpetual upward curve of his beaked snout, the dragon smiled.

Chapter III

JOSÉ MARÍA

"*Ya lo sabía. Ahora traes la basura de la calle en casa!*" Mamacita's voice was high, but not shrill. She eyed her first-born dubiously, trying for the thousandth time to comprehend the bizarre mental quirks that compelled him to bring every stray cat and mangy alley dog he could find into the house. She had grown used to dealing with the animals over the years. Now José María was thirty-five, a father in his own right, with a good wife, fine children, and still he brought in the strays. But this time he had gone too far.

"*Qué quieres*, Mamacita?" José María shrugged. "Did you want him to die in the gutter?"

Mamacita crossed herself and exclaimed, "*Ay! Qué cosa decir!* I only mean to ask you what you think your wife is going to say when she sees him. And, *por Dios*, where are you going to put him?"

José María exchanged a sheepish glance with his mother over the body of the knight and shrugged again. To shrug was in effect his philosophy of life. Either you had the answer to a problem or you didn't. If you did, *bueno*, you did. If you didn't, you shrugged and waited to see if someone would come up with the answer for you. It was all a matter of how long you had to wait and how many times you had to shrug before you found the person with the answer.

"Papá, papá, ya parió la gata negra!" little Elena shrieked, racing into the kitchen with the good news. She had watched the black cat carefully from the day her beloved Papá brought it home, half-starved and badly mauled by life in the streets. Now, grown sleek on scraps and attention, the animal had repaid José María's thoughtfulness by a gift of four kittens.

"Válgame la Virgen," sighed Mamacita. "Now she'll want milk." She left her son in the kitchen with Elena and the knight.

At six, Elena was all eyes for anything new or interesting. A piece of news that would make her a real someone at school was always good, and this looked like the perfect thing. Her Papá had brought home a drunk. How had he done it? Why? And a crazy drunk, too. He was wearing a dress and stockings, a real weirdo. Yes, that was just like Papá. He brought home what no one else would look at twice. The scrawny mud-colored dog he had rescued just two days ago came out from under the kitchen table and sniffed at the knight's feet, whining.

"Jesús, Papá, where did you find this one?"

"You, don't waste your breath asking silly questions, and go put clean sheets on Sanchi's bed," replied José María gruffly. Elena was delighted. That was her Papá, talking tough but letting her be part of this new adventure. Sanchi's bed? That made sense. Before Sanchi, it had been the nursing corner for all the homeless creatures that had the good luck to find Papá.

Together father and daughter stretched the knight out on the mattress and examined the alien clothing he wore. José María stood with arms folded across his chest, shaking his head and shrugging his shoulders helplessly. Elena was more practical. The man had managed to get that clothing on his body somehow, and what goes on comes off. Her nimble fingers found clasps, thongs, buttons, and fastenings for which she had no name. All of them came open. Her father had to stop her before she stripped the poor man naked. José María believed that even the mad have their own modesty.

Mamacita came back, raving about the perfection of the black cat's litter. There would be no trouble, she said, finding good homes for them. Bobby and Sanchi had already lined up a law student at Columbia to take the mother cat, and kittens were always easier to place.

"If it were only so easy," she added meaningly, "to find homes for people and dogs."

José María ordered Elena to bring a basin of warm water, a washcloth, towels, and first-aid supplies. In his house they might occasionally go short a light bulb or ask for a week's extra grace on the rent, but you never knew when one of God's poor creatures would show up with a cut or a bite or a wounded paw. Always they had enough bandages and salve. Always. It was a matter of honor with him.

"He was attacked in the street last night," said José María while he washed the knight's lacerated face and studied the cuts to see if a trip to the emergency room would be necessary. Thank God, the man had only shallow hurts and one big bump on the side of the head. He'd be all right, once he woke up.

"Who attacked him?" demanded Mamacita. "Did the police come?"

"I had no time to wait for the police. Three of those *mocosos* were stripping him naked in the street. I chased them halfway to Jersey, but they took a lot of stuff. God knows what. One of them could hardly run, so loaded down. And the way he lay there, he looked like just another drunk, sleeping it off in the gutter. So I brought him home. When he's better, he can go with Sanchi and me around the pawnshops and find his stuff. Shiny. I saw the streetlights on it. Maybe a horn. Maybe he's a musician. They stole his horn."

The knight groaned and opened his eyes.

"Look!" cried José María, triumphant. "How about that? Better already!"

"Now he'll have a hangover," opined Mamacita. Her son took offense.

"You still say he is drunk? *Por Dios!* Smell him! Do you tell me he smells from booze or what?"

Mamacita leaned so close her nose touched that of the knight, and sniffed. "Horse," she said. "He smells like a horse."

The knight shook his head to clear it, trying to sit up, but José María was a firm believer in keeping the patient still. Gently but surely he pushed the knight back down against the pillows. It was a mistake.

Mamacita screamed and Elena fled to fetch her brothers as the knight overturned José María and pinned him to the mattress, a short dagger in his hand. They had left him his undershift when they undressed him, and while there was a layer of clothing left, the knight would carry some small weapon hidden in its folds. Simple good sense and long experience prompted him. He was not dead until they took his last weapon from him.

Elena's brothers were big and streetwise and not pleased to see their father being manhandled by some derelict. The three of them noted the dagger, but they'd seen knives before, and they weren't afraid of dealing with one armed man when there were all three of them together. It became a kind of ballet. They circled the knight like wolves in the snow will cut off a stag from the herd and finish him.

The knight did not wait for the end to come. He read their purpose with the same glance that took in his surroundings. Willingly he offered them the dagger, his head low with shame. José María, stiffly indignant, shoved the knight off him and strode away to comfort Mamacita.

"I'm calling the cops," spat Manuel, grabbing the dagger. "You've done it this time, Papi. This one's Bellevue. You guys keep an eye on him until the man comes."

Elena peeped around the doorjamb as her brothers began the great debate. Manuel was firm about calling the law, but Mike and Roberto had other ideas. José María said nothing, still glaring at the discourteous guest.

"You call them, man, you get more trouble than help," said Roberto. "They gonna wanna know who this dude is, and then what are we gonna tell 'em? Just look at him, man. Got a face like—like—"

"Like one of those saints down at church," put in Mike. "Yeah, Berto's right. You know what the man'll ask. What's a *gentleman* like that doing in a dum—a place like this? I mean, you think they're going to feature that Papi brought him home to help him out? No way."

"Hey, you two, so what do you think the cops *will* think? That Papi mugged the man and brought the body home with him? The cops aren't that smart, but they're not so dumb either."

"They'll still wanna know what a man like that's doing here. We don't need trouble," declared Roberto. "Papi, let's give him his stuff and show him the way out, *de acuerdo?*"

For his answer, José María shook himself loose from Mamacita and stalked back to his three sons. With silent grandeur he demanded the dagger, which in turn he coldly presented to the knight. The knight looked up at him and slowly shook his head.

"Take it," ordered José María. "But don't try anything like what you did again. We want to help you."

"I know," replied the knight gently. "I am your debtor. And I am ashamed." The words lilted exotically on his tongue, as if he were trying hard to imitate José María's intonations. His hands lay folded in his lap.

José María sat next to him and patted him on the back. "I understand. You didn't know where you were. You were afraid. I know what it is to be frightened. But you're safe here. You rest, and in a while we'll go after the things they stole from you. It may take a little money, but don't worry. If you need a loan—" José María hesitated. It was one thing to comfort this man, another thing to blithely promise him money when there wasn't that much of it to go around under this roof. He felt the knight's eyes on him, took a deep breath, and gallantly said, *"Pues*, if you need a loan, we will find a way. Now say, are you hungry? Thirsty? You want to wash up or—whatever?" The knight shook his head no to each question. José María shrugged.

"Then you sleep," he said. "Things will look better after you rest. Sanchi can share with Roberto. Come, *m'hijitos*, give the man some privacy." He led the procession of his family out of the little room. Mamacita shut off the lights and closed the door.

The knight sighed and lay back on the mattress, feeling the fingers of a hundred aches probing his muscles. The room was no room, but a cross between a pantry and a walk-in closet. Light came from a crack under the door, air from a dusty vent in the wall, but it was the closest thing to a private room in the apartment. Everyone had agreed that when Sanchi first came he needed a place to be alone, but that was long ago. He was part of them now, and he could give up his place to the sick man for one night.

In the dusk around him, the knight listened for voices, and the sounds of the old apartment building filtered back to his ears. Water gurgled in the pipes. Hot air soughed in the vent system. People argued, laughed, spoke in whispers, spoke with hands and eyes and smiles, and all of it flowed in to him, washing over his mind, his feelings, his soul.

It is always like this at first, he told himself. This time of waiting. And it always aches so much! How many times have I done this? There have been times when he didn't give me the chance to do this. I made mistakes, but in the long run I think I should have been grateful to him for rushing me. It always hurts so much when I come to know them. Each time I think it hurts more.

The voices faded and he sent out questing thoughts to bring more voices in. Like the spokes of a spider web they shot out from his mind, searching other minds around him for clues, questions, dreams, taboos. It was important to take the time on each new world to do this. It was imperative to meld—in a few moments—with the ideas that had evolved in a world over centuries. Brick by brick he built his knowledge, and each brick was a mind.

"Hey, mister," a voice whispered. "Mister? You asleep?"

The knight turned onto his side, wincing with pain from a bruised rib. The door was open slightly. A small shadow stood waiting, a darker shape against a background of darkness.

"Mister?" it whispered urgently. Without waiting for a reply, it slipped inside and closed the door behind it. The knight was aware of rapid breathing.

"You are Sanchi," he said. "Come in. I'm awake."

"Hey! How do you know—? Oh. Papi musta told you, huh?" The little figure sidled nearer and sat on the edge of the bed. The knight waited patiently. "He tell you this was my room?" Sanchi asked at last.

"I think so," replied the knight. A longer silence.

"So, you feeling better?" asked Sanchi. The bed began to sway slightly as the boy swung his legs rhythmically back and forth on the edge.

"Yes. Thank you," added the knight, wondering when the inevitable question would come. He would be asked to leave. The boy was young, and the young seldom knew how much time they had ahead of them. He expected this Sanchi to tell him to clear out, and not too politely. To his surprise, the order didn't come.

"Well," said Sanchi after a long while. "Well, I guess I better get to bed, or Bobby gets all the covers. You want anything? An extra blanket? You know where the toilet is?"

"Thank you," said the knight again. The boy got off the bed and dragged his feet to the door. "Wait! Come back here. Please." Sanchi returned. "Is there nothing else you want to ask me?"

"Oh, I dunno," answered Sanchi. He started to shrug his shoulders but stopped himself. He didn't want to imitate José María. He felt that imitation was a kind of insult. If you weren't good enough at it, you became a walking caricature, and that was lack of respect to the one you admired.

"But this is your room," pressed the knight.

"Yeah. It's not much, is it?" said Sanchi, flashing a nervous smile. What was it with this guy Papi picked up? It was like he was trying to get Sanchi to say what he was thinking. Hey, it was worse. It was like he knew what Sanchi was thinking without Sanchi telling him, and Sanchi wasn't thinking anything too nice right now.

"Sanchi, I won't be here long," said the knight. "I'll give you your room back tomorrow. I know it's important to you, a room of your own, and I understand why you need—"

"What do you mean, man?" Sanchi yelled, springing up from the bed and flicking the light on. "Who told you anything about me? And don't you say that Papi told you, 'cause Papi wouldn't do something like that to me!" The knight tried to answer, but Sanchi shouted him down. "You don't understand nothing, man! Nothing! I don't know you, and you say you know me? Well, you lie. Who are you anyway? How do you—"

José María, rumpled and grumpy from interrupted sleep, confronted them. "Why are you out of bed, Sanchi?" he inquired, his voice dangerously quiet.

"Papi, this man he's some kind of freak," wailed Sanchi.

"Has he done something to you?" demanded José María, his large hands clenching fiercely. Not for the first time that night he found himself re-

gretting his good deed. If this strange one was up
to no good with his Sanchi, he'd fix him for it.

"He doesn't do anything to me, Papi," said Sanchi
quickly, reading José María's thoughts. "But he
talks funny. He talks like he knows me. He maybe
knows all about me, Papi. You didn't tell him
anything, did you? You wouldn't—"

"Go to bed," said José María evenly, and when
Sanchi made no move to obey, he thundered, "To
bed! Now!" Sanchi scampered away. "Forgive him,"
José María addressed the knight. "It's his age. When
they get to that age, they like what's theirs to stay
theirs. Stubborn."

"But this is his room."

"He must learn to be accommodating to guests,"
said José María. "I apologize for him." Before the
knight could speak, his host was gone.

In the morning the family gathered at the breakfast table, where the knight joined them. Sanchi
glared at him, then spent the rest of the meal
looking at his bowl of cereal. José María's wife
was in a corner, trying to coax Elena away from
the new kittens for a bit of breakfast before school.
Roberto, Mike, and Manuel exchanged furtive
glances as they whispered about the bizarre way
their unexpected guest acted at the table. His food
grew cold, lying untouched until the women were
seated.

The household dispersed after breakfast. There
was a great scraping of chair legs and the kitchen
emptied out, leaving only Mamacita at the sink
and the knight seated at the table. He watched her
sloshing the suds over the dishes, then got up and
tried to help. His linen undershift looked like a
soiled white housedress, and the sight of him dab-
bling in the sink made Mamacita laugh before she
rounded on him and launched a tirade in Spanish.

"I beg your pardon?" asked the knight, not troubling to hide a touch of exasperation. He had spent most of the night in learning this world, and while he knew that there was more than one language spoken here, he concentrated his efforts on learning the tongue most common to the immediate area.

"She says it's her kitchen and you get out," a sullen Sanchi said from the doorway. "Leave her alone. You don't impress anyone but Papi with your fancy manners. Papi wants you to do something else, anyway, and I have to help you. When you're dressed, we'll get started."

The knight wiped his dripping hands on the dish towel Mamacita offered him. "You want your clothes?" she asked. "I put them on the bed, the big one."

"She means Papi's bed. I'll take you," said Sanchi dully. The knight followed him to the master bedroom where he found a neatly folded pile of bright-colored garments. To Sanchi's eyes they were no more than a stack of bedsheets. This guy was weird. He watched the knight slip on the tunic and tabard, then the close-fitting hose and thin leather shoes.

"*That's* what you had on?" demanded Sanchi, momentarily forgetting to hate the odd visitor.

"Almost all."

"What were you, playing at a masquerade party? Ah, never mind. Say when you're ready and we'll check out the pawnshops. What did you have, a trumpet? Sax? Trombone, man?"

"Where is it?" murmured the knight, paying no mind to Sanchi's questioning. He darted his eyes around the master bedroom, then fell to his knees and peered under the bed. "Where is it?" he repeated, a bit louder. He opened the closet and rooted through the shirts and dresses hanging there. "Where is it?" he shouted.

"Where's *what?*" Sanchi matched shout for shout. "Hey! You come outa that closet! You're messing it up. What you looking for? Hey, I said stop!"

"Where is it?" roared the knight, tearing the covers off the bed, toppling the mattress from the springs. *"Where is it?"* His face was red with rage.

Sanchi went chalk-white with indignation and threw himself at the knight, pummeling him with his small fists. "I-said-you-*stop*-messing-Papi's-things!" he panted. "You-*stop*-that-God-damn-it!" The knight seized Sanchi's wrists and the boy kicked viciously at his legs. He dangled Sanchi an inch off the ground until they both were calmer.

"My sword," said the knight. "Where is my sword?"

"Say what?" said Sanchi.

"My sword, please," repeated the knight. "I need it. My magic is strong, but not quite strong enough to battle him with only sorcery. I need my sword, and it is only fitting that I use it. They called it Belgor. Dragonbane. I need a sword to slay a dragon."

Sanchi stared. Then he began to titter. He laughed and laughed until he thought the world itself had turned to laughter. And through his laughter he could still hear the madman pleading on and on for his sword, his magic sword, a magic sword to slay a dragon.

Chapter IV

DIANE

The day came, or rather the evening, when they all admitted that they had run out of things to do. They had discussed the New York political situation, with the smart young lawyers dominating the conversation. They had made a serious analysis of the coming fashion trends, Lysa wading into the middle of the row to tout her own line of signature belts, which were not doing well commercially because the public had no taste. They had talked about the arts, the advisability of joint custody, the rights of the poor, and the merits of French over Northern Italian cuisine. They drank neat liquor before dinner, wine with dinner, brandy afterward, and those who felt like it got into a corner to smoke a little grass and maybe try something a little stronger. Diane was cool about it.

"If you're going to do that," she told Richard, pointing to the traditional rolled-up twenty-dollar bill in his hand, "I don't want to know about it."

"Afraid we're going to be raided?" he teased.

"Don't be ridiculous. But I don't like it."

"Killjoy."

"Look, I didn't say you couldn't do it, did I? Do what you want. We're all adults. But don't feel

33

obligated to tell me what you're doing, because I couldn't care less."

"Except it frightens you," said Richard. "Grass is fine, it's hardly even illegal anymore. All the best people say so, right? But nothing stronger for our dear Diane. It makes her nervous."

"You sound like you're trying to dare me," Diane told him. "I don't take dares."

"Who's daring you? I'm just telling you what you are," rejoined Richard, looking smug. "Self-knowledge is a wonderful thing. Now if you'll excuse me—" He joined the group in the corner, hunched like cavemen around a fire.

Diane let him go, but she felt a poignant touch of regret to see how easily he gave up her company for his other friends. The scratch-and-sniff crowd, she liked to call them. He was so handsome, so perfect for her, and he could simply walk away like that because—because—

Because she bored him. Diane got herself another drink and took a slab of smoked salmon to her pet lizard, who paced his cage irritably. The creature snapped the pink tidbit to shreds with his horny jaws, then cocked one golden eye at her.

"Are you bored with me?" she asked him. "Not while I feed you. God, I don't blame Richard. I feel like a clone of every damn woman here, and this party—it's like I give the same stupid party over and over again, and before that I was invited to parties that were this party all over. The only things that change are the weather and the menu. Want some more salmon?"

The dragon opened his mouth and roared. It sounded like the creaking of a rusty swing. "Greedy bastard," said Diane. "Come with me." She hoisted him out of the cage. "I'm sick of being your slave, monster. I'll put you down on the buffet table and you can help yourself. That'll teach them. Serve them all right if you step in the quiche." She plunked the dragon down on the Hepplewhite sideboard among the bowls of dip and trays of raw vegetables.

"You daft woman, what are you doing?" piped Lysa. "Get that abomination away from my food this minute."

"Until you eat it, it's my food. I'll do what I like with my food and my monster. You liked the poor beast well enough the last time you were here."

"I was pissing drunk the last time. No sober person should be forced to look at something that ugly."

"Ssh! He'll hear you," Diane said in a burlesque stage whisper.

"Goody. What will he do to me? One false move, and I'll make the little beggar into a belt. Maybe that would sell; genuine monster-skin. He *is* a monster."

Diane gathered the dragon to her in an exaggeratedly tender embrace. "Insult my monster to my face, will you? Then the curse of the Loch Ness monster will strike you down."

"That thing is hardly Nessie."

"A cousin," returned Diane. "A cousin once removed."

"What are you two scrapping about now?" demanded Richard. Privately Diane smiled. There was nothing to lure Richard like a good, loud argument. Whether it concerned him or not, he was always ready to join in.

"I insulted her monster," said Lysa, "to its repulsive face. I'm doomed."

"She wanted to make him into a belt," protested Diane, appealing to Richard. She knew that this was a situation he adored. He was just an associate with a well-established old New York law firm, but he looked forward to the day when he would be a judge. The law was the means to the end, and the end was Richard Walters, resplendent in black robes, giving judgments worthy of Solomon.

"Ladies," said Richard, ponderously stoned, "I have the one peaceful solution to your ills. Remove the cause of conflict and you remove the conflict itself. Hence, in the name of the court, I impound Exhibit A, not to be returned to you until the space of forty-eight hours has elapsed." Neatly he plucked the dragon from Diane's arms and settled it to ride precariously on his shoulder. Diane's objections were summarily overruled.

"One more outburst and I'll clear the court," he said. "The monster in question stays with me. Besides, I want to take him home to show my sister."

"Scare her with, you mean," mumbled Lysa.

"You take good care of him!" cautioned Diane.

"The best," replied Richard.

He called her the next night and asked if he could see her. She felt misgivings, fearing that something had happened to her new pet.

"Did you lose him?" she asked.

"A vote of confidence," said Richard dryly. "Thanks, I needed that. No, your precious beastie's fine. I want to give him back to you." She could almost see the frown creasing his handsome face. Vaguely she wondered whether he would ever think of her as more than just another member of their cozy social set.

"Before the sentence is up, Your Honor?" she simpered. She hated herself for it the second after those miserably kittenish words left her mouth. Why did she always make a fool of herself when dealing with a man she wanted? And it never worked. They always ran, and she was left knowing she'd made them run.

"He got time off for good behavior. Can I come?"

She made a swift change of clothes, selecting a chic at-home robe whose silky material clung smoothly around her, setting off her fair hair and brilliant eyes. When Richard arrived, the dragon riding his shoulder, she had a bottle of white wine and two glasses waiting. She might have saved herself the trouble. Richard refused to drink or even to sit down.

"Diane, listen," he said, his voice hard. "This is important. I'm at a loss for how to say this well, so I'll just try to get it out and what happens, happens. Diane—Diane, you know that I know how much money you've got."

Her eyes narrowed. "I didn't know you were so up on my finances," she said.

"Oh, for God's sake, if you're going to be like this—!" Richard turned as if to leave. Twined around his neck, the dragon tightened its pearly claws once. Richard stopped and looked at Diane again.

"I'm sorry," Richard mumbled. "This is hard for me. I'm observant. I can see the way you live, Diane, and I've got a good idea of what a lifestyle like this can cost. Satisfactory answer? Well, I'm not hurting for money either, so it's not a question of money. I want to marry you."

Diane's expression remained unchanged. She was waiting for him to go on, to say, "April Fool," to talk about something else so she'd know she had only imagined his proposal. Richard leaned toward her, waiting. The dragon's breath rasped in his ear.

"Well?"

"Well, I—I'm speechless," she managed to say.

"Isn't it a cliché for me to say that this is so sudden?"

"Look, either you're ready for an adult commitment or you're not. I know how I feel about you. I'm ready. You've got a pretty basic decision to make. Yes or no?" He moved closer and kissed her in the way she had always dreamed he would kiss her. "Yes or no?" he asked.

"Yes," she said, still dreaming. She felt his arms drop away from her limply. He was taking the monster off his shoulder, handing it to her, heading for the door once more.

"Where are you going?" she cried.

"Sorry, but I've got an important appointment. I should have been there fifteen minutes ago. I'll come back tomorrow evening and we'll go someplace for dinner." He blew her a kiss from the door.

"Just like that," said Diane to herself. "What got into him? Probably nuts. Too much time with the law books cracks a man's mind. Oh, but I hope he stays insane!" She threw back her head and exulted, calling up every detail she could remember of that mysteriously sudden proposal. "Love at first sight," she rationalized, addressing the dragon. It blinked. "Love at first sight always lasts the longest."

Love. He knew about love. It was important, to a greater or a lesser degree, on all the worlds he had visited, but never important to him. Well, perhaps indirectly so, for he had learned early to turn everything he encountered into a tool for his own purposes, and love made a very handy tool indeed.

The dragon closed his eyes and dreamed, feeling the borders of his flesh grow larger. It was a distant, tingling feeling, barely noticeable, that heralded each new world. How reassuring it was, he mused. It meant he had already established the foothold of his power, for there could be no strength for the transformation without power.

Diane put the dragon back in its cage, then looked at it and took it out. "That's funny," she said. "Well, I guess the food around here's good for iguanas. You're getting cramped in there. Now where the hell can I put you?"

The dragon's sides swelled and collapsed with each breath, flecks of gold glinting on each scale. So soon, he thought. So soon she notices the change. This is a fruitful world, then. I was wise to make my first move quickly.

Diane searched the apartment for a likely new home for her pet. Finding none, she dropped the dragon on the coffee table and manned the telephone. The dragon pressed his belly against the wood, learning the touch of polished mahogany, reading the history of the tree from which the wood had come. There would be no time for dreaming. Soon, he thought, soon I will regain all the power that deserts me in each passage between the worlds. And once I am myself again, I'll take this world—this lovely, life-filled world—for my own.

Against his shuttered eyes he saw orchards hung with the ripe fruits of harvest. Grainfields stretched away to meet the hills. Cattle and stupid sheep lowed and bleated, rumbling through the passages of the slaughterhouse. People milled through narrow streets, jostling, sweating, swearing, teeming across his vision.

The dragon's claws appeared to melt into the table as he probed deeper into the speaking grain of the wood. He saw the jungles of another land, and through transparent layers saw a vanished time. Shapes of dead men made the night shine with the fiery spit of rifles, the yellow-throated roar of cannon, the fields in flames. The dragon smiled, feeling for the heart of the world with his claws, and dreaming of the richness, the feasting, the amusement he would derive from these creatures. For they could be very amusing. Once he had been driven to a world where there were only trees, rooted in their thoughts, spanning a galaxy of peaceful stars. He had fled that world of his own free will. His enemy had not even found his trail before he was gone.

But these beings will be different, thought the dragon. Quite different. He twitched his tail, impatient to cast off the fetters of his small size. A necessary disguise, but constricting. He must be free. He hungered for this world. And he hungered for more.

Lysa did her best to help Diane, but all she had come up with was an empty liquor box, begged from the wineshop on the corner. She followed Diane into the living room, where the dragon kept his private vigil on the coffee table.

"Jesus, he did get bigger," said Lysa. "Uglier too. Do you think he'll fit in here?"

"We can try," said Diane. "I'll shred some newspapers."

"You'll need the whole damn Sunday *Times* for this crawler."

Diane giggled. "Maybe I should just give him the run of the house. He doesn't look like he'd do anything bad, like claw the furniture."

"Swell. How do you housebreak a lizard?" asked Lysa.

"You're right. I'll go get some old papers. You mind him. Don't let him mess up the coffee table."

"What do you want me to do about it? Diaper

the goddamn thing?" shouted Lysa, but Diane was out of earshot.

The dragon opened his eyes and looked at Lysa steadily, relishing the little start she gave when she knew he was staring at her. Delightful, thought the dragon. I need amusement, just a little amusement before I must apply myself wholeheartedly to the coming task. This one will entertain me very nicely, and without too much trouble. She is as shallow as a leaf holding rainwater.

Lysa looked at the dragon, and when she tried to look away she found that she could not. Slowly the thought came like a bubble gracefully rising to the surface of a pond that she did not want to look away from those slitted golden eyes. It was peaceful to be free of Diane's unbearable chatter, and even to let her mind drift along aimlessly, thinking of nothing at all.

She felt a great sense of freedom as she abandoned all effort to think, because it was nicer to forget that terrible news she'd had last week about how poorly her designs were selling. It was sweet to think of nothing, sweeter than seeing the face her mother would make when Lysa told her about her latest failure at making a name for herself. And Mother would shake her head and explain for the thousandth time that it wasn't the money. God knew the family had enough to see Lysa through a dozen more harebrained schemes. It was only that Lysa should realize by now that she was not talented, that she lacked the creative gift, that she was wasting her life trying to make a name for herself against people who did have the ability, that she should admit defeat at last and get married before all the suitable men were gone.

Lysa floated in the dragon's eye, and now the currents took her along, faster, faster still. Her mother's face loomed up out of the golden shadows, mouth prim, telling Lysa that her problem was she thought herself better than she was. You're a fool, and you'd realize it yourself if you weren't so busy giving yourself airs. And for what? For your friends? Do you say you don't need a husband because you have friends? Well, my girl, those friends of yours are laughing themselves sick at you behind your back. They buy your belts to give you false encouragement. They praise you for that stupidly affected device of thinking you could change your life by turning blond hair red, switching Lisa to Lysa, flitting from poetry to pottery. I want to laugh at you myself, but I find you pitiable.

Thoughts spun of sunlight reflected in golden eyes that were older than the mountains. They swirled through her head like sparrows, and each with a woman's face. Each twittering with the cold, cold sarcasm that Lysa's mother had mastered long ago. Their wings joined in flight, and hard words came from the golden eyes.

You are nothing. Listen to me well when I say that you are less than nothing. In a matter of years you will be dead, and no one will know that you ever lived. You have no name that will survive, and even if you marry and have children, your memory will die when they die.

You wanted to walk with the titans of Earth, didn't you? You wanted the sanctity of seeing your name printed where others could read it and envy it. But you've only come as far as you have riding the back of money that another person earned for you. Parasite. Leech. All you are good for is spending what others, better than yourself, have earned.

Give up. Why bother searching for the one thing you can do well? We both know what that is.

Spend what you have on making the short, dismal days more pleasant. Make the world seem beautiful. Only seem. There are ways to purchase illusion, and you have the means. Go.

Lysa felt a hollow, sick sensation in the pit of her stomach, as if every daydream and aspiration she had ever had were melting into derisive laughter. Give up, said the eyes. Your mother was right. You have nothing to hope for. Live for yourself and for the day. It's the one thing you do best. Give in. Don't struggle with the world anymore. Rest.

Diane was shaking her shoulder, but she was unable to respond. It took every bit of her drained will to drag herself away from the spell of the golden eyes. Diane was asking her if anything was wrong.

"Wrong?" she echoed. "No. Nothing's wrong." Her voice was dead. The dragon lolled his tongue in a soundless laugh. Really, this had been too easy.

A stray thought leaped from his unguarded mind into hers as the two pulled painfully apart. Lysa shook her head violently, fighting for light, and latched onto that sliver of alien thought.

"Diane!" She gripped her friend's arms tightly, eyes wide and wandering. "Diane, get rid of him! He's a monster, a real monster. He wants you, your money, the power of it. He knows about these things, and he needs it for—"

The dragon stamped his paw. Lysa released Diane and sat back, slumping like an old woman. "Oh, what's the use?" she muttered. "In the end, we die the same." She left without a word of farewell.

Diane was still puzzling over Lysa's extraordinary outburst later that day when she had an

unexpected and unwelcome caller. She was antici-
pating seeing Richard, but when she opened the
door, there stood Lysa's mother.

"I thought you should know, dear," the thin
woman said with a sardonic smile. "You were
always *such* a good friend to my daughter. *So*
generous to buy those pitiful scrapwork belts she
wasted her time with. So *kind* in the way you told
her all that delightfully liberated rigmarole. So
utterly charming all the time you gave that perfectly modern line about women not needing to have
a man to be worth something. Only I hear that you
preach a better line than you practice. She said
you're engaged. Such a primitive, sexist custom,
isn't it? Wasn't it *good* of you to spare Lysa the
humiliation of marriage!"

"Mrs. Grant," Diane took a deep breath, "I'm
expecting guests and I wish you'd get to the point.
If you want me to convince Lysa to get married, I
think you're mistaken. Lysa's a grown woman and
she'll do whatever she wants. I never told her not
to get married, you know. She has a mind of her
own, if you'd only take the time to realize it."

Lysa's mother laughed with the mechanical sound
of iron gears clashing. "Oh, I do realize how inde-
pendent Lysa could be! To the last. I'm only her
mother, after all, and a mother's good advice counts
for nothing with you people. But I don't mind. I'm
just there to pick up the pieces that you and her
other *friends* never have to deal with. Here." She
thrust a piece of paper into Diane's hand.

"Wh—what's this?"

Mrs. Grant hugged her purse and said, "Conso-
lation, I suppose. Her last thoughts were with you
and your happy, happy marriage-to-be. Lysa's
dead."

The words hung frosty in the air long after she

was gone. In a trance Diane closed the door and sat down, the note crumpled in her hand. Absently she stuffed it into the pocket of her lounging robe.

The dragon climbed the side of the liquor box and crept across the rug to wind himself around her ankle. When she looked down he was there, golden eyes unblinking.

Chapter V

SANCHI

"**I**'m telling you, man, Papi should call the men with the nets for this one, but you can't talk to him about it," said Roberto, tossing a baseball from hand to hand as he and his brothers leaned against a big green Cadillac at the curb.

"*Qué va*, you know Papi," said Mike, snatching the ball and passing it to Manuel. "You tell him to do one thing, he does another, just to show you who's boss. You gotta go slow and easy with him, Berto. You gotta bring him around."

"Listen to the expert," sneered Manuel. "Talks like he can make Papi jump through hoops."

"This time, I wish he could." Roberto was serious. "Man, someone's got to get that *loco* out of the house before he does something bad. You know how tough it is to keep an eye on him? Making sure he don't get a chance to be alone with Mama or Mamacita or Elena? I don't trust him."

"How many lunatics do you trust?" Manuel grinned. "Maybe we can look them up and get them to talk ours out of the house. *Aquí se habla loco.*"

"You want him out?" asked Mike. "Easy. Just give him his magic *sword!*" The brothers broke up into hysterical laughter.

"Psst. *Ojo! Aquí viene Sanchi*," hissed Roberto, elbowing Mike in the ribs.

"So what? Who made him God? You hit me like that again, man, and I'll—"

"I'm sorry, I'm sorry, OK? But cool it with talking about the *loco*. It gets Sanchi mad."

"Yeah, Sanchi's a real fan of his, I forgot," Manuel snickered. "We should tell him we saw the sword for sale in Alexander's toy department, mixed up with the *Star Wars* light sabers. That'd get the *loco* out of the house. And maybe Sanchi too."

Roberto's punch came too suddenly for Manuel to duck. Sanchi came along just in time to see the two brothers pummeling each other while Mike tried to separate them. Manuel's nose was bleeding and Bobby had a purple bruise under one eye when they were finally pulled apart.

"Man, I am fed up to here with you defending every goddamn stray that Papi brings in the house!" shouted Manuel, wiping at his nose. "You're such a champion for them, *you* go get yourself a job after school to help feed that pair of parasites!"

"You call them that again," returned Roberto, "and I'm gonna mess up your face so good that Mama won't know you. *Vete al diablo!*"

Manuel made a well-known gesture at Berto and fled. Berto dusted himself off and smiled at Sanchi. "He's sore because he can't play rooftop Romeo when he's got the job at the *bodega*. Don't mind him, Sanchi."

Sanchi didn't meet Roberto's eyes. "He's right, Bobby. He wasn't just talking about the *loco*. He meant me too. No wonder I dig him, huh? Pair of parasites. Hell, I never knew Manuel ever learned a word that big. Saved it for a special occasion." Sanchi's voice blurred with suppressed tears. "A real special occasion. Like me finally packing up and leaving!'' He lurched away from Roberto's outstretched hands and ran as fast as he could, putting three blocks between him and the brothers before he let the tears flow.

There wasn't much time for crying. He got it out of his system in a few short, fierce bouts of sobbing. Wiping his face on the sleeve of his jacket, he swaggered homeward, trying to look cool in case he ran into Bobby and Mike.

The green machine in front of the apartment was deserted. Good. Sanchi had been thinking as he walked, and a definite plan was fixed in his head. It was Saturday. Papi and Mama would be taking Mamacita to visit her husband's grave. It was a fine day, sunny and cold. The three brothers wouldn't come back to the apartment at gunpoint on such a day. That left Elena and the *loco*, and Manuel had insisted that Elena spend the day with Aunt Rosa. Never take chances with the *loco* alone in the house. Perfect.

No one home. No one to stop Sanchi from packing his things, taking his bread, and getting away. It was something he should have done long ago. No wonder Manuel resented him, called him a parasite like the *loco*. The *loco* had an excuse for hanging around. He had no money, no place to go, and anyone could see he was still a very sick man. But Sanchi had no more excuses. It was time to get the hell out.

He kept the money *she* had left him in a special place, a jar lined wth red beans. He'd made it himself, so proud of it. The beans were glued to the bottom and sides of the jar, the money slipped inside, the lid screwed down. It was plenty safe on the pantry shelf. The brothers wouldn't be caught dead touching food before it was cooked, and if Mama or Mamacita came across the cash, he knew they'd leave it where it was. Elena was too small to reach that shelf yet. Safer than in the bank.

He snagged the money first, then tiptoed into his room to pack. The house was quiet. Dust motes hung motionless in a sunbeam on the kitchen floor. Every step he took echoed. It was strange. Not even the sound of breathing.

Sanchi felt suddenly cold as he crouched over the cheap overnight bag that was his suitcase. Holy Jesus, what was the matter? he asked himself. I feel like a goddamn burglar or something. I got a right to take what's mine, don't I? What's giving me the creeps like this?

Then he realized what was chilling him. There was too much quiet. It had a voice of its own, that unnatural silence, and it gave him an awful message. There should have been some noise. At least the sound of a floorboard creaking. At least the sound of breath. At least the solid feeling that there was one other person in the apartment with him. The *loco*. But there was nothing. It was like living in the house of the dead.

Sanchi knew that feeling. It wasn't one he was likely to forget. Old times came back to his mind. He was little again, living with *her* and the big guy, his uncle Carlitos. There was this ridiculous yellow-flowered wallpaper in the room, and a thin green carpet on the floor. *She* was out somewhere. *She* was always out somewhere. The kid was old enough to take care of himself, he imagined her saying. You worry about him too much, Carlitos.

But Carlitos continued to worry, and he picked up the habit of coming home unexpectedly during the day. One day Sanchi heard someone in the kitchen, someone fooling with the lock that led to the back-hall stairs. He was little, but he was no dope. If it was *her* or Carlitos, they'd come in the front. Anyone else, they didn't want to be disturbed with whatever they were doing. Sanchi was smart enough to hide, smart enough to realize that whoever was there would eventually finish what he was doing and go away.

He hid under the bed and heard the intruder get the kitchen door open. Then there came the indistinct sounds of whatever unknown errand had brought someone to break into Sanchi's house. There were whispers, too. Two of them. Giggles. Scrabbling.

Then Uncle Carlitos turned his key in the front door and burst through the apartment, surprised them in the kitchen, shouted something, the gun— Footsteps running away, and then total silence. Sanchi trembled under the bed until he couldn't bear it anymore. He crawled out and crept into the kitchen. Uncle Carlitos was dead.

Maybe someone had come into José María's house and surprised the *loco*. Maybe the *loco* was dead too, like Uncle Carlitos. If he was, he'd have to lie there until the others came back. Sanchi wasn't going to look for him. Not this time.

"You won't find it."

He was there the way a tree is there, always there but unnoticed until something makes you recognize its presence. But a man is harder to overlook than a tree, especially when he seems to spring up out of the floor. Sanchi jumped.

"Did I frighten you? I apologize," he said. "You are going away. Why?"

"Hey, man, who made it your business?" muttered Sanchi, hunching his shoulders and going back to his packing. No wonder he'd had the creeps. This guy was bottom-out weird. The sooner he got away from this madhouse, the better.

"Where will we go?" asked the knight. He was

calm. He was so matter-of-fact that the words glided over Sanchi's head. The boy didn't grasp what the knight had said until he thought it over.

"Are you out of your *mind?*" he yelled.

"You think I am," replied the knight. "And since I seem to be in your power on this world, I suppose we shall have to accept your opinion. I hear what you call me. You think I am insane. Well, I must accept that. In fact, I confess I feel as if I'd taken leave of my senses when your father so kindly insisted that I wear this costume instead of my proper clothes." The knight made a comic gesture to sum up the brown polyester slacks and striped tan shirt he wore. "I look like a clown."

Sanchi sat down on his traveling bag and took a good look at the knight, all gotten up in Papi's finery. The slacks were way too short, clearing the ankles. Black sneakers, borrowed from Mrs. Santí's kid, were too big.

"You shoulda gone back to wearing your old stuff," said Sanchi.

"I intend to," said the knight. "I've wasted too much time as it stands. You understand, I'd hoped to make your father realize that my mission is serious; deadly serious. But he refuses to believe me. I had better luck talking to the trees."

This dude *is* nuts, thought Sanchi. I should dump him in Central Park and let him talk to all the trees he wants.

"Gratitude," the knight went on, "is important. I am more than grateful to your father, but he is a simple man. The higher knowledge will always be beyond him. I don't condemn him for his ignorance. He was born to it, the way a dog is born to learn only so much and no more. The kindness of his heart makes up for the lack of his mind. If he would only—"

Sanchi lashed out with his foot and found himself seized by the ankle and flipped backward onto the floor. The knight gave him a withering glance. "Poorly planned, poorly executed," he stated. "You would not have lasted a week among the other pages. You haven't the spark."

Stunned, Sanchi listened as the knight coldly evaluated him. Too hotheaded. Too quick. Too— what was he saying, that crazy man? Too stupid?

"Hey, you call me stupid, man, you got a nerve. Call Papi dumb too, when you don't have the brains to save your own skin if Papi wouldn't have brought you in. You lie here in his house, you eat up his food, and then you call Papi dumb?" Enraged, Sanchi scrambled up and made as if to try a second kick at the knight, then thought better of it.

"Oh no, man, no way you catch me that way twice," he said. "You must know karate, huh? Big deal, so that makes you a man. But you remember this, *loco*, you call Papi dumb one more time and I'm coming for you with more than my foot!" He whirled around and went back to packing, stuffing the clothing into the bag with all the fierce hate he couldn't use on the knight.

The knight kicked the bag away from Sanchi. "To run away like this, with no destination and no cause, brings you closer to her," he said. "You run right into her arms. That's what you want, isn't it? To find her again without seeming to look for her?"

Something went off in Sanchi's mind like a firecracker. His black eyes sparkled. "How'd you know," he asked hoarsely, "about *her?*" The knight had nothing to say. "How'd you know?" Sanchi persisted. "Who told you? Papi's the only one knows, and he wouldn't tell. Never. Come on, man who did it?"

"No one told me," said the knight. "If I always had to wait for people to tell me things, I'd be dead."

Sanchi opened his mouth, ready with a smart remark about how this nut must think he's got ESP, but a look silenced him, bottling up all the confusion deep down until the only place it could come out was his eyes, angry tears he unsuccessfully tried to blink away. He drew a breath and it came as a sob.

"Damn you," he whispered. "Damn you!" he wailed. And Sanchi cried on his bed the way girls cry, the way he'd cried when he knew Uncle Carlitos was dead, when he heard *her* talking over running away with her boyfriend, the way he swore he'd never cry. He hadn't cried like that the day he woke and she was gone. He'd cried since then, but never like this, so deep, and with someone he despised to witness his downfall.

When he at last lifted up his face he saw the knight still standing there as if nothing had happened. "What you staring at?" Sanchi demanded between gulps of air.

"Myself," answered the knight. "Myself as I once was, and can never be again." The way he said those crazy words had a bizarre effect. His voice reached out and held Sanchi fascinated, and the boy neither moved nor protested when the knight gazed into his eyes and touched him lightly with two fingers between the brows.

"Open the third eye," said the knight, "and see."

This is crazy, thought Sanchi. This guy's a flake. No, he replied. I'm the crazy one.

He was seeing and not seeing. Sight came inside his head, radiating out from the spot where the knight had touched him. Light bloomed like flowers, one vision bursting from the bud of light to be followed by another. His past loomed up and sank down into darkness with a sigh. The faces of people he knew and people he had seen passing on the street wavered and nodded in the shifting patterns of light and shadow. There was a film of blood, and the light snaking through it, blood and light embracing, ebbing and flowing like the sea.

Then he saw that he was standing beside a tall man in armor. Torches flared against brown stone walls in an endless tunnel. Shields of enameled silver glinted between the torches, with huge swords suspended above them. More torches burned in the distance, and from the gaily lighted end of the tunnel there came song, laughter, the sound of cups and plates clattering, a sudden storm of applause.

They stood in the center of the hall, a long room lined with tables that groaned under the weight of wine and steaming platters of food. Sanchi stared at the men and women who feasted there, each as gaudily dressed as a peacock, each face as wonderful as a star. A company of men leaped over the banquet tables and surrounded Sanchi's escort, thumping him on the back and telling tales that made them all laugh uproariously. Sanchi they ignored.

Then a slender hand the color of new roses rested on his shoulder and Sanchi looked around to see the sweetest woman of his imagination. Her hair was dark brown, caught up in a golden net sewn with pearls, and her smile reached out to hold his heart. She spoke to him, and not understanding a word of her language, still he understood her meaning and returned the smile.

Her face rippled and trickled away as he opened his mouth to speak to her. He was looking at the dingy walls of his room and the knight, abominable in the tacky shirt and slacks, was standing with him looking sad.

"They are all gone now," he said. "That fair, bright company. They are gone, stolen away, destroyed. Not even the elves are left alive to sing of them. The world lies black and bare, dead for all the ages of all the worlds born and unborn, and there will never be another world exactly like it." He gazed at Sanchi earnestly. "I am the only one who survived."

Sanchi shut his eyes tight and tried to summon back the vision of the merry court, the handsome knights, the beautiful women. Nothing came but the spinning, starpoint circles behind his closed lids. The knight shook his head.

"I've done for you something that I've never done before, for anyone. Never before on any of the worlds I've seen. It wasn't necessary. But your doubt was so deep and so firm that I had to do this much for you. You had to see with your own eyes what was lost. Now you've seen it. Think it over. I must rest. The journey was a worse battle for me than any I've had with him." The knight started to go, paused at the door, said, "I'll be waiting for your answer."

Sanchi took a few moments to get back to reality, then sprang up and ran after the knight. He found him in the kitchen, head pillowed on his crossed arms on the kitchen table, just like Elena when she got sleepy over dinner.

"Hey!" demanded Sanchi. "Hey, how'd you do that?"

The knight lifted his head and quite reasonably asked, "How did I do what?"

"That. You know. Hypnotize me. Make me see all that stuff. The party. Those people. It was like—like—" He struggled to pick something from his limited life with which to compare it. "Like *Monty Python and the Holy Grail*," he settled, "but serious."

The knight sighed. "I don't understand," he said. "I thought you'd accept it by now. I never hypnotized you. Of all the minor arts, that one alone is beyond my skills, which is ironic. He is the master there. I'm highly susceptible to hypnosis myself. Perhaps that's why I can't master it."

"But what *was* all that?" Sanchi persisted. "What kind of place were we at? Who were those people?" He hesitated, then added softly, "Who was she?"

"You saw her?" The knight's reply took Sanchi aback. "Was she there? A small woman, dark-haired, very lovely?"

"Yeah," answered Sanchi, getting nervous again. "Sure. She touched me. She was gorgeous, but real nice. She had pearls in her hair. She smiled at me."

The knight's hand shot out and seized Sanchi's wrist in a grip so tight and urgent that the boy cried out in protest. "Did she speak?" begged the knight. "Did she say anything to you? Anything at all?"

"Well, yeah, she—hey, let go of me, will you? I'll tell. She said something to me, but I couldn't get what it was, not really. But it was like I could get it inside, the feeling of it. I think—" He struggled to recall the sensations of her words. "I think she was saying thanks to me and Papi for—for looking out for you?" he finished uncertainly.

Leaning back in the kitchen chair, the knight smiled, but his eyes were distant, looking past Sanchi to vanished things.

"Hey, man," said Sanchi at last, "you still didn't tell me. Who was she?"

"She was my lady," answered the knight. "She's dead."

"Oh," said Sanchi. "I'm sorry." The other questions he had meant to ask about her, about the others, about the feasting hall, all seemed stupid now.

"You wonder," the knight's voice invaded his thoughts, "how you could see her if she is dead? That's something that must wait for another time. We have no time, Sanchi. I've lost too much of it since coming to your world, and he walks here, and Belgor is still lost. Will you give me your answer?"

"Answer?" echoed Sanchi. "You mean about . . . you and me taking off together? Hey, before you said, 'Where'll *we* go?' like sure, I'm gonna go with you, no problem—no questions about it. Think maybe you want to ask *me* first? *Direct?*"

The knight clapped Sanchi on the back much the same as the phantoms of the vision had done to him. "By the Seed, you're right, boy! My mind's a muddle. I am leaving the kind hospitality of your father's house, you see. Leaving it today. Too much time lost, didn't I say that? And I must regain my things: armor, horse, sword, shield, all scattered. To tell you the truth, the thing I want from you just popped up in my mind the moment I saw you making ready to leave this place too. Why not leave together? I thought. Why not ask the boy to come with me? For I need you with me, just for a while. Will you come?"

Sanchi didn't answer right away. Go with this dude? Go where? Back to that crazy, beautiful, wonderful place where he'd dreamed that lady? It had to be a dream. Too much double-talk for Sanchi to understand. And hadn't he said the lady was dead?

"As my squire," said the knight. "Page and

squire both, unless we can find another to help us. You're small to be a squire. No insult meant, but you'd have a hard struggle with my arms, once we'd regained them. If only there were someone stronger who believed me . . . Well? Will you come?"

"Let me get this, man," said Sanchi, slinging himself into a chair. "You want to go, leave Papi's house, and take me with you? Swell. I was leaving anyhow. Man, am I ever fed up with them, especially Manolo. Call me a parasite, that son of a bitch. I'll show him. Sure, I'll go with you. I'll play. You want a squire? You got a squire. You just tell me what you want done, and I do it. But if I do, I get paid. No such thing as a free lunch," he finished with a grin.

The knight frowned. "So that is all," he said. "You'll come with me for money. He's picked his world well this time. You seem to be familiar with his very words."

"Whose very words?" asked Sanchi.

"The one I seek. The one I'll have to slay." The knight shrugged. "I thought you understood."

"Hey, I can dig it," returned Sanchi. "You mean the—uh—you said you want to kill a dragon, right? Talking dragon, huh? Great. Swell. He talks, I'll hear him, you can slay him. *Perfecto!*" He looked slyly up at the knight. "Now about my wages . . ."

The knight tried to suppress a laugh, but failed. "By the Shield, so young and already so wise! Cash on the barrelhead or I'm out a squire, is it? Well, I followed him to this world, and we'll play by his rules for the time being. You'll be paid, Sanchi. I need a squire too much here to haggle. What would you have? Gold? Jewels? A kingdom of your own to rule? I'll win you one. Name your own wages."

Sanchi, who had been hoping to hear something

like an offer of five bucks an hour, turned mad. "Who you jiving?" he demanded, as belligerent as his size would allow. "Everybody on the street knows big talkers don't pay nothing. How you going to give me gold and jewels and like that, man? You don't own the clothes you're wearing!"

The knight traced circles in the air between them and each airy outline filled itself with shining metal until, like ripe plums, they dropped jingling to the floor. Sanchi pounced on one and held it up to his eye. It weighed at least an ounce and was as slick as a mirror.

"This real?" he whispered. The knight continued to trace circles that grew golden until there was a small heap of coins at Sanchi's feet. The cat came in and batted at them, dancing in the glittering shower.

Only when the last coin fell did the knight speak. "I know they are real," he said, "but no doubt you won't take my word for it. The thought of gold is too rich for your brain. I intend to leave these coins here, in gratitude for all the hospitality I've had from your father."

"He's not my father," Sanchi said at last. "He just took me in. Like he took you in."

"And what are you leaving for him to find?" asked the knight. He looked around the kitchen as if he were searching the entire apartment from where he sat. "Not even a note."

"I was going to write him one," Sanchi mumbled. The knight's bright eyes made him squirm in his lie. "Well, I was!" he shouted.

"As you like," said the knight, very dry. "It's of no consequence to me. I suppose you'd prefer your wages to be in . . . dollars?" He fanned a stack of bills out of nothing. Sanchi was impressed. Not even Brother Jimmy who ran the card con down on 110th Street had faster hands. But that money was real. Sanchi could tell a real bill from a queer a mile off.

"Yeah, sure, that's fine," he said.

"I am so pleased that you approve," said the knight, giving Sanchi a look to make his skin feel itchy. "Here." He thrust a twenty at the boy. "A down payment on your services. You'll probably run off the first chance you get, but I may get some honest work out of you before then."

He arose and went into Papi's room where he rummaged in the closet until he found his own clothes, nicely washed and tenderly ironed by Mamacita. Never had she felt such fabric! So soft, so fine, so colorful. He stripped to the skin and stood naked beside the bed while Sanchi watched, waiting. His body was burned brown all over, except for the odd spot here and there where the skin showed the color of cream. Sanchi's eyes traced the path of long scars, some brown with age, some still white and puckered, one glowing faintly red. They laced themselves across the knight's chest in cruel designs. His back was untouched.

"Well? What are you waiting for?" snapped the knight. "I paid you in advance. Are you stupid as well as greedy? Help me dress!"

"You mean I'm supposed to—" Sanchi faltered.

"The simplest duty of a squire!" barked the knight, tapping one foot impatiently. "The most basic. By rights a page should do it, and pages are only six years old when they learn how. Come on, stop gaping. I'll tell you how to do it, step by step."

Dumbly Sanchi obeyed the instructions he was given. He helped the knight don hose and tunic, belt and tabard and shoes. It took a long time.

"Praise the gods that my armor's not here for

you to bungle," said the knight, impatiently tugging and straightening his clothes. "I had a blind boy serve me once and he did a better job for less pay. Well, you'll do until I find someone better. Come, we have no time to waste here. Get your bag and we'll go."

Sanchi wanted to tell him to take his scorn and shove it. Hey, he was trying his best, wasn't he? So what if he didn't get it perfect the first time? So what? Did that give this dude the right to look at him like he was a roach? He'd really turned uppity since he passed Sanchi that money, like Sanchi was beneath contempt for wanting to be paid. Screw him if he was too good to pay a man for his work. Sanchi didn't need him. Sanchi didn't need anybody.

But the money crinkled in his pocket and the pile of gold shone on the table where the knight had placed it. Sanchi remembered the rest of the money, too. You could buy a lot with that kind of money, and the dude was willing enough to pay. So what if he maybe looked down on Sanchi for wanting pay, so long as he paid him? It takes all kinds.

And he needs me, thought Sanchi. He goes around acting like that, flashing that kind of bread, he'll get his head bashed in before he goes a block. And if that happens, no more money for Sanchi. Sanchi could use money. It was the green and golden bridge to everything he wanted.

Everything.

Because when Sanchi got enough money, he'd be rich, and when he was rich, he could hire men to find *her* and bring her back and make her sorry she'd ever gone away. He liked to imagine how it would be when he saw *her* again. He was always up on some kind of throne, and she was down on the floor, crying and saying she was sorry.

It could happen.

Why not?

All he needed was enough money, and now he thought he'd found the way to get all he wanted. It was only a matter of time.

"Hey, Boss! Boss!" he hollered after the knight, hearing the hiss of those weird pointed shoes going down the stairs. "Wait for Sanchi!"

Chapter VI

RICHARD

"I'll tell you what it is about the law," said Richard, momentarily shoving a stack of documents for a murder case aside. "The law is a defense of what folks want to believe."

"Oh, God," said Avery. "Spare me." He was very young, younger than Richard, and full of ideas that were—well—fine in the classroom but rather uncomfortable in the real world.

"For instance," Richard went on, "what's evidence? Anything you can make of it. Take this case we have coming up, Delgado versus Sawyer. What have we got? An assault complaint by Carl Sawyer's wife, typical case of wife-beating, only she wants to take him to court."

"It would seem pretty obvious," said Avery calmly. "The doctor who set her jaw didn't think she imagined that fracture."

"Wrong, wrong, wrong." Richard thumped his desk for emphasis. "See, this is where interpretation comes in. Yes, she had a real fractured jaw. Yes, she had a lot of other injuries, bruises and what not. OK, but as Sawyer's attorneys we've got to make the jury realize that just because she's hurt doesn't mean he's the one did the hurting."

"Excuse me," muttered Avery, trying to get away.

He'd met Sawyer and taken an immediate dislike to him. When the man admitted he'd "brushed that woman" a few times "to keep her in line" and now wanted to get off the hook, money no object, Avery had prayed to be taken off the case. It was no use. The high-and-mighty of the firm insisted that Avery be taken under Richard's wing for this very difficult case. Richard knew the ropes. Richard understood the law. That Avery, he was a genius, a top graduate of Yale Law, but he didn't understand the real world. Never mind, Richard would break him in.

"Hold it," said Richard, detaining him. "I just want to run this by you, because Sawyer's your baby. I'm just in the wings. The honor's going to be all yours. Right, I know you're thinking he as good as confessed he did it. But so? Did he *say* he fractured her jaw? Did he say it in so many words? Maybe he just slapped her once or twice, and she decided to make him sorry, so she engineers a few injuries of her own to make a good case against him. I mean, hey, there weren't any witnesses, were there? She says he threw her down the stairs. Whose word do we have on it? You see, Avery, it's all a matter of how you approach the evidence you've got. Then you help the jury approach it that way too."

"You're going to sit there and try to make me swallow that Ms. Delgado threw *herself* down the stairs? Just to make it hot for her husband? Are you crazy?" demanded Avery.

"Ah! There's something else we can use for Sawyer. *Ms.* Delgado. Did you hear what you called her? Yes, her husband's name isn't good enough for her. I'll bet we could get a few brownie points with the jury, some of them, for that alone."

"Gotta go, I'll miss my train," said Avery quickly,

breaking away from Richard and disappearing out the door. If he stayed any longer he was going to shove Richard down a flight of stairs.

Richard let him go. If Avery could have read the young jurist's agile mind, he would have found a similar wish to shove *him* down a flight of stairs. But such tactics were too heavy-handed for Richard. Instead he simply made a one-line entry in a small brown notebook on his desk. In certain circumstances it could be just as effective as a sharp push at the head of a steep flight.

The working day was almost over. Richard watched it end reluctantly. He loved the law. He loved his own vision of it, his own idea of what the law should be, a black-velvet backdrop to set off his own brilliance in the office or the courtroom. Already there were hints whispered about how far he could go if he wanted to, and Richard knew he wanted to. It was all a matter of timing and organization, of knowing which side to show to the cameras, which way to jump.

He checked his watch, got his coat and sports-car cap, and bid a beaming good-night to the office girls, never quite condescending, but never giving them the idea they were even vaguely his equals.

An evening's enjoyment beckoned, and Richard was eager to meet it. Diane's place, newly decorated, newly liberated, and his second home. All of a sudden, he mused, she's changed. No sense knocking it. God knows it's better than the milky-blooded little girl she was before.

Something had changed her. Richard didn't much care what, but all the knowledgeable people said it was poor old Lysa's suicide. How distressing it had been for Diane, especially when Lysa's mother called her up and practically swore she'd take Di-

ane to court for murdering her kid. But Lysa wasn't
a kid anymore, and as for why she'd killed herself
. . . it was a topic even less interesting than why
Diane had changed.

"I could almost take her nonstop, now," said
Richard. "Married to Diane. There are worse things,
and a good lawyer needs a wife to make him repu-
table. A lady who won't cramp my style is all I
want, and I do think Diane could do that; respect
my needs. Well, we'll see."

His cab let him off at her place. The doorman
recognized his face and let him in before bothering
to announce him. Diane was waiting, her lithe
body shining pale and silvery beneath a tawny
gauze caftan. If she was beautiful, even if she was
very beautiful, very desirable, he was too wise to
let her know it.

"We'd get along," he remarked after dinner.

"What did you say?" she asked, passing him a
crystal bubble of brandy.

In his favorite hiding place under her bed, the
dragon listened, not yet ready to reach.

"Nothing. I was just thinking." Richard smiled.
His teeth were bone-white, perfect, his face ready
to be photographed and used to sell anything to
anyone in a full-page color ad. "About us. Funny,
isn't it?" he chuckled. "I'm completely out of style.
I'm thinking that maybe I should get down on one
knee to you and ask you to marry me, the whole
Victorian bit. We're pretty far gone from then,
though."

"I don't hear you complaining," she teased. Her
eyes were warm and hard, fixed on him, waiting
for him to say it was all a joke. Just another one of
Richard's jokes. There were so many!

"But I am complaining. Things have gotten to
the point where I *think* the woman's supposed to

be the one to say, 'Hey, let's live together awhile and see how it goes.' I don't hear you asking me."

"I asked you to dinner," countered Diane, mouth still smiling without her eyes. Inwardly she cursed them, wayward eyes. Cooler, please. Please. One wrong step and we lose.

No, said the dragon.

"And breakfast. It's not enough. I want to marry you, Diane!" The words flew out so suddenly that they frightened her, startled him. "We—we could do a lot together."

She had intended to make him wait for an answer. She always had a fine supply of noble intentions, and never kept a single one. She was in his arms, hugging him, kissing him, letting all her joy lie open to him. Carefully he put down the brandy glass before returning her caresses.

With her money and my brains, there's nothing beyond us, thought Richard. He gently pushed one side of the caftan from her shoulder, brushing her tense skin with the heat of his breath. Fire-breather. She was aflame. He knew what was expected of him. It was wrong to cheat the lady you deceived.

The dragon crawled out from under the bed and crept behind the potted plants that veiled the terrace. Strands of light fell in burning dewdrops on his scales.

Don't love, he counseled Richard. Never love. The best-beloved betrays. I know. I have had that lesson. I have lived that lesson. The best-beloved betrays.

Calmly, without regret or passion, he watched them act out a shadow play. His golden eyes became cups to hold the shallow sighs, the murmured words dutifully said, the sound of skin to skin.

How primitive, he mused. How limited. Yet maybe they are more fortunate this way.

Memory drew him down a dark time-funnel into a labyrinth of stone tunnels where a proud green-and-gold beast lay sprawled on a heap of treasure, watching a naked boy playing jacks with diamonds. Wordlessly he called, and the young one left his game to answer his lord's summons.

Do you know, he poured his message into those dark-lashed, frank, believing eyes, that I have never loved another soul as I love thee?

The boy smiled and stroked the harsh scales, tickled the black spots on the reeking gums between the slashing rows of half-moon teeth. He would not answer.

I love thee, insisted the dragon.

"You'll change," said the boy, without sorrow. "I've heard of how it always is. That's just the way you are. And when you change—"

Yes?

"They say you'll eat me. That's what *they* say. But I think you'll only let me go free when you're tired of me. When I don't amuse you anymore."

"Amuse me?" the dragon repeated aloud. "Is that all you think you mean to me? *Amusement?*" The roar of his indignation filled the cavern and sent chips of gray rock rattling down like dried beans in an empty clay pot.

The boy was unafraid. On the contrary, he seemed to be rather amused himself, sitting cross-legged like a ragged tailor and looking up into the flashing golden eyes merrily.

"I'm no reader of minds, great one," he remarked. "That is for you to do." He paused, scratching his toes where they peeped out of his soft leather sandals. "That must be fun."

The dragon shook himself, amazed at the boy,

the almost-child. It was not a good feeling, amazement. It made him forget the sheer power in his claws, the bone-snapping might of his mouth, not to mention those other powers he had made his on a long-gone day of blood and betrayal.

"It is . . . fun," he admitted. "They can't keep me out. Their minds fall open as easily as an overripe pear splits when it hits a rock."

"Pretty wasp, pretty wasp, tell me a tale. Will Mama have any pears for sale?" chanted the boy. He was still fascinated by the shape of his own toes. Finding no willing ear, the dragon turned away and curled up on the heap of gold, coins rattling against scales, flecks of bright metal embedded in the horny skin.

You shall come to me, thought the dragon. They all do. You are no different than the others.

Yes, he thought. Yes, you are different. I love thee.

Never love, Richard, my new pet, my dragonling, my key. Never love. The best-beloved betrays.

Chapter VII

GEORGE

Who let all these street kids in here anyway? Wasn't it hard enough trying to study *and* it was a gorgeous spring day outside distracting you *and* it wasn't safe to sit outside by yourself if you were a woman *and* you had to study these heavy art history books because Professor Talbot was such a stickler for getting atmosphere *and*—

Where was I? thought Sandra, pushing her glasses up her nose.

It was no use. She'd fought and lost another round to the monster distraction. She was getting so scatterbrained that she couldn't summon up a thimbleful of concentration anymore.

Both Sandra's elbows rested on a full-color plate of a fourteenth-century Madonna as she surveyed the reading room. No one else seemed to be having her problem with diligence. God knew what all of them were reading so avidly. She recognized two French doctoral candidates, one English postdoc, and a screwy number from the classics department. You had to be screwy to imagine you'd get a job in classics. Or English, for that matter. And the French Ph.D.'s were happy if they snagged a post teaching junior-high-school students how to sit on chairs.

And what about me? History! I should have gone to law school. Right, or get an M.B.A. You can get anywhere you want with a business degree.

And you don't have to put up with these punky street kids all over you. Didn't student security mean more than that empty phrase, "community relations"? For the love of heaven, hadn't a student been attacked right here in the university library last week? And don't tell me another student did it!

Angrily Sandra flipped the page, trying to immerse herself in her chosen century.

Some things are not meant to be. She felt the short curls on the back of her neck stir in the breeze-breath behind her. If the kid leaned any closer he would topple against her.

"Do you mind?" she grumbled, hiking up a wall of shoulders against him, and hunching over the book.

Impervious to the chill in her voice, Sanchi persisted, bobbing up and down to steal a glimpse of the painting before her. It was of a man armed with sword, shield, and lance, riding a white horse. He was a very seriously occupied young man. It took a lot of concentration to slay a dragon.

"Think he'll make it?" asked Sanchi.

"I *beg* your pardon?" snarled Sandra.

"Him." Sanchi's grubby brown finger stabbed the knight. "Think he'll kill the dragon?"

"It's only a painting," said Sandra, speaking up a trifle too loudly. The screwy classicist made a gargoyle's face at her across the table.

"Yeah, so what? So if the guy did another painting, you think he'd kill it?"

"Young man," Sandra tried to sound desperately old and cold and dignified, "I could not care less. I suppose he will kill the dragon. It's a typical representation of St. George slaying the dragon, so it's safe to say that St. George wins. The legend does not change. Now, is that enough for you? I have important work to do." She turned the page, writing finis to the saint's painted battle.

"Mind if I have just one more look at it, huh?" asked Sanchi. "Please. It's important."

Sandra sighed deeply, the last gasp of exasperation. "Look, kid," she snapped, leveling her eyes with his, "you want to look at St. George and the dragon? Fine. Go get another book. This one does not, repeat, *not* have the one and only picture of it."

Sanchi's smile twinkled in reflection on Sandra's glasses. "I'm not let in the stacks," he said, trying to explain things rationally to this short-fused lady. From her put-on snooty accent when she was talking down to him and her real voice when she got mad, he'd guess she was from— "Brooklyn, right?"

Sanchi's Sherlockian powers were not endearing. Sandra preferred to forget Brooklyn, and even if she was compelled to live in a not-so-hot part of Manhattan, the day would come when she would get enough cash and class to live there in proper style.

On what? The salary of an assistant professor of art history? her shrewd side asked her. Don't make me laugh!

So instead of laughing, she let her rage out on Sanchi. "If you're not supposed to be here, get out or I'll call a guard," she declared.

"Huh!" snorted Sanchi. "Sorry I asked for blood." He thrust his fists into the pockets of his jeans and gave every sign of walking off in a huff. But he didn't move. Plainly he was offering her a second chance for good community relations.

"Wait a minute," said Sandra, gentling her tone. "Look, look at it all you'd like. I was bored with it anyway, and I've got time."

Sanchi seized the halfhearted invitation with both hands. He slung himself into the chair next to Sandra and hauled the huge folio closer to him, staring at the old painting with such hunger that Sandra began to get a creepy feeling in her legs. The screwy classicist made one last grimace, slammed his book shut, and stalked off to a less community-oriented table.

"So that's a dragon," whispered Sanchi. "Wow." Raising his voice a bit, he asked, "Is that about how big they get? Or do they come bigger?"

Sandra shrugged. Where did it say she was majoring in dragons? And this kid seemed too old still to believe in that fairy-tale stuff, asking considered questions about dragons and unicorns and all the flotsam of broken legends as if they really existed. Something had to be wrong with him.

"How old are you?" she asked.

"Twelve, I guess," said Sanchi.

"You guess?"

"Hey, it's an honest answer, OK? At my house, we didn't stand up and cheer every birthday, y'know," explained Sanchi.

Well, at least that sounded closer to reality, thought Sandra. Friends of hers who did tutoring with the neighborhood youth told her they'd come across more than one kid who couldn't have told you his birthday unless he looked it up at City Hall. But twelve years old and asking about dragons? How much of this kid was for real? This high up in Manhattan, twelve years old was worth twice that in street wisdom and hard cunning. You don't get streetwise chasing fairy tales. What was with this kid?

"So that's about average for a dragon, huh?" Sanchi was nudging her.

"Uh—I think so. That's about the size they are in most of the medieval paintings, although at times they're smaller in the sculptures of St. Michael defeating the dragon, for the sake of balance in the artistic composition," Sandra lectured. Inside her a shrill, outraged, bewildered presence demanded, *What are you doing, Sandy Horowitz? What the hell are you doing, telling some ghetto kid about artistic composition, for God's sake?*

"You mean they'd make the dragon bigger or smaller than he was just so the picture'd look good?" demanded Sanchi. Ghetto kid or not, she'd never seen such indignation.

It matters to him how big they made the dragon, she thought. It really, truly, actually matters. Oh, Sandy Horowitz, you have been spotted by a loon.

A young loon, she countered. And I know karate.

"I believe so," she replied. "Most artists do that. Are—are you familiar with the work of Salvador Dali?"

"Hey, lady, don't give me that," hissed Sanchi. "I'm not crazy, and I don't know any Salvador Dali."

"Good," answered Sandra quickly, "because his stuff almost drove *me* crazy. Kid, I'm sorry, but if you're not crazy, I've got to be. How many guys from your neighborhood come slipping into the Columbia U. library and ask about dragons like they were tomatoes at Food Mart? How big do they get? How small? How come the artists didn't do them the way they were? Just listen to yourself, kid! How many sane people think you can sketch a dragon from *life?*"

* * *

Sandy Horowitz, in all the glorious years of the Horowitz family we have been asked to leave houses, neighborhoods, cities, countries, and continents. For what? For what we believed. But Sandy Horowitz, never—not in all those centuries of persecution and despair—never has a single member of the Horowitz family been asked—nay, compelled!—to leave a university library for being too damn noisy.

"Sorry," said Sanchi, sitting next to her on the bench.

"My own fault." Sandra grinned weakly, pushing her glasses up her nose. "I've got a bad temper. You know what they say about redheads."

Sanchi gave Sandra's paprika-colored curls the once-over. "Nice," he said, "Is it real?"

"Twice as real as you and your dragons, and the temper's real too. Where did you get your nerve, kid?"

Past master of the eloquent shrug, Sanchi let his shoulders rise and fall once, dismissing the question. "First time you get thrown out of there?" he asked.

"It isn't a favorite habit of mine. I have to get my work done, and I have a feeling your company is not quite conducive to good research. Why don't you run along home now?"

"What's that mean, conducive?"

"Leading to. From Latin, *conducere*," Sandra replied glibly. She had never deliberately enjoyed a word of Latin in her life, no matter that it was required for her coveted degree. Any one of her fellow students would gladly have lectured for thirty minutes about the word conducive, its roots and offshoots. Sandra found the whole spectrum of linguistics boredom in many hues.

"No kidding. Like *conducir* in Spanish," Sanchi provided. "Far out."

"Very far. Now if you don't mind, I have my work to do." She tried to leave her new admirer on the bench, but he tagged along, more questions on his lips, and none of them about Latin verbs, or history, or even Spanish. For some arcane reason, this chatty guttersnipe seemed to think that modern small talk should be solely and entirely about dragons.

"Could you go back in there and take out that book?" he asked her, loping at her side.

"What book? The art book?"

"Yeah! The one with George and the dragon."

"What the hell do you want it for? It won't get you much on the open market," Sandy snapped. Mental calculations told her she had four days left in which to complete two long papers, one of which she had not researched yet. Professor Carmody was known to forbid extensions.

The kid had thin hands, but a good grip. He got her by the arm and made her stop while he glared at her. "Hey, look, I'm no rip-off artist. And don't you call me one. You don't got the right to talk that way."

I should yell, thought Sandy. *I should scream and get a cop over here . . . if there is a cop.*

I should say I'm sorry, thought Sandy. *What's got into me? These kids don't steal art books. I've been in New York too long. I'm seeing my own brand of dragons.*

"Sorry, kid," she said humbly. "I guess I'm just unhappy with getting tossed out of the library. I do have a lot of work to do, honest and—well—you know."

Sanchi nodded as solemnly as any sage in blue

jeans. "I know. I get the same thing at home a lot, these days. Everyone's too impatient, man. They never get enough time for what they got to do. That's why I came up here, to get away from him. He's been on my case like crazy lately. He says we gotta hurry and find the horse next. I mean, you can wing it without armor, but you gotta have a horse."

"So true, so true," said Sandy, not listening until the boy's last word echoed back inside her head and she woke up asking, *"Armor?"*

"I got the breastplate easy," Sanchi confided. "I knew I would. The kid who took it was some kinda fool, man. You can't unload a chunk of steel like that in a pawnshop, and where the hell you going to drag it, up in Harlem? Maybe some pimp buys it for laughs, but they're no fools. A sword, a helmet, a big old shield, that's something classy to hang up over the fireplace. In Khwarema they always hung their swords over the fireplace, but it wasn't for show. It was so they'd have them ready if the lord sounded the alarm and needed armed men fast. But where you going to stow a breastplate? Looks bad over the fireplace, man. And would you believe I picked up the leg guards—they got a fancy name, but I forget what—in another joint only two blocks past the breastplate. Got them for five bucks apiece, more than I paid for the breastplate, but I guess it's because the old man figured they were some kinda fancy shin protectors for playing hockey. Hockey in Harlem! Pretty funny, huh? Huh? . . . Hey, what's the matter?"

Sandra Horowitz was backing away, trying to escape step by step from the first honest-to-God dangerous lunatic she had yet met. Beside this one, the weirdo from classics paled to sanity. Who taught this grubby slum kid to prattle of arms and the man? And what else? Pawnshops, dragons, horses, and the market value of breastplates, swords hanging ready above fireplaces, waiting for the battle cry. . . .

Where did he get all this? asked Sandy Horowitz. Drugs.

It has to be drugs. Don't try to tell me otherwise. What else is there to believe? What else *can* I believe? You don't get the stuff of knighthood on the streets of New York. You get pimps in Lincoln Continentals, not Sir Galahad on a white horse. You don't even get the horse, unless you count those tired specimens that drag tourists around the park in hansom cabs. If it's not drugs, it must be because he's read *Le Morte d'Arthur*. The Grail legends. Chrétien de Troyes. Monmouth's *History*.

Sure.

Right.

Makes sense, doesn't it?

The kid's on drugs. Or crazy, free-lance crazy.

The maniac stuck his hand out at her, smiling. "Hey, if you're worried about me, calm down. I'm Sanchez Rubio, but all my friends call me Sanchi. See, I used to live with the Sanchez family, so they liked the nickname for me instead of confusing them when Mamacita had to yell for me to come upstairs using the family name. What's your name?"

"Sandra Smith," said Sandy Horowitz. Never give them your right name. They look you up in the phone book later and come after you.

"*Smith?*" All the scorn in the world was in Sanchi's voice. "Sure."

"There are people named Smith, you know," said Sandy, trying to sound haughty.

"Yeah, thousands. More every time someone checks into a motel, right? Hey, it's cool with me. You don't want to say who you are, I understand.

Look, to this day I don't think George gave me his right name, and we're partners."

"I'm going to hate myself for asking, but who is George?"

"Can't you guess?" grinned Sanchi. "He's the guy's gonna kill the dragon."

"Uh-huh," said Sandy, taking a step backward.

"You want to meet him?" offered Sanchi. "He's real nice."

"Uh-uh," said Sandy, taking another step away.

"Who knows," Sanchi persisted. "He's not bad looking. You might like him. Maybe if he had a woman, we could forget about the dragon."

"Uh," said Sandy, getting ready to spring for it. In her mind, if not on her tongue, her parents' Yiddish was getting a good workout. *Even by the meshugganim they got yentas, and every one a shadchan.* Loose translation meant that even the crazies have matchmakers.

"How about it?" pursued Sanchi.

"Bye," whispered Sandy, and ran like hell.

"So you didn't want to come here? Why? Did you fear me?" asked the knight.

Sandy nodded her head, trying not to gape at the clean, comfortable, highly respectable surroundings in which the strange boy and his equally odd companion lived. It wasn't the sleazy opium den she had expected.

"If you were afraid, why did you come?" the knight asked.

Sandy shrugged. She was getting as expressive at it as Sanchi. "Your friend's very persuasive," she said. Being honest with herself, she had to admit she didn't know why she was here. She hadn't the vaguest idea. In fact, she drew a blank when she tried to conjure up anything that had happened to her between the time she had tried to run away from Sanchi uptown and the moment she had awakened to find herself walking with the boy through the lobby of a sleek East Side apartment house close to the river.

"I've been drugged," she mumbled to herself. It was impossible, of course, unless the kid had pulled a blowgun on her. So what had really happened to her? A blank, pure and simple.

"You should have seen the picture, George," said Sanchi. He hovered behind the knight's chair doing a stationary two-step on the balls of his feet. He looked like a cross between a servant and a runner on the mark. "Some dragon, man! And the knight took him easy, one stab of the lance right on the nose. Is that how you're going to do it?"

The knight smiled indulgently and leaned forward to pour Sandy a glass of wine. "Sanchi is persuasive," he said, ignoring the boy. "Also persistent, resourceful, imaginative, and a little free. I ask you to excuse him. Will you?" He offered her the glass.

Gingerly Sandy took a sip, her tongue searching for the telltale trace of barbiturate. Was Sanchi imaginative? He had nothing on Sandy Horowitz, now dreaming of drugged wine and white slavery. She swallowed the wine and felt nothing but the normal warmth from the alcohol.

"He—piqued my curiosity, I'll admit," she said. "I never expected to be doing anything like this in my life."

"Anything like what?" asked the knight, enjoying his own crystal bubble of sherry.

"Why—this apartment, for one thing. For another—you."

"I don't match the apartment?" The knight was amused. For the space of a brief laugh his face softened, his eyes grew bright. Something lifted from him like a dark, winged shadow, and Sandy saw a face that seemed to brush her heart by a secret path of magic. "Or don't I match your ideas?" he asked. The shadow fell again.

"My ideas?" Sandy repeated, confused. The bright eyes probed her mind. She could feel them, chill and efficient, and she knew that her thoughts were being searched like old dresser drawers. A comic idea, but she had no taste for laughter. He was inside, walking the whorls of her brain like garden paths, seeking her memories. The worst part of it was, it was unnecessary. He was doing it because he wanted to do it. A stray slip of his mind touched hers as he passed through her thoughts.

I must test my powers. It is not good to let them go unused too long. In the final meeting, I must have them all about me, sharp, like my sword. You are as good a testing ground as any other.

"No!" shrieked Sandy, bolting from her chair. "Get out! Let *me* get out! No, please! *Please!*"

You are a husk, an empty hull. All that matters to me is me.

"Ah!" Lights crossed in her brain, branding an unseen sky with hidden lightning. Sanchi gaped as the red-haired girl lurched backward and crumpled to the floor. Her shoulders trembled like butterfly wings.

"What did you do to her? Goddamn you, what did you do?" Sanchi knelt beside her, lifted her face. Her breath stirred across his fingertips. She was still alive, he thought. He had expected to feel death.

The knight moved quickly, scooping her from the floor and stretching her out on the sofa while Sanchi made futile grabs at her clothing, trying to wrench her away from him.

"What did you do to her, man?" he demanded. "I brought her here like you told me, but you never told me you were going to kill her! I don't want anything to do with this, you hear me? I stuck by you, I helped you, I got back your things for you, but this is it! You never told me you were going to kill people. You said you were going to help them!"

"Be quiet," said the knight grimly, touching Sandy's clammy hands. "She isn't dead and you know it. I don't know what's happened myself."

"Look, George my man, don't lie to me. I'm just your whaddayacallit—squire?—but we're together. I stuck by you, remember, and I got you every piece of your old stuff back that we got so far, and I know what you can do. You did it to me, remember? And I saw you do it to other people. Remember that old man in the hock shop who wasn't going to sell me the belt with those silver seashells on it?"

"Scallops," corrected the knight.

"Whatever. Remember him? I went out and got you, and you just stood there, looking him in the eye for maybe five minutes straight, and all of a sudden he was ready to *give* us the goddamn belt for free."

"I paid him a fair price," said the knight. He stopped looking at Sanchi, kneeling by Sandy's side and stroking her brow, tracing patterns on her face with his fingers.

"*Now* what are you doing to her?" yelled Sanchi. He grabbed the knight's wrist and yanked his hand away from the girl's face.

"Let go, Sanchi," said the knight without raising his voice. "I'm not hurting her. I'm only looking for something."

"See, that's what I mean! How can you—? *What*

can you be looking for that way? What did you look for with the old hock-shop man? Hell, what did you look for with *me?* I could feel you looking through my eyes like you were on the inside with me. You do it to lots of people, I've seen you at it. On the street, even, just walking by. They kind of shudder and duck into stores to get away. You did it to a waitress in a restaurant one time. She dropped a tray and ran."

"If either you or I were better cooks, we wouldn't have to bother waitresses," said the knight, trying to lighten the air. The effort fell flat. Sanchi continued to scowl. Sandy groaned and made a feeble attempt to squirm away from the questing fingertips that fluttered over her face like windblown reeds.

"I said leave her alone!" grunted Sanchi, and he smacked the knight's hand away. The sharp noise roused Sandy like a pistol shot and she came to her full senses in time to see the knight turn a look of unbelievable outrage and power on the boy.

"Do you dare . . . ?" he whispered. Their eyes locked. A spear of unseen force seemed to have transfixed the two of them in a moment frozen in eternity.

"Let him go!" Sandy heard herself shouting, echoing what Sanchi had said and done for her not five minutes before. She grabbed the knight's shoulder and dug her fingers in hard, forcing him to break his gaze and look at her. Like a ghost just glimpsed out of the corner of her eye, she saw the last wisp of what he had been directing at Sanchi, and she shuddered.

"At least," said the knight coldly, "you are loyal to one another on this world, if not to me. There is something to build on, at any rate. But be warned,

Lady; do not interfere again. What happens between him and me doesn't concern you."

"In a pig's eye!" retorted Sandy. She hadn't been alive very long, but already she had an extensive list of things she hated, and topping it was being told what to do. "I'm not going to just stand by and let you—*hypnotize* some poor little street kid who doesn't know what's going on! I'll call the cops!"

"Hey, honey, you don't call nobody, OK? Who asked you, huh?" Sanchi waded into the fray. "You lay off of George, you got me? I mean, what he and I do, that's our business, like he says."

Sandy was speechless in the face of this unexpected burst of ingratitude and—could she call it devotion? She liked to think that there was nothing that could shock her. She knew all the possible permutations of personal relationships in the city, but this one . . . She looked from Sanchi's pinched, intense face to George's cool, handsome one and wondered if there was some kind of sexual bond at work. Her instincts told her no, yet could she trust instincts? They were the products of man's natural state, and there were few things as far removed from the natural as New York.

"No, we are not lovers," said George with a tight, amused smile. "There are other bonds stronger than love, my dear."

"What?" Sanchi squealed his protest. "You mean she thought we were . . . ?" His sternly macho upbringing would not allow him to say the despised word. The look he rifled at Sandy was pure boiling rage. "You got a filthy mind, man," he said.

Sandy pivoted her head from man to boy to man again until she felt dizzy. Her mind was losing all traction in reality. She could feel rational thought slipping away, like water going down a drain. What had that man done to her? How had the boy brought her here? Why couldn't she gather enough strength to get up and get the hell out before they tried something else, although God alone knew what they wanted from her? The questions fell, stinging like hail. She bowed her head under the downpour and cried.

Gentle hands touched her hair with all the reverence of a holy relic. She sobbed and sobbed while cool fingers stroked the tears from her cheeks and strong arms cradled her close. Behind closed lids she dreamed she saw the knight standing with an upraised sword glowing white, fending off the nightmares of her world, his armor shining. She stopped her tears.

"Forgive me," said the knight. His voice was husky. "I've been fighting alone for so long, so very long. I've forgotten that there are some things more important than pride. Forgive me, Lady."

Sandy snuffled and accepted the tissue that Sanchi hastened to provide. She blew her nose loudly. "It's all right," she murmured. "Honestly, I don't know why I took on like that."

"You had every right to, in the face of our unforgivable rudeness. I've seen men lashed for less of an offense against a lady," said the knight, then added with a grin, "I trust you won't insist on a similar punishment for me?"

"I don't feel much like insisting on anything," said Sandy, dabbing at her eyes. "Except maybe an explanation. Whoever you are, you're too weird even for New York, and that's saying something. I'm fresh out of guesses. So who are you, already? And who's the kid playing Tonto to your Lone Ranger? Your sidekick," she tried to clarify when a look of puzzlement covered the knight's features.

"Well," he said. "An explanation. I have been

trying to give an explanation from the moment I set foot on your world, but first I was prevented from doing so by a mob of hostile folk, and ever since Sanchi has consented to serve me as squire, he has made me swear never to explain my mission to another soul. His exact words were, 'You do and they lock you up in Bellevue forever and throw away the key.' "

"They would, too," said Sanchi, on the defensive. "But go ahead, you tell her. You let her in on it, George. Then you see what she makes of it. And if she don't run like hell, I'll buy you a pizza. Pepperoni," he added, naming his personal favorite.

The knight threw his head back and laughed, and again the oppressive, invisible mantle of gloom seemed to leave him momentarily. "How can I resist an offer like that?" he chuckled. "If the lady is willing to listen . . ."

"I don't know about willing," said Sandy, "but I don't feel up to doing much else. Go ahead, only go easy on a poor girl who's sure she's cracked up, OK?"

"Hey, don't worry." Sanchi poked her in the arm. "I thought I was going nuts too, when he first told me. But the way he told me! He took me there, back to see where he came from. Man, it was something else! You could almost taste it. You gonna take her back there, George? If you do, can I come along again?"

The knight relaxed on the plump biscuit-colored sofa and reached for his drink. "What price pepperoni?" he sighed with feigned weariness. "I suppose we must all go."

"Go? I don't want to *go* there!" objected Sandy. "I don't even like where I am now! I'm not—"

"My lady, forgive me," said the knight, his hand closing warmly around her own, his eyes glowing

with green fire. "You must. It has already begun."
He clutched Sanchi with his other hand and the
boy instinctively reached out for Sandy's free hand
to complete the circle. The ring wavered like rain
and they slipped past the edges of one world into
the next.

Chapter VIII

FIRST BLOOD

They moved because Richard preferred it. She paid the stupendously overinflated rent because Richard assured her they could ill afford not to. They sold or gave away all of her old furniture because Richard opined that the modern look would not go well with the small, compactly elegant townhouse a block from the Metropolitan Museum of Art. They shopped for antiques together, but they bought only the ones that Richard determined were worthy of their new image as a happily married couple whose future joy was entirely dependent upon their continued good fortune and good taste.

And now Richard was dead.

Diane sat on the edge of the heavily carved black-oak bed and stared out the window at the little garden behind the house. She felt numb, her brain incapable of bringing anything into focus. Her grief removed her from the world, and she had hardly had the chance to establish her liking for her new life, her new home, her new furnishings. She was totally adrift, entirely at sea, with nothing familiar for her to grab onto and save herself. All she had was Richard's brother Lionel, and he wasn't here this morning.

She looked down at her lap and saw that she

had fallen asleep while still dressed. Her jeans and silk shirt were hot and felt like they had adhered permanently to her flesh. She stared at the telephone beside the bed, remembering . . .

Richard hadn't come home last night. That was nothing new. From the day of their marriage, from the moment he had begun to initiate his bold new plans for where and how they would have to live in the future, coming home at a decent hour had never been a part of the grand design. At first she believed it was law-office work that kept him, but the one time she called the office they told her he left promptly at quitting time. Rather too promptly, his superior stated huffily.

"Richard," she confronted him when he trailed in that night, after eleven, "where have you been?"

"Not bad, Diane," he replied. "Not bad at all. I was expecting a scene, but thank God you've got the good grace to keep it simple. No tacky outbursts of a woman scorned? Marvelous. Good breeding always shows."

"You're not answering my question," she said, hearing her voice grow harsh. From underneath the black-oak bed the dragon lugged his constantly growing bulk and stared at the two players in his latest drama with detached amusement, precisely the expression on Richard's face.

"I know. Nor will I answer it," said Richard. "I suppose you called my office? Suburban of you, but perhaps it's excusable. Just let me say that no, I am not seeing another woman. And no, I am not stealing away to gamble all your hard-earned inheritance at the track or elsewhere. No one knows better than I that gambling's not in our budget. So. Will that satisfy you?"

"No, it will not!" The words tore in ragged sobs from her throat, and she hated herself for letting the tears come so easily. It was admitting defeat, to cry.

Richard made a disgusted noise. "Well, it'll have to do, because that's all the explanation you're getting. I didn't get married to you to make you my warden. Or my conscience. Now if you don't mind, I'm tired and I want to go to sleep." He began to undress.

"You're not sleeping with me!" Diane shrieked at him, and her own image of herself as she wished to be was revolted by the shrewish note in her voice. "Not until you tell me where you've been."

Richard raised one eyebrow and his lips curled. "I'm sleeping in this bed," he said flatly. "If you don't want me sleeping with you, it's your move. Make it and shut up." He finished undressing in a few neat, efficient moves and was under the covers with his eyes closed before she could do anything. The dragon wheezed with laughter and clambered up the blanket to lie across Richard's feet.

That night seemed to have taken place ages ago, thought Diane. She recalled clenching her fists in impotent anger and despair, pacing the bedroom, starting to say half a dozen crushing things to him and giving up on them all. Then she saw the dragon looking at her with cold disdain and she knew that she would stay because that was all she was capable of: surrender.

Since that night she never asked Richard where he had been or commented on any of his decisions. She became a doll who smiled and frowned and wept and loved in order to please her master. Everyone made their own world of happiness in marriage, she thought. This is the way I must make mine.

So perfect, so easy to give in, and now it had all been for nothing.

The doorbell rang and she pressed the admitting buzzer mechanically, not caring to use the intercom and identify her visitor. Richard's brother Lionel looked at her closely when she opened the door to admit him.

"Diane, are you—? Stupid question. Of course you're not all right. Didn't you call anyone to come stay with you last night?"

"Who would I call?" she asked. The words came out of a hollow shell.

"I don't know. A friend, maybe a relative. You shouldn't be alone. Not after the shock."

She managed to laugh in his face. "Isn't it always a shock when it happens to someone in your own family?" she asked with a death's-head grin. "I must've read in the papers a hundred times about crime in the streets, but when it happened to Richard. . . ." She laughed again. And again. Short, sharp, ghastly explosions of laughter that shook her like the final throes of love. Lionel was horrified, helpless. If this was the state she was in now, did he dare to tell her what he knew about his brother's death? Her mind would snap like a celery stalk, her reason collapse like a house of cards.

He had to tell her. It wasn't Lionel's way to hide anything, and he felt she had the right to know. "No one killed Richard," he said softly. "He killed himself."

The room was silent. From the garden below came the sound of pigeons in a panic, making noises that were almost screams. Something outside was chewing.

"No," said Diane.

Lionel nodded. "I'm telling you what I saw when the police called me in to identify him. The wound was self-inflicted. You could still see the powder burns and—"

"No!" Diane stamped her foot. "Richard wouldn't do a thing like that! He wouldn't!"

Lionel tried to hold her, but she jerked away. "Diane, please, I felt the way you do. Richard was never the kind you'd expect to—to commit suicide, but God! How can you ever know? Maybe we thought he'd never do something like that when all along he was heading straight for it."

Richard's faintly supercilious smile flicked into Diane's mind. Was that what he had been trying to do by his odd behavior? Trying to get a rise out of her? Trying to provoke her to fight him until he brought all the inner sickness out into the open where they could combat his personal demons together? And she had only surrendered, doing what was easiest for her. She had killed him as surely as if she had put arsenic in his soup or used the small automatic .22 left conveniently available in her bedside-table drawer, "security" for all those nights when he stayed out so late, so very late.

"I'm getting your things packed," announced Lionel. It made him nervous to look at her when she was like this. He thought of Diane as she had been when he first saw her and felt guilty because that recollection brought back how envious he had been of his brother's choice. How like Richard, who triumphed easily in everything he undertook, to marry the kind of woman other men lacked the imagination even to dream about. "You're going to stay someplace else."

Diane gave him the same vacant, acquiescing look she had so often given to his brother. "Where else is there?" she asked. "Your place?"

Lionel blushed at the thought of Diane, glorious, sophisticated, elegant Diane lodged—however chastely—in his somber apartment. What would she make of the obscure little rooms, the jumble of medieval relics, the clutter of his books and class notes for his courses in Medieval Studies? It would be like persuading a butterfly to take up housekeeping with an owl.

"A hotel," said Lionel. "We'll check you into a hotel near my place until you're feeling better. Where's an overnight bag? I'll pack for you."

Diane shrugged and let him do what he liked. She was childlike in her unquestioning cooperation. Only when her things were packed and Lionel had her almost out the door did she stiffen suddenly and refuse to take another step.

"Oh, what am I thinking of?" she cried. "I forgot him! He can't be left behind, Lionel. Richard was so fond of him, and he loved Richard almost like— well, like a dog. He's in his enclosure in the back. Please, we have to get him.

A pet? thought Lionel. He tried to remember his brother showing anything like interest in a living creature from whom he could not extract some benefit. "All right, but we're going to have a tough time finding a hotel that takes pets," he conceded.

There will be no need for a hotel, said the dragon. I am not leaving this place. And neither are you.

Lionel gazed into the fathomless eyes of the dragon, the eyes that sparkled just on the other side of the window, the eyes that were each as large as a windowpane. Scraps of feathers and flesh, traces of blood clung to the hard, scaly lips. The dragon was sitting comfortably on its haunches in the garden to peer into the second-story window. Its smooth belly blocked the garden door.

"Oh," said Diane, toneless. "There he is now. He's right, you know. We can't leave. He likes it here. It's so convenient to the park. He likes the park. Richard used to take him there."

This is New York City and the twentieth century, thought Lionel, and a good neighborhood. And there is a dragon in this woman's trim, expensive, sooty rear garden. A dragon.

You aren't going mad, the dragon's thoughts leered at Lionel. But you aren't going anywhere. Don't try to leave by the front door. I don't feel like pursuing you, and if you anger me, my reach is very long. Your brother found that out. He learned it the hard way, when he would defy me. For that he died.

Diane was weeping silently, the tears simply brimming up and spilling out of her eyes. The windowpanes melted like ice in sunlight and the dragon slipped his taloned paw inside with absurd gentleness to caress her cheek.

Pretty, he said. So pretty. So fit for all my purposes.

"Please," said Lionel, turning aside so that he no longer had to watch the revolting spectacle of the dragon's caresses. "Please, let her go. If you have to eat something, take me, but let her go. She never hurt you."

Ridiculous, stated the dragon without bothering to look at Lionel. As if anything on this paltry world could hurt me! But you may set your mind at rest, little man. I have something else in mind for her. Something quite else.

The dragon slowly shifted his gaze to Lionel and sent the image in all its force burning into the young professor's brain. The ancient book smoked and crackled like a common log of wood in the heart of the bonfire while formless creatures leaped and capered in the eerie black shadows cast by the flames. The rocks stood firm against the blaze, the old, old manacles still firmly anchored to the heart of the towering green stone. The whirling demons howled and chanted in a tongue whose lightest curse could bring screaming madness to mortals, calling upon the thing they served, the thing they feared and worshiped.

The girl, robed in white, struggled against the iron gyves until her wrists and ankles were rubbed raw and spots of blood stained her silky robes at cuff and hem. The wreath of snowy flowers on her brow looked grotesque, like a jester at a funeral. And then the dragon came.

He was at full girth and growth, his rainbow crest magnificently arrayed down the length of his back and his tail like the crest of a sunlit wave that rises from the lost depths of the ocean and sweeps away cities in its path. The fiends prostrated themselves in abject surrender, the girl's screams lost in the unholy litany they sent climbing up the spirals of smoke to the icy moon. The dragon surveyed their quivering ranks with contempt, then turned his attention to the girl.

She had given up screaming. There was no longer any room in her aching mind for terror. She waited, past caring what would become of her, like a sheep about to be slaughtered. She was sure he would devour her, that she would feel one snap of those titanic jaws and be dead. Somehow it seemed like a relief, to know that the end was almost upon her.

But she did not die. The manacles fell from her wrists and ankles, shattered by the dragon's power, and she stepped free into the circle of firelight. Her heart began to thud uncontrollably. To be so ready for death and to still be alive—! Then she looked into the dragon's eyes, and she saw what he had in mind for her, and the most piteous scream she could ever call up out of the recesses of her soul was a feeble, insufficient thing to express the sheer unthinkable horror awaiting her.

Lionel witnessed it all, the final moments of that long-gone sacrifice. The world where it had taken place was gone now, and the demon-things that offered up the girl, and the gentle race the girl came from; all swallowed up in the never-ending hunger of the dragon. And that girl was only one of many, and Diane would be the first of many more.

You may leave us, said the dragon indifferently. She will stay, but you may go.

Lionel gripped Diane's arm and tried to drag the woman away with him. Even knowing any attempt to evade the monster would be futile, he still felt compelled to try. But Diane was wood. She never responded to the pressure on her arm or to the more and more violent tugs. The expression on her face was almost one of peace. The dragon laughed inside Lionel's head.

Go, he said. You will say nothing about my presence. Not until I call you to me again, Lionel. Little lion. Toothless, clawless little lion, what a splendid tool you shall make for my use. No, you will say nothing of me . . . yet. You know what will happen if you do not obey.

The hard, low, roaring sound of the dragon's mirth followed Lionel out of the house and in his despairing flight back to his own modest apartment. Waves of laughter dogged him, sounding like the cry of hounds, until he slammed the door and sank into his lone leather-covered armchair. An old Thuringian triptych displayed its glories on the wine table beside him. The side panels showed stolid German burghers waiting for their lords while these same lords knelt in feigned humility under the guidance of patron saints, facing the central panel. There the Fall of Man was shown in all its implications, and the gimlet eye of the artist had hung the crucified body of Jesus from the branches of the Tree of Knowledge. Of course the snake bided near, mocking.

Lionel stared.

You will say nothing of me, the dragon spoke with the snake's painted mouth, his massive evil seeming even more terrifying when reduced to the miniature size of the painting. Nothing. You see how far I can reach. You shall see more, little lion.

From the dusty shadows of Lionel's morocco-bound books the five mighty claws came closing in to tighten around the young professor's chest. Tighter and tighter they squeezed, claws like swords biting into his flesh, and it was overwhelming to realize that the dragon was not even expending the tiniest fraction of his true power to destroy the man.

Abruptly, at the point when the room around was beginning to slip away into darkness, Lionel was released. He rolled from his chair and gasped for breath on the floor. His brain was echoing like a brass bowl with the dragon's parting thought.

The lure. I have the lure at last.

Chapter IX

KHWAREMA

In the forest of Beltrani the dew fell from the leaves of the aged beech trees and sparkled on the massed blue-and-purple flowers that sheltered at their roots. Small eyes peered out of the mists to watch the travelers pass and to marvel at their garb. Few folk dared the forest of Beltrani without the protection of a sworn knight, yet none of these wanderers resembled a true fighting man at all.

"When," whispered Sandy, fighting off the fear that kept coming back, "is he going to explain?"

Sanchi was feeling just as nervous, but he would sooner have died than admit it. Now he put on a solid front of unconcern and said, "I don't know, man. This isn't like he explained it to me. You must really rate. This looks like the royal treatment." He essayed a grin, but something cried out of the forest shadows and a creature with naked red wings dipped and chittered around his head, tiny teeth grinding furiously.

"Denars," snarled the knight, swatting at the thing. "I should have known. They're all over the forest at this time of year. Don't touch them if you can help it. They're more dangerous dead than alive."

Sandy shivered as she watched the small beast

flutter back into the shelter of the leaves. Its face was almost human, its wings such a wet, shimmering scarlet that they seemed to have been flayed. A drop of something red fell from the limbs of the beech trees with the dew.

"We haven't a thing to fear," the knight went on, his long strides taking him easily through the tangle of small growth on the forest floor. "I've chosen this time for just that reason. They'll all be together, the lords of Khwarema and the lords of Elfin." He chuckled reminiscently. "Too bad if Conchobar's not there. I'd like for you to meet him. He's the one who taught me everything I know about a sword. Well, maybe it's best if he's gone off on one of his endless sulks. He always hated what he called useless fraternizing with the lords of Elfin, and if he hears that I've lost Belgor, he'd have my finger-bones for tossing-sticks."

"Stand!" The order was barked, but barked in a voice such as Sandy had never heard before. So musical it was, so sweetly lilting even in a single syllable that she deliberately disobeyed the command and marched forward, seeking the speaker.

The knight's firm hand seized her and dragged her back. "Are you out of your mind?" he hissed in her ear. "Haven't you eyes? There's an arrow aimed right at your heart, woman! I didn't bring you this far to lose you."

Sandy peered into the forest darkness and saw nothing, no arrow, no one. Then there came a rustling of leaves and a tall, limber, grim-faced man blocked their path, holding an ivory-colored bow as tall as himself, nocked with a white-fletched arrow.

"Who are you?" he demanded, keeping the bow trained on the three. A flat quiver of mother-of-

pearl bristled with more shafts. Sanchi took one
look at him and understood that he could probably
send a flight of arrows in the time it would take an
ordinary man to fumble out his Saturday Night
Special and fire.

The knight seemed untroubled by the archer's
belligerence. In fact, he laughed in his face. The
archer dropped his dour look momentarily, but his
taut grip on the bowstring never faltered. In spite
of that, the knight stepped ahead, placing himself right in the path of the arrow, shielding Sandra and Sanchi with his own body.

"You're a poor excuse for an elf, Rimmon," he
said. The archer frowned. Slowly he lowered the
bow. "You always were and you always will be,"
the knight went on. "How long before your masters learn that your sight fails you by night? You'd
better tell them, friend, before they find out for themselves. The lords of Elfin aren't known for their
sweet tempers."

The bow fell to the forest floor and the tall man
leaped with outstretched arms to embrace the
knight, making the shadowed air beautiful with
his laughter. "Persiles! May all the gods you follow
damn you black, you sharp-tongued bastard! By
Sel, it's good to see you again. I thought we'd
never see you again. And what"—his eyes slued
around to observe Sandy and Sanchi—"do we
have here?"

"Stand back, Rimmon. Your ugly face'll scare
them off. Then they'll get lost in the forest and I'll
waste what's left of my life finding them. You
know I've got better things to do. Sanchi! Come
here." Reluctantly, Sanchi obeyed. At close range
the tall one called Rimmon began to look a trifle
less than human, and therefore a trifle more up-
setting. His long russet hair, as fine as cornsilk,

hung shining to his shoulders while through it Sanchi could just make out the tips of his sharply tapering ears. Rimmon let Sanchi scrutinize him, maintaining an arch expression the whole time. The colors of a cloudy summer sky whirled and tumbled across his eyes.

"This is my squire," said Persiles. Rimmon tried to repress a laugh.

"Hey!" objected Sanchi. "I'm getting pretty good at it, man! Don't you laugh at me! You ask my boss if I'm good. Ask!"

Rimmon fought a losing battle with his amusement. "Is he," he asked between spurts of merriment, "a worthy—*squire*—for the noble Persiles?"

"Shut up, Rimmon. You were raised by corvels and denars and your mother ate tree-spawn. Bad blood shows."

"Friend," said Rimmon, suddenly serious, "don't presume too far on my good will. You've said in one sentence enough to get yourself slain four times. And for what? To defend the honor of a cub you picked out of the rubbish of another world because there was nothing better on hand to be your squire."

Sanchi made a choked sound in his throat and would have lunged for the elf, but his master's hand held him back and shoved him into Sandy's arms. She was staring at Rimmon like one in a trance.

"Rimmon," said the knight just as severely, "my good will has limits, too. You know me well enough to realize that if the boy weren't equal to what lies before us, I would have done without him. I would have done without a squire entirely. You are blind in the third eye if you believe that only Khwarema can give birth to heroes."

"We were talking about squires," said Rimmon, jocular again. "Not heroes. Come with me. The tables are already set in the banqueting tent, and my lord Yralind has lent his personal corps of minstrels for the evening. The ceremony will be brief, praise Sel, and then . . ." He let his eyes rest warmly on Sandy. She felt them as surely as if they had been the questing, gentle hands of a man enamored.

They followed Rimmon through the beech-tree glade, sometimes sprinting to catch up with the long-legged elf. Not a blade of grass was bent beneath his feet, and his passing was as light as the warm breeze that scattered the dewdrops from the branches.

At last they cleared the last of the forest of Beltrani and found themselves on a hillock overgrown with wild wheat and poppies. The false dusk among the beeches had deceived Sandy into thinking the hour later than it was. Now she saw that the sun—pale as a ripening peach in this strange world—was only just beginning to dip behind the horizon, its final rays picking out the silhouette of a tumbled, abandoned castle. Something about those ruins made Sandy shudder, even though the evening was not that chill.

At the foot of the hillock was a meadow, and sprawled across the meadow were the tents. The fading sunlight glowed on silk pavilions held up by gold-topped poles. Gonfalons snapped and fluttered in the breeze that came out of the west, and a menagerie of fantastic beasts ramped and growled and menaced the innocent bypassers from the thicket of emblazoned shields set out in rows before the pavilion entrances.

"You're surprised to find us here?" asked Rimmon, cocking one eyebrow. The knight merely shook his head, a confusion of emotions on his face too interlocked and intense for the casual viewer to separate or fathom. "Well," the elf went on, "it has its disadvantages. The echoes still plague us here, but so they would in any corner of the world. So we might as well make our stand here, near the ruins. We've grown fond of them. They keep your people and mine well content."

"How?" mumbled the knight, his eyes veiled. "How could Conchobar bear to dwell so close to the scene of—?"

"Oh, well, *Conchobar*—!" Rimmon interrupted. He made a sweeping motion with his slender hands. "Conchobar's a law unto himself. Always was, always will be. He never comes to the tents unless he has to, and he says the only reason he'd have to would be when you—and I quote, so don't hold it against me—when you came to your senses, if you ever had sense, and called on him for the help you've always needed but are too mud-pig blind and garsem-stubborn to demand."

"Yes." The knight smiled ruefully. "That sounds like Conchobar, all right. Just as well he's far from here."

Sanchi gave his master one of his peculiarly penetrating looks. He was mulling over the sword again. Yeah, that was it. Stupid sword. Hadn't Sanchi scrounged him half a dozen good blades—everything from yataghans to damascened Iberian court-swords—from every goddamn pawnshop in Manhattan? Half a dozen, did he say? Half a hundred. And each time he had been turned back by a frown and a curt shake of the head by good old George. Hell, what did he want? A sword's a sword, isn't it? Maybe he expected Sanchi to go over the bridge and rummage through Queens and Brooklyn pawnshops too? The hell he would. There were some sacrifices that weren't in his contract. Brooklyn! Jeezus.

Now a stirring came from the tents below. People dressed in the ornate livery of high-placed servants and tall ones of Rimmon's race garbed as greenwood hunters came from the pavilions bearing torches. The evening breeze brought a tantalizing hint of the fragrant wood of the blazing links, and the scent grew headier as the lighters hastened to thrust their torches into the footed braziers scattered throughout the encampment. Small chips of sandalwood incense were mingled with the coals.

"Shall I announce you?" asked Rimmon with false deference.

The knight patted him on the back and said, "None of your gibes tonight, Rimmon. You know what it costs me to come here like this. And you know what's in store for me."

The elf shrugged. "I thought you'd put an end to it once and for all, this time. You could, you know. I thought you'd come for us at last. But I see by your looks that you're still the stubborn fool Conchobar always said you were."

"You don't understand!" the knight exploded. At the sound of his voice the lighters paused in their tracks, frozen into a pattern of flames that winked and gleamed in lesser reflection from the flaunted shields. "Why can't you see what's tormenting me, you who always boasted about how much more *sensitive* your people are than mine!"

Rimmon suppressed something—it might have been a laugh, but Sandra didn't think the beautiful, strong, elfin face could harbor that sort of cruelty. Abruptly Rimmon's expression sobered. "There is no further talk of your people or my people now, Persiles," he said. "I only wish it had come earlier. Then we might have had a chance.

But we don't dwell on what's past here, unlike you. Open your eyes, Persiles. It may save you."

He would have said more, but the approach of a company of men forestalled him. They were shorter than the elf, but more substantially built, and their faces wore smiles of untarnished welcome. Servants flanked them with flambeaux, for the sun was completely down and night came swiftly out of the beech wood.

"Persiles! By all the gods, it's good to see you!" boomed the foremost man. He wore a light tunic that grazed his knees, with an alien beast embroidered across his chest in an attitude of watchful awareness. On his legs were sandals of soft buff leather with long thongs that crisscrossed up his sturdy legs until the tunic hid them. The men who came after him were similarly attired, differing only in the colors of their tunics and the heraldic devices emblazoned there.

"And it's good to see you, too, Cham," said the knight, but Sanchi saw something besides happiness in his master's look. Regret. Deep sorrow and regret beyond words. "I see you've stolen yet another leaf from the elves' book." He pointed to the sandals.

The one called Cham looked shamefaced. "Well, they are more comfortable," he mumbled. "And it's summer. It was stupid to cling to our heavy riding boots in summer. It always was, but we were stubborn, weren't we? Stubborn about more things than wearing boots in the heat." He looked the knight straight in the eyes.

"I am not among you an hour and already I'm beset on all sides with object lessons against stubbornness," the knight replied, trying to make light of the entire matter. "Come, Cham, escort us before His Majesty, won't you? I've a lot to tell, and damned if I'll tell it without a drink. Oh, this is my squire." He pushed Sanchi forward. The boy put on a bold look under the curious stares of Cham's companions. To his chagrin, they didn't waste much time surveying him before giving the knight their full attention once more.

"Never mind the stripling; who's the wench?" roared a daring voice from the back of the crowd. "You'll have hell to pay for her tonight, Persiles!"

"Wench yourself, you son of a—" Sandy Horowitz checked herself in mid-curse. Somehow she had the feeling that she was in a place where women were neatly divvied into two sorts, the ladies and the wenches. And while she was pretty sure that loving didn't mark the border between one class of girl and another, foul language did.

The knight smiled gently and led her into the torchlight delicately by the hand, as if he held something very precious.

"The lady Sandra could boast as much knowledge as a lesser mage, if she chose to boast. But her discretion exceeds her knowledge and her beauty exceeds her discretion." Then he dropped the flowery niceties of courtly speech and added, "The next corvel who calls her a wench answers to me."

"You'll still have hell to pay for her," reiterated the voice, somewhat less boldly. "Or have you forgotten your lady as well as your sword-mates?"

"Be still, Gundar," came a second voice, soft and sweet and strong as the breathless arc of a blade. "Persiles will never forget either his sword-mates or me, to the gates of death and beyond."

The torches parted and Sanchi gasped. He recognized the infinitely lovely woman who came through the flickering gauntlet. Even by firelight her skin bloomed like a flower newly opened to the dew and the sun. Her dark hair shone like the starlit sea. No one told him to do so, by word or gesture, but still Sanchi awkwardly knelt at her approach. He wished he had something to offer her. Desperately he plucked a tuft of poppies at his feet and proffered them clumsily, keeping his eyes averted.

He felt a smooth, cool hand take them, but she said no word of thanks. She didn't need to thank him. He could feel her smile as clearly as if he saw it by broad daylight. Out of the corner of his eye he glanced at his master, half-expecting him to be kneeling also. He was not. Not physically kneeling. But Sanchi believed that someplace inside his master was humbling himself before the lady just as sincerely as his squire.

"Come," said the lady, drawing her light-green cloak about her shoulders. "We must welcome Persiles back in proper style. Why do you all stand here chatting on a hilltop when civilized beings live in tents? His Majesty knows you are here, Persiles, and waits for you."

Silently Persiles came to take his lady's hand and let her lead him down the hill. The others stood back a few paces and let the lovers go, giving them the courtesy of solitude. Only when they were well away did Cham start down the hill after them.

"Who is she?" asked Sandy, half-aloud, her voice confused with admiration and envy. "Who is she?"

"That," Rimmon was suddenly at her side, "is Persiles' lady. I thought it was obvious."

"But what's her name?" demanded Sandy. Her bitterness made her strike out at the elf for no reason. "I thought that my *question* was obvious to an intelligent being."

They were face to face, woman and elfin archer.

The last of the torches was trickling down the hill to the camp, leaving them with only stars and faint moonlight. There was a great emptiness inside her that Sandy struggled against now as she had many times before in her own world when she had seen lovers pass and feared that she would never share that special certainty that nothing else mattered more. Only the beloved, only the love.

Rimmon's eyes glowed softly, like a cat's, but immeasurably more spellbinding. "My people," he said, "were never famed for our intelligence. We are the despair of mages and enchantresses who have sought to teach us things over the centuries. We cling to the small magics we were born to, the powers over wind and water and the lives of gentle things. I'm sorry if my blunders have upset you, my lady."

For answer, Sandy began to cry. The elf took her gently into his arms and let her cry. There were few tears, only wrenching sobs. "Persiles is lucky," murmured Rimmon.

The way he said that made Sandy jerk her head up and confront him. "Lucky! My God, if that's not an understatement. Did you ever see any woman that beautiful before? Lord knows I never did. There's no one who can touch her!"

Rimmon smiled. Sandy could see the thin, white line of his teeth by the moon. "That wasn't what I meant," he said. "Never mind. I hate explanations almost as much as Persiles does. Our nights are not especially warm. We should go into the camp. You'll want to see His Majesty, won't you?"

"I hear an awful lot about His Majesty this and His Majesty that," said Sandy as Rimmon escorted her toward the massed tents. "But who is he? I mean, he must be king, but king of what? King of whom? And why king in a tent, Rimmon? I saw something on that other hill that looked like a tumbledown palace. Have your people forgotten how to build?''

Rimmon chuckled before answering. "By Sel, you ask a plagued lot of questions, woman! And you know I hate explanations. Persiles obviously brought you here to show you what he means rather than to tell you. That's wise, I'd say. You strike me as the sort of lass who demands proof.''

"I see," said Sandy grimly. "You think I'm some kind of child who has to see it before she'll believe it. Thanks a lot.''

They were among the tents. A banner of green sarcenet sprinkled with a pattern of golden bees waved languidly above Rimmon's head. They were still a ways from the largest pavilion, from which the sounds of celebration spread over the entire camp. The knight was receiving welcome home. An intricately wrought brass stand held a shallow dish of fire high, casting changing shadows over the faces of elf and woman.

"Talk is useless," said Rimmon, his mien grave. She had hurt him with her outburst. "You had better rejoin Persiles. You don't want to hear what I have to say." He wheeled sharply and vanished into the tent of the green banner.

Sandy stood alone in the aisle between the tents. The echoes of revelry called to her; called fruitlessly. She could picture what she would find in the large tent. Music and feasting, most likely, and Persiles—she had heard the knight called this too often for her to doubt his name—certain to be seated in a place of honor near the king. And on his other side, the beautiful lady, and nothing but her presence would fill his eyes and his heart. He would not notice whether Sandra was there or not. While he held his lady's hand, he inhabited a closed world where only two could pass.

She lifted the flap of the elf's tent and went in.

She expected to find primitive arrangements. She had been prepared for what most people would call "barbaric splendor." Instead she found herself in an atmosphere of refined elegance and sophisticated appointments fit to rival the classically simple yet luxurious country manors of old England. Silken carpets in subtle hues of blue and cream covered the floor, and she saw that they lay on wide, well-hewn boards rather than raw earth. The tent was star-shaped, the central pole of silver carved to resemble the light spray of a fountain. Cressets of carven rock crystal hung suspended at intervals by fine golden chains to light the room. In one corner was a well-arranged library in miniature, in another a careful tumble of musical instruments. Finally, where she had thought to find a rough pallet covered with animal skins, Rimmon stretched at his ease on a delicately fashioned beechwood bed whose pillars curved up and inward to meet in a tangle of perfectly depicted vines and flowers.

He swung his legs off the bed and sat up the moment her feet brushed the carpet. A scroll was in his hands, one he had obviously been reading, although he had taken it up in a very bad temper. The parchment was crumpled where he had been too angry and impatient to unroll it properly.

"My lady does my humble tent an undeserved honor" he said with a cutting edge. "Or have you simply come to see how one of my kind lives? Well?" His gesture took in the whole tent. "Are you impressed? Or disappointed?"

Sandy lowered her eyes. "I came to apologize," she murmured. She refused to look at Rimmon, although she suspected he was gazing at her with that funny, mischievously questioning look he had so often given Persiles and his companions.

"An apology," repeated the elf. She heard the light sound of his barefoot approach over the silky rugs, the breath of a dragonfly. "Why?"

"Because I was rude to you," she said, her voice still low. "It was unforgivable. I felt so unhappy, I just hit at the nearest thing." She ventured to raise her head. "That was you." She smiled ruefully. "I'm sorry."

Rimmon laughed and touched her chin. "Accepted. I've had worse things said and done to me in my lifetime. In fact—"

He never had the chance to finish what he was saying. The sides of the silk tent began to sway, slowly at first, as if a strong wind had sprung up outside. The cressets shook and tinkled against one another at the end of their chains, and from somewhere far away an eerie wailing rose and whipped itself into a shrieking that grated through the skin down to the bone. The earth underfoot trembled.

Rimmon seized Sandy and dragged her from the tent just as the slender silver central pole tottered and collapsed against the pile of fragile musical instruments. The crash also brought down the cressets along with the rest of the tent. Little flecks of flame began hungrily to devour the green pennant sewn with golden bees.

They ran through a camp that had been turned into a rout. Everywhere around them men and elves were running, screaming, cursing, dragging out their swords and lances and bows. They ran without watching where they went. They ran down their companions and were in turn jostled and sent sprawling by them. The shrieking in the heavens sounded louder, and Sandy turned once to see a dull-red glow beginning to edge its way sluggishly over the ruined stone lip of the crumbled castle. Then Rimmon and she gained the safety of the forest of Beltrani and she could see nothing but leaves.

Rimmon threw himself down on a thick pile of beech leaves. She sank down beside him, panting. "What is it?" she asked when she got her breath back. She had to shout. The winds whipped through the thick branches overhead and the cries of the others left behind in the encampment mingled with a sound more awful than the death-cries of the innocent, more irresistible than the baying of winter-famished wolves.

"The echo," said the elf. "It is the echo of his passing."

"Whose passing? For God's sake, what kind of an echo could turn that camp into chaos?" demanded Sandy. Her voice was full of anger, but underneath there ran a note of panic. Rimmon himself looked paler. The forest floor shuddered, then heaved spasmodically, sending her tumbling against him. He held her close while the woods themselves grew even darker than the night and the leafy canopy could account for. The wildness of the coming tempest wailed and whimpered malevolently, slithering through the thickets, tearing at the tree limbs with claws of icy rain.

"The shadow of evil," said Rimmon while Sandy buried her head gratefully in his shoulder. "The shadow of the dragon."

She looked up at him then, and she gasped when she read a hurt and a sorrow in the elf's ever-changing eyes that ran threads of pain like electric wires through him from feet to fingertips. His slender hands clenched and she realized that he was just as fearful as she was, and suddenly nothing else mattered to her but that together they must fight the fear and the encroaching evil by any means they could.

They had only one sword for such a fight. Something made them look hard at each other and see the terror neither one would admit, and cover that terror deep in the burning heart of a kiss. Rimmon's mouth was sweet on hers, sweeter than any she could recall out of all the kisses she had known. Her fears melted away one by one and her hands touched him shyly, then gradually became bolder and bolder still while the winds slashed down at them with hail that burned like fire.

He loved her without haste, without urgency, and yet with a hard, hungry wanting that transformed her until she dreamed that she and he were streams of living water coming together in a glorious light, so natural, so burning, meant to happen from the first. He murmured words she could not understand yet sensed, and she reveled in the strength and pleasure that coursed between them, seemingly without end. Their clothes lay scattered like windblown petals and the rain that penetrated the beech woods made their bodies sleek and lissome as young otters. The winds groaned and drew the echo of the dragon away with the storm before the lovers fell away from each other to whisper a last tender name before sleep came.

Sandy awakened in Rimmon's arms, his russet hair falling across her face in gossamer strands that fluttered with her every breath. Wonderingly she reached out to touch the incredibly translucent skin, soft as a baby's, beneath which ran his supple young muscles. Her touch woke him. Sunlight dappled his face. He smiled and began to make love to her again while the daylight grew stronger and the sun warmed the earth.

At the last of their embrace, Rimmon cast his eyes about and said, "Here's a fine state of things! Forgive me, my lady, but it looks as if sometime while we were—sometime during the night, your clothes were discovered by a most discourteous corvel." He reached out and held up a tattered blouse for her inspection. "Corvels," he explained, "claw things."

Sandy stared at what was left of her blouse and began to giggle. "I guess it'll be pretty plain what we were up to," she said. There was not a touch of regret in her voice.

Rimmon looked stern. "I won't have the men making jests at your expense, my lady. My own people have enough grace to pretend momentary blindness, but yours—" He considered the matter while he pulled on his breeches. The questing claws of the corvel had been foiled by the butter-soft elfin-cured leather. His leather shirt was also untouched, and Sandy's skirt had been overlooked in the dark. Bare-chested, he dressed her in his shirt as reverently as if he were decking an idol.

"That must do," he stated firmly. "And if any man opens his mouth about it, I'll see to him." He kissed her tenderly and started back for camp.

"I wonder how much is left standing after last night," mused Sandy. Rimmon squeezed her hand.

"At least now there's no need for me to explain why we live in tents. The echo comes less and less frequently, but still often enough. And it will continue to come so long as the dragon lives. All acts leave imprints of themselves on the worlds of being, sweet lady. Our loving will leave it's little mark, and our quarrel. But nothing leaves so strong a print as evil, and the ghosts of great evils return time after time to reenact their tragedies. The dragon knows. Even on your world, he knows when the echo comes on this world, and on the other worlds he's marked. He grows fat on it, my lady, fat and powerful each time the echo comes, and the echo will never stop coming until he is dead."

They emerged from the forest and Sandy gave a delighted gasp. The camp stood as perfect and as beautiful as she had first seen it. Even Rimmon's pale-yellow tent flaunted its green banner.

"We are used to the shadow coming now," said the elf. "We've learned how to wipe out all traces of it as soon as it goes."

Few people were abroad in the camp. They passed one or two elfin equerries who acted as if they saw a half-stripped archer and a mortal woman garbed in his leather hunting shirt every day. Inside Rimmon's tent, evidence waited to prove that the events of the previous night had really happened. Two of the crystal cressets lay smashed past repair. The musical instruments were a pile of splinters and a tangle of broken strings. Scorches defaced the silken carpets.

Even Rimmon's magnificent bed had suffered minor damage. A few of the sculpted flowers had been badly chipped, but that was all. The lovers sprawled on the downy cushions and enjoyed each other once again. The sun wandered through the sky unheeded and it was nearly evening before ordinary hunger compelled them to part.

Rimmon knelt at the corner of one of his prized rugs and began to pry at the floorboards. A square of wood came up easily. He reached into the hole thus revealed and drew out a green-and-crimson-figured clay bottle.

"Wine?" asked Sandy.

"The best," replied Rimmon. He produced a pair of wafer-thin glasses overlaid with tiny silver trails of seaweed. Mermaids and hippocamps sported in a sea of wine. A plate of strange, tantalizing fruits materialized from a hidden cupboard to complete Rimmon's offering.

The first flask of wine was gone and the second well-started when Sandy noticed something that intrigued her. It was part of the silver tent-pole—now slightly battered—and the brightly limned medallion portrait seemed to follow the watcher with large, haunted eyes. It was the semblance of an elfin woman.

Rimmon saw where Sandy's eyes had wandered. "That is Jelana," he said quietly. "My wife." Before Sandy could speak, he laid his fingers on her lips. "She died long ago," he said. "We married young and she died young. It was in the days when the dragon's raids were only short, infrequent shocks. When he ambushed her in Beltrani Wood she was gathering flowers and sweet herbs to perfume our home. My sovereigns were very sorry, of course, but what could they do? It would be impossible for elves to carry on the way that mad mortal, Sir Persiles, was doing. He made too much of a dragon, they said. We would watch for it and kill it if we found it, as we had killed other dragons. Ridiculous to think it was more than an ordinary worm."

The portrait inlaid on the tent-pole seemed to smile, an aura of serenity mantling the long yellow hair, the gleaming white shoulders. Sandy felt no pang of jealousy, only a blurred sorrow and an impossible wish that Jelana were still alive.

"I shall never see her again," murmured Rimmon. "Our deaths were severed." He drank another cup of wine, then stretched his empty glass toward Sandy, who held the flask. She gazed at him without moving, her lips pale.

" 'Our deaths'?" she echoed.

Rimmon looked puzzled. "Have I said something wrong? Have I offended against your gods, perhaps? We believe that when the dead go one by one, in the natural order, they find a second life where we may one day join them. But on the day that the dragon unfolded his wings and spread his claws across the sun, he slew a world and all on it. At first," the elf went on, unconscious of the wild look creeping into Sandy's eyes, "we thought we were held under another of his black spells. But little by little we came to know that we and everything around us had been wiped from the physical universe. Our world was plunged into annihilation, our world as it was in life, and so we dwell here as we always have done, but this is the death we are bound to, and we can never hope to find the world where our loved dead walk."

"No," said Sandy in a strangling voice. "Why are you saying this, Rimmon? You're not dead! How can you love me like that and be—?"

"I still can love as I loved in life, my lady," said the elf. His eyes grew dark as the sky before a storm. "And I do love you."

"And—and the knight?" Sandy scarcely recognized her own words. She felt removed from her body, watching it move its lips to let the sounds come out. They meant nothing to her. "Persiles. He's dead too."

"No, not he. Before the end came, the dragon lured him from this world, then hastened back on his own tracks to destroy us. Some say he did it because he knew he couldn't strike the final blow while Persiles was near. Others say he did it because he deliberately sought to spare Persiles. Because of what he once was to the monster. Because he loved him."

"Impossible." Sandy shook her head. A dry beech leaf fell among the airy bedsheets and she crumpled it. "How can I love you so, and you're dead? Impossible."

"More impossible than loving a living elf?" Rimmon teased gently. "Or less?"

"An elf!" Sandy gave a false laugh. "God, I've been making love to a mythical creature, haven't I? Any second now I expect to wake up under observation at Bellevue." Her laughter sounded shrill, metallic. Rimmon let his wine cup smash to broken glass and crumpled silver on the floor and took her in his arms. Her laughter changed to tears.

She never noticed the fragment of blood-red stone that the elf fastened carefully around her neck by a silver cord. When Sanchi came to fetch her back to their familiar world, she went wrapped in the soft white dress that Jelana had once worn, and a silver flower was in her hair.

Chapter X

LIONEL

He felt the usual tightening in the pit of his stomach as he brought his last class of the day to an end. It was Friday. The students were fidgeting; even the graduate auditors were under strain to keep up their masks of dedication. Their minds were on the weekend.

His mind was on hell.

He dismissed the class coldly, going through the familiar motions of gathering up his papers, getting his always-there umbrella from the corner, marching down the hall and into the street, avoiding the more hostile routes to the subway. He was going to Diane's place. He always went to Diane's place after work, every day, without fail. There was hell to pay if he failed to come. Painful hell. But the ritual awaiting him in that sleekly furnished townhouse came close to hell by hairs.

He had been given his role and he was expected to play it. He knew well what it was. He was a toy, a plaything. He amused the creature that wrapped its horny bulk once around the building with ease, yet had the power of illusion great enough to go invisible to human eyes. Or to appear as Diane's pampered pet lizard when in the mood. Or to take any form it chose, to animate precise replicas of living beings, and dead.

No one bothered him on the subway in spite of the fact that he had lately begun to seek out the cars most closely packed with the hating eyes, the envious eyes, the malicious eyes. There remained a corner of his mind that the dragon could not reach, and from that still-smoldering bit of self left to him by his tormentor, Lionel knew that he was seeking freedom, even if it could only be the freedom of death.

But death turned away from him. He could walk the streets of the city anywhere, at any hour, and no one would touch him. When the small, nearly smothered voice within cried out for liberty, he plunged into the midnight caverns of New York, and came out unharmed. They shied away from him. In the subway, on the street, they shied away. The mumbling crazies and the hot-eyed youth would sum him up, gauge the possibilities, start to move in, then freeze as if transfixed on the point of a spear. They ran away.

Lionel arrived at Diane's front door and let himself in with the key. It was no duplicate. He held the original, and his dead brother's copy had never been found. Diane never left the apartment except when it pleased the dragon to release her for a brief walk through the park. As with Lionel, a halo of revulsion seemed to cling to her. Go, said the dragon at any hour of the day or night, and Diane went into Central Park, exchanging empty glances with furtive men who reached for their guns and then, for no reason they could think of later, ran away from her. When she wanted to get back inside, the dragon's will alone was the universal key.

Today, noted Lionel as he came into the living room, the beast was in a fey mood. He had willingly dwindled down to the size of a field mouse, and he scampered up and down Diane's naked arms and legs briskly, nervously, while he addressed Lionel. His rainbow crest was a sliver of brightness against the woman's pale skin, a moving sickle of blood.

Welcome, manling. It was the usual greeting, almost a ritual. What followed was indeed part of their evening rite. A copy of the *Daily News* lay on the floor. Chuckling, the dragon flickered down to perch on Lionel's instep. He knew what was expected of him. He got down on his belly and began the methodical turning of pages.

That one, said the dragon, his tongue tickling Lionel's ear. No, beside it. Yes, that one. That was my doing.

It was the story of the murder—robbery suspected—of an old diamond broker on Canal Street. So the dragon had already begun to make himself a proper bed.

Turn the page, he said. That one. And the one next to it. In the subway, as you call it. Fascinating. And entertaining. Most entertaining.

A young couple on their way home to Brooklyn were found dead in the car at Hoyt Street. A child was missing, feared kidnapped. No news of ransom demands. The dragon leered.

Most entertaining.

So it went, from page to page, the dragon gleefully underscoring the crimes that bore his mark and that went unnoticed among the raft of shootings, stabbings, gangland slayings, and unsolved deaths decorating the newspaper pages like the medieval illuminations of saints. At last they closed the paper. It was time to go on to the business of the night.

Diane sat cross-legged on the sofa, her only gar-

ment a clinging teddy of black lace and satin.
Lionel winced. Her face was heavily painted. She
looked like a whore, a cheap one. The dragon was
laughing. He was in rare good humor tonight to
let Diane play the clown for him. Normally that
was Lionel's task.

*Isn't she lovely? Do you want her, little man?
She won't turn you away. As a token of my gratitude for your continued cooperation I will guarantee the sincerity of her kisses, the heat of her
embrace. I could even make her want you. If you
like.*

Lionel shook his head. "Not tonight," he croaked.

Tonight or never, manling, smiled the dragon.
*Very well; never. But I trust you will still continue
to serve me?*

Lionel didn't answer. The tiny clamoring light
inside his skull hurled curses at the dragon, but
Lionel himself couldn't even open his lips to reply.

Excellent, said the dragon, just as if Lionel had
given a flowery oath of eternal devotion to a beloved master. *Then listen to me, and listen well.
Tonight there is something you must do.*

Lionel shuddered. Diane was watching him carefully, leaning forward on the couch so that the
curve of her breasts was clearly visible above the
froth of black lace. He would do whatever he was
commanded, he knew that already. He only hoped
it wouldn't be something touching Diane.

There, said the dragon. *On the mantel.*

Lionel scanned the marble mantel and saw nothing. Nothing beyond the Dresden shepherdess and
the goggle-eyed pair of blue-streaked Staffordshire
dogs. Yes, and the small, round pillbox perched
between the shepherdess' dainty beribboned feet,
blue-enamel sides and a bouquet of late-summer
flowers delicately hand-painted on the lid.

Take it. Open it.

It warmed his hand when he touched it. He half-expected to find a lump of live coal inside. Or perhaps a demon in miniature. On the inside of the lid was a tiny black-and-white drawing of a wide-belled horn and scrolls of music surmounted by the words "Forget-me-not" immortalized in fanciful calligraphy.

There was a single lump of white sugar inside.

Tomorrow, said the dragon, you're going to feed it to a horse.

A wave of seeing curled invisibly high over Lionel's bent head, hung there a moment, then crashed down upon him. His eyes were flooded with sight, and the small bit of him still stubbornly free of the dragon seemed to howl dismally as it was swept away by the force that invaded his vision.

Darkness. The glow of fire. An old man bent over an older book. Obscure clutter in the shadows behind him. Outside the soothing sound of warm autumn rain on crowns of ancient trees. A blazing fire of fragrant pine in the circular hearth freestanding in the center of the room; the cave.

It is a cave beyond doubt. A naked boy comes creeping to the doorless rocky entrance, his dark hair pasted in curved spikes against his high forehead. His eyes are too full of hunger and cold to fear the old sorcerer. And they are full of a greater fear and a greater knowledge. The sight of the old man's book freezes the boy half-in and half-out of the cave. He stays so until the mage looks up, sees him, and shuts the ironbound hasps.

There are thin leather sandals on the boy's feet and a limp leather bag in his hand with a small bulge at the bottom. The wizard rises from his studies to coax the child closer, but he is the first to perceive that he is not addressing a child. The boy's thick-fringed eyes hold knowledge, and knowledge always brings a dark ending to any childhood. Knowledge and fear, the fear of knowledge.

They are speaking, but Lionel cannot understand what they say. The tiny spark of his selfhood strains toward the words, fighting the currents of the dragon's power to draw him into an alien world and an alien past. And then he knows what they say—not word for word, but thought for thought—and new visions dawn behind the captive teacher's eyes.

A sword. In all the worlds only one sword whose iron holds the destiny of a dragon's death.

A shield. Plain oak-wood overlaid with flashing silver, gem-bright, marked with battle-runes, and yet those runes are only chicken-scratchings, the silver only empty show. It is the wood itself that will stand against the breath of dragons, the wood hewed from a bearded oak beneath whose branches the pale-green egg first hatched, the wood that witnessed its own death when the newly born worm infected the old oak's roots with its poison. Shelter repaid with treachery, but the wood was strong and would not forget.

And the last, a horse. White and trembling in the straw at his mother's feet, tottering upright, roaming the hills of the north wind, defying all comers, all would-be masters, until one should come whom the steed would recognize. The only horse fit to bear a knight into battle against a dragon.

The old magician smiled at the boy with his eyes. He had recognized the boy, even if the fabulous stallion had not yet found him. He looked at slim brown hands and imagined them closed around the pommel of the sword. He saw the skinny arms and dreamed the fated shield on them. All this had been written long ago. With sword, with shield, with steed together, the boy could not fail to triumph.

Without one of the three, gloated the dragon, the chances grow dimmer. Take the sugar, Lionel. You will go with it where I tell you. You will do with it what I now say. The white horse will look larger than any of the others with him, although the city grime has turned him streaky gray. You will feed it to him.

"It won't work," protested Lionel. The sugar cube was beginning to dissolve around the edges in his sweating hands. "If he—if the horse isn't . . . ordinary, he'll know why I've come."

The dragon switched his tail back and forth, the golden eyes chilling. You are clever, manling. But you are a fool to think so little of me. I will lift my touch from you before you go. No scent of my presence will be on you. You will be—the dragon smiled coldly—like other men. But you will still do my bidding whether I hold you mindlinked or not. Because you will remember me, and my power, and the one I still hold.

Automatically Lionel looked at Diane. How long had he been walking through the dragondreams? She had scrubbed her face clean of makeup. She had covered the black lace with a rose-colored summer robe of sprigged muslin. Her bare feet and hands struck Lionel with their simple beauty.

"Lionel," she said, her voice seeming to come from far away, through clouds. "Lionel, only you can save me."

And he saw himself mounted on the big white horse, splendid in armor, holding the shield and brandishing the sword against the dragon, slaying it, cutting the bonds that held Diane linked to a cool, seaweed-shrouded rock while the waves of a different sea lapped about her naked feet. He wiped the dragon's blood from his sword and embraced her.

Then the seaweed smoothed itself into emerald scales and the gray rock sent out paws and claws and fangs and golden eyes. It smashed one heavy paw down and broke the sword. It roared flames, and the shield fell to ashes. It snapped its ponderous jaws once, and the stallion was a mangled heap of blood, torn flesh, cracked bones.

Manling, hissed the dragon. See that you do not forget me.

Inside his head Lionel heard a screeching sound, like a rabbit in a snare, and the room swam. He thought he only closed his eyes for a moment, but when he opened them he was stretched out on Diane's front steps, clutching an enameled copper pillbox in his right hand. And immediately he knew that he was free. There was no sense of the other crowding his brain, no feeling of being watched, no weight on his shoulders where an invisible dragonling perched and curled its tail around his neck. Free.

Lionel leaped to his feet and stretched his hands for the heavens. Free. Nothing impossible to him now. He could pluck the stars like apples. He could cut the moon in two like a melon and swallow it down. He could—

Obey, whimpered the newly liberated scrap of himself that had survived the dragon's imposed captivity. You know you must obey him. Find the horse. Feed it its death, guarantee that the dragon shall live forever.

But there are other horses, Lionel told himself.

And other swords? And other shields? And other women like Diane? his voice mocked gently, kindly. You know how you used to hate jigsaw puzzles.

The pieces all looked so similar, but there was only one place for each piece to fit. Only one.

Then I'll throw this away, thought Lionel. It would be the easiest thing in the world to let the enameled box slip from his hand and roll into a sewer opening. Easier to let the sugar cube itself fall underfoot and be crushed to powder.

The dragon's left me, said Lionel to himself. And—I don't know why, but—but I think there isn't any way for him to take me again.

Lionel felt exultant. Even the gritty night air tasted fresh and cool in his mouth. The steps of the New York townhouse towered into a clear-blue mountain peak where Lionel stood untouchable, ruling the ways of the winds.

The hollow clip of hastening footsteps on the street brought him down from his mountain stronghold. His watch's glowing face told him the lateness of the hour, yet here came a lone woman, trotting smartly toward him and heading in the direction of Central Park. But no, the park wasn't her destination. She was looking at the numbers on the row of townhouses. She was scurrying along like a little mouse, darting her bright eyes from one building to the next, always checking back to the slip of white paper in her hand. And she stopped right in front of Lionel.

"Excuse me, sir," she asked in musical, slightly accented English. "You are standing in front of the house number. I am looking for an address. Do you know if Mrs. Walters—? Ah! Never mind." She had glimpsed the iron numbers behind him. "This is the place." Politely she edged past him and rang Diane's bell. The door buzzed and she slipped inside.

Who was that? Lionel wondered. He thought about going in after her, but the uneasy breath of cowardice blew across the back of his neck, making his hairs prickle. If he went back in so soon, without having accomplished his mission, what would the dragon do? To him? To Diane?

Maybe Diane's hired a maid, he shrugged. Or a companion. Maybe she's advertised for a roommate.

Did she look like the kind of woman Diane would have for anything but a servant? asked his voice. The plain nylon-print dress, the battered sandals, the vinyl pocketbook—are they the marks of Diane Walters' chosen companion? There is another hand in this, a taloned hand. He grows restless. He wants more room, more of this world. He wants to feel the limits of his strength, but he is too wise to risk losing Diane while he is gone.

A watchdog, thought Lionel, and he wondered whether the black-haired little woman who had just disappeared into the townhouse realized what awaited her. Well, what did that matter? Once she was there and her eyes met those golden eyes, she would have no choice. And to come answering a summons at this hour of the night indicated just how much she was willing to risk for the possibility of a job. She might submit willingly. The perfect watchdog, a loyal one.

Something cold and moist brushed Lionel's cheek, something that bore the reek and tang of dark places.

Here, said the dragon. He was clinging to the wall behind Lionel, down to iguana size again. His breath enveloped the young professor's face in waves of nauseating fetor.

"What do you want?"

To set your mind at ease, manling. You waste your time in needless worries. I have summoned another to keep Diane company. To serve her. And to serve me. For you see, manling, I may have need of you again, after you have carried out this mission. And since I can—do not choose to bring you to me by the old ways, I will send the woman for you. Also I will send her for you if you disobey.

The dragon looked amused. No protests? he asked archly. Do you think you have no reason to fear such a small thing as that little woman? Well, manling, believe that and you will find yourself dead.

Lionel could hardly stay on his feet. Never had he felt the overwhelming sensation of suffocation from the dragon's breath before. His eyes clouded, then the mists parted as the dragon sent him a final vision. He was only vaguely conscious of the effort the monster had to expend to pierce his eyes.

The small woman sat in a cramped apartment reading a romance magazine. Lionel caught sight of a few Spanish words on the glossy cover. The room was neat but shabby. The woman wore the same dress he had seen her in, but her feet were stuck into terry-cloth slippers. Suddenly she heard something—again Lionel was shut out of hearing what he saw—and sprang from the chair, hurrying into a shadowy corner. When she turned toward Lionel again, she held a brown-haired infant in her arms, its mouth open in silent squalling. She smiled and offered it her breast.

She will be happy to bring the child here, the dragon stabbed through the peaceful vision. Such a kind employer, Mrs. Diane Walters. A widow with such a large house, and no babies of her own. Bring the child, live here with me, Diane will tell her. And she will. She will because I will have it. And then, with the child here, there will be nothing that tiny woman will not do, if I command her, to protect her son.

The dragon chuckled. It sounded like the clicking of a black beetle.

Not that it will matter in the end, he said. The reek grew thicker as the monster felt the thrill of anticipation flow through his body like a warm tide. Nothing will matter in the end but my will.

Tiny wings spread themselves from the dragon's shoulders, wings radiant with a dull, sullen glow. The dragon sprang from the wall and fluttered around Lionel's head like a bat, then soared between the blind rows of townhouses, seeking the sky. He grew as he climbed higher, and the beating of titanic wings sent a muffled roaring through the huddled trees of the park. The dragon rose up to his full majesty, black against the moon.

Nothing will matter but my will.

Chapter XI

SANDY

It was an education for Sanchi, was the letter. He had never seen a letter like this one before. Sandra Horowitz was amazed. Incredible, just incredible! Her mother could be twice as sulky, self-pitying, and put-upon in print as she could orally.

The letter had been waiting for her in George's mailbox. She and Sanchi still called him George, the alien syllables of Persiles sounding out of place in the way they chose to live. Persiles, pick up some milk at the store. Persiles, have you seen my left shoe? Persiles, take out the garbage. All wrong.

Sandra:

(Nice touch, that colon, and the lack of "Dear." Mom was loaded for bear. She had typed the letter. Maybe she had even gone down to Dad's office and conscripted his secretary. Who kept the file copy?)

You can imagine my shock and great disappointment when your father and I received a letter from your dean informing us that you had not been at school for three whole weeks.

(Mom had been unable to resist underlining certain choice phrases in red marker-pen.)

God knows what would have happened to your

poor father if you had not finally <u>deigned</u> to drop
your own parents a note telling us where you are.
You know how your father's <u>pressure</u> is, and I don't
even want to go into what Dr. Sanborn said about
his <u>heart</u>. Even with your <u>incredibly short excuse</u>
for a letter to your own parents, I was only just
able to restrain him from going <u>straight</u> to the
address you gave us and <u>horsewhipping</u> that George
creature to within an inch of his life.

Don't bother to thank me. Thanks are the very
last thing I'd expect from you. I've never had them
and I never asked for any, so don't start now or the
shock might kill me. The only reason I kept your
father calm and at home was for his own sake, <u>not
yours</u>, and certainly not for that George bum you've
decided to throw your life away over. God alone
knows how a creature like that would have treated
your poor father, after all he's suffered and with
his heart the way it is!

Sandra, we have tried to be good parents to you.
Somehow we have failed. Maybe there is something to Darwin after all. God forgive me for men-
tioning the dead disrespectfully, but your Aunt
Mona was never exactly <u>right</u> in the head. Of course
she only married into the family, but <u>blood will
tell</u>.

All right. You probably think you are showing
us what a <u>big girl</u> you are by breaking our hearts
this way. When did I ever treat you like a child?
But enough. If you want to talk about this whole
<u>terrible situation</u> you have put me in, where I can't
even hold my <u>head</u> up when people ask how you
are, then you can meet me at the Plaza Hotel in
the Palm Court for lunch on <u>Friday</u>. Don't bother
<u>straining</u> yourself to write a civilized reply. I will
<u>be there Friday</u> from noon on. If you come, you

come. If not, I sit. Don't worry about me. Worry about your poor father instead, while you still can.

Your loving mother.

Sanchi finished scanning over Sandy's shoulder. She folded the letter shut. Sanchi shook his head and sighed, "Oy." She stared at him and he shrugged, "Hey, man, I'm bilingual."

Sandy folded the letter into a butterfly shape and leaned back with her eyes closed. "What am I going to do about this?" she asked the ceiling. The red stone at her throat glowed like a coal.

"Gee, I dunno," said Sanchi. "Maybe you should go see her and explain things, you know."

"Marvelous," growled Sandy. "I'll take you and George along with me. That'll really comfort her! Not only am I living with a *goy*, but we've got a Puerto Rican kid! And then, even supposing she swallows that bone, I tell her *why* I've shacked up with you two." Sandy leaned across the coffee table toward an invisible Mother Horowitz. "Mommy," she said brightly, "you mustn't worry about me. There's nothing sexual between George or Sanchi and me, darling. I'm only staying with them until we slay the dragon." She moaned and sank back into the sofa cushions.

"What's not to understand?" asked Sanchi innocently. "That's the truth."

"The truth shall set you free," replied Sandy. "Only in this case the truth will send all of us straight to Bellevue." She rested her head in her hands. "I don't know, Sanchi. It's been so long! Mom must know by now that I applied for leave of absence from school, and for what? What have we accomplished? Have we even set *eyes* on a dragon? He could be in Peoria by now. He could be three worlds away and heading west!"

"He's not," said George, leaning against the doorjamb. Now he strode into the room and sat beside Sandy on the couch while Sanchi perched on the back.

"Well then, where is he?" challenged Sandy. "What proof do you have he's within a mile of New York? Maybe he landed here, but why would he stay?"

"He is tired," said the knight quietly. "The hunt has lasted longer than you can imagine. It did not begin in Khwarema and it might not end here." He gazed out the window. A long ship was passing down the river. "He means to make a stand. He hopes to kill me."

"Only we're gonna kill him first," announced Sanchi brightly. "Hey, come on," he prodded Sandy, who still looked morose. "I been waiting for George to do something longer than you. But look, we haven't just been sitting on our butts around here. We've been getting ready, and we're set to roll now!"

In a corner of the living room the suit of armor twinkled in the weak beams of sunlight. On the helm in low relief a unicorn curvetted on the left side, his mate and foal stretched at full gallop on the right. The cuirass was undecorated, but the beauty of the silvery metal needed no useless embellishments. It was, thought Sandy, cast of no mineral known on earth, at once thin and flexible yet strong enough to withstand almost anything— including the charge of a dragon. In a certain light it shimmered with hints of bronze and gold.

"Get a load of this!" shouted Sanchi. He slung the resting shield over his left arm and seized the lance in his right. It had been straight luck finding the lance. None of the pawnshops would've given a nickel for something that far out, but Sanchi backtracked all the vacant lots near where Papi said he first found the knight and it turned up sticking out of a pile of rubbish.

"I'd put that down if I were you," said the knight, smiling. "My enemy has many ways of finding me, when he wants to, and that shield is only one of them. Would you like to be mistaken for me? By him?"

Sanchi shook his head vigorously. "No way, man." He replaced the arms with all proper respect. He'd made excellent progress in performing the duties of a competent page. It was therefore decidedly odd that the shield, once firmly leaned against its makeshift stand, should topple to the floor with a resounding clang. Fall, then inexplicably right itself and roll at a leisurely pace toward the sofa where Sandy and the knight sat.

The shield was wobbly in its rolling; it wasn't circle-shaped, after all. End over end it went, but as it went its outline began to melt and change, shimmering the way the desert will through waves of heat. The shield was gone; a rounded shape of gold-and-crimson light rolled over the floor and shone with a hundred flashing lesser lights down into a vortex whose heart was blackness.

The roundness moved like a living thing, a creature pulsing with primitive life, yet without fixed shape. Sandy watched aghast as tentacles of light curled languidly out of the heart of the thing and trickled into changing patterns. She felt a fear she could not name, and then there was a name for it, just as the roving strands of light wove themselves into a solid image, an image green and gold and rainbow-hued, death-clawed and doom-eyed.

Sanchi cowered, trying to back away. The dragon's sending ignored him. This was a hundred times worse than when they'd been in Khwarema and that force—what did George call it?—that echo of the dragon hit. Here was the real thing, no echo, and Sanchi wanted to run.

He saw George then. He accidentally met his master's eyes. His master wasn't looking at him, but straight at the burning phantom, and there was hate in his eyes, and strength, and a little fear, and a great recognition. All these, burning with a fire greater than the transformed shield in dragon shape.

Sanchi knew then he was never meant to run; not run out on George; not ever.

Challenge, said the dragon. The words boiled out of the flaming shield and rolled like storm clouds to fill the room with their thunder.

"Accepted," replied the knight. "To the death."

What need to set the terms? mocked the sending. You decided them long ago when you betrayed me, manling.

"You made them yourself," returned the knight, "with the souls of a dozen slaughtered worlds."

The dragon chuckled. Sandy clapped her hands over her ears. There was neither humor nor malice in the sound, but an emotion so evil and alien to all things human that she could not bear it. Sanchi paled slightly, but fixed his eyes resolutely on the ensorcelled shield.

You play the hero, said the dragon. But what did you ever care for worlds? It was only when I brushed aside the life of your favorite slut that you swore death against me. You are a lecherous creature, like all your miserable kind. Come, call me a truce and I'll give you and the wench I see beside you free life, passage to a rich world I swear I'll never touch, and treasure.

The shield glowed, flaring brighter into a cascade of diamonds that spilled into the room from the lower lip of the shield. Sandy scooped up a handful in wonder.

"When we meet," said the knight steadily, "when my sword drinks your blood at last, then you'll have my answer. And my lady's vengeance."

The fire in the shield grew dimmer, a heavier brilliance. The dragon's face clenched inward like a fist, all pride and rage.

What a pitiful thing you are, Galaor, it hissed. Ah! That startles you! It has been ages since anyone called you by your true name, the name with which you were born. But I know it. I know many things about you that no one else can know. And I know how to hurt you. What a naked worm. I have wasted too much time fleeing you. The end comes, but you will never see my blood. You will never even have the pleasure of seeing me.

The shield fluttered with a ripple of color and the dragon's face shrank, changing, shifting, dwindling down. But it did not vanish. It blew into a mist that traced a new face, pale and perfect, framed by wings of dark hair. The knight stared at the face and his heart perceived something in those large, sad eyes that pierced him like a bolt. Beyond the rim of the world a lady wept, sensing the moment of his betrayal.

The woman's face disappeared. The shield was again a patina of mutating colors, the colors of flame—fire and flame, smoke pouring over the edge of the shield and choking them, fire that was real reaching out to lick away their lives.

"*Jesús!* The goddamn place is on fire, man!" yelled Sanchi. "That bastard set us on fire! Man, I ever catch him, I'm gonna—"

Sanchi's threats against the dragon dropped to pantings and mutterings as he proceeded to beat out the flames with a heavy throw rug. Sandy ran for water. Wisps of smoke from the smothering fire curled around Sanchi's ankles like serpents.

They were. Hoods spread wide in menace, fangs shining starbright, they rose up out of the ashes and swayed back and forth before the terrified boy as they obeyed an invisible flute-player. Green death and brown, banded death and black, they twined themselves up his legs and wreathed his arms in the coils of poison. He was a garden of snakes, a living tree weighted down with deadly fronds.

Sandy froze in the doorway, water slopping out of a red-plastic container. It was the instant that always comes, the moment to say *it cannot be* while at the same time a sense you never knew you had affirms *but it is*.

The snakes dipped their heads to unseen gods, their small black eyes bright with silent thanksgiving. They gathered their heads into a horrible bouquet, stretching their fluid bodies until all of them were staring with cold glee directly into Sanchi's eyes. Sandy set the pitcher down quietly on the carpet and drifted along the wall. Beside the knight's suit of armor lay the pile of discarded swords.

Her hands were very white when they closed around the pommel of a neglected saber, its engravings dull but its edge sharp. It looked like a fit weapon for a cavalryman. Sandy breathed deeply and drew nearer, every nerve of her tensed, determined to strike, determined not to let her aim miss or her hand tremble. A clean, quick arc, a kill, the heads of the snakes hewn from their necks at one blow. She dreamed it. She prayed it. It would have to be.

What am I doing? she wondered, her old self trapped behind the cool glass of her eyes. I'm no swordswoman! I've never swung one of these! God-

damn it, I shouldn't have to do this! If I miss ...
Oh, Lord, I can't miss, I mustn't miss. . . . Damn
the man! The slayer of dragons! The shining knight!
And there he sits, like a rag doll, while Sanchi—
Sanchi—!

She cleaved the air, the narrow isthmus of air
between Sanchi's stony face and the gathered flicker
of forked tongues, the gape of fanged mouths. And
she killed some of them; only some.

She sobbed as the ones left alive reared back in
their fury and struck at Sanchi. They arched in a
slow ballet, each fang a mocking scythe to cut a
grown man down. They struck for his eyes.

Force crackled through the room. Force given
form of purest white light that sheathed the boy
and broke the fangs of the serpents. They recoiled
and tumbled to the floor, stunned and still more
furious because they were afraid, and no snake is
more dangerous than when he fears. Sandy gave a
strange cry and leaped into the center of the writhing mass, hacking at them with her sword, blind
or perhaps uncaring of what they could do. Her
feet were bare. A coral snake twisted itself around
her ankle like a grotesque bracelet and clung to
her as she stabbed and thrust at the others. Their
blood left stains like smoke marks. She killed them
all. The coral snake released its hold and trickled
between her toes, seeking escape. She sliced it in
two with her sword.

She looked up, seeking Sanchi, expecting to find
him trembling uncontrollably, perhaps collapsed.
Instead he smiled at her, a serene smile. She wiped
a trickle of sweat from her brow. His calmness
irritated her, but not as much as the knight's re-
poseful looks. Still he sat on the sofa as if nothing
had happened, nothing at all.

Sandy threw the bloodied saber down in disgust. "I'm getting out of this!" she declared hotly. "Damn it, I have had enough! You two sit grinning like a pair of constipated cats, and I just—I just—" Her hands flew to her face and she began to cry.

Sanchi and the knight twined their arms around her. She could smell the mingled warmth and spice of their hair. "You were wonderful, Sandra," said the knight. "I've traveled through many worlds, and I never saw a woman as brave. Not even in lands where they forge a sword for each daughter. Not even on the icy world where they raise none but shield-maids."

"Hey, no kidding, man," added Sanchi brightly. "You were terrific! But listen, George wasn't just *sitting* there. He—heck, I don't know what he did, but all of a sudden it was like I felt *safe*, you know? Even with all those snakes on me, I knew he wouldn't let them hurt me." He spared an angry glance at the now-innocent shield. "I'm gonna get that mother for it," he mumbled. "And if it takes a sword all the way from Jersey, I'll get it for you, George. He doesn't get me like that again."

The knight looked glum but resigned, his eyes fixed on a point beyond the river. "We may not have the time to find my sword, Sanchi," he said. "This is the beginning of the final contest. He has grown strong enough on your world to challenge me, and he knows where we are."

"Can't you," gulped Sandy, controlling her tears, "find out where he is?"

The knight shook his head. "When I served him, when I was a child playing amid the horrors of his lair, then I could hide from him, but he could never hide from me. I always knew where he was, just knew it without seeing. There was a taint to him that never let go. But then I found the book that had given him his power, and I read it eagerly." His face paled as he remembered all he had seen in the book, the unfolding of a knowledge and an enchantment so strong that it could destroy a myriad of living, green, shining worlds on planes that ordinary men could never imagine.

"It was too much for me. I ran away. But what I knew would never desert me, and I could never forget it. There was the start of evil in me, and the first faint scent of it came out of my skin like sweat."

"I don't get it," said Sanchi. "If you had this—like a *smell?*—all over you, why did he let you go? Why didn't he go out after you and bring you back? I mean, he must've known what you learned, and if he knew that, he could guess you'd use it on him."

The knight seemed to pay no attention to Sanchi's words. He released Sandy and walked over to where his armor awaited him. He was dressed simply in jeans and a short-sleeved shirt. They had planned to go out together later that morning and examine the antique stores on Third Avenue. And Sandy had said something about having a hunch on where they could find his wandering steed. . . .

"Robe me," said the knight, his voice low. He stretched out his arms.

Sandy and Sanchi exchanged a look. "I must be crazy," she said. The boy grinned.

"You were nuts before he got you," he replied. "He can sniff out the real crazies the way a dog can sniff out garbage. Even in New York, man, he can pick the cream of the crazies."

Sandy glanced at the knight. He had not said a word, nor had he reprimanded them for dawdling. Suddenly she had the impression that this was it, the end of playing, the true beginning of a contest older than dreams. The knight's shadow, arms extended gracefully as a dancer's, cast a cruciform of shadow over the brilliant metal shells.

Sanchi sensed the change too. His grin faded. Without another word he was at his master's side, his nimble fingers darting here and there, removing the earthly clothes.

Sandy brought the tunic and hose from the bedroom and stood patiently by while Sanchi finished his first efforts at attending his master. The knight stood naked in the sunlight, his fair skin blemished only by the threads of old scars. For the first time Sandy noticed the golden down on his broad chest, the ironhard muscles of his thighs, the high arches of his feet, smooth as a lady's. Sanchi drew on the hose and tunic, hiding all.

Now he brought his master's armor. Piece by piece he girded it on, the fastenings slim silver chain-and-button, a strange device. The knight placed the helm on his own head. Sanchi knelt before him, offering the magic shield.

Fully armed, the knight at last spoke. "My friends . . . my companions! If you want to turn back, now is the time. This is not your fight and I won't think less of you for retreating. You've seen the kind of enemy we face, and you are both so very young. . . ."

Liar, hissed a voice. Neither Sandy nor Sanchi heard it. The knight clenched his teeth and tried to shut it out, but the sender was determined. Weak as a whisper in the desert, still it tickled his brain. *Hypocrite. How many children have you bound to your cause, your worthless cause, with words like that? Tell them to turn back and they are ashamed because that was exactly what they wished to do. But now they cannot. Now they will be cowards if they abandon you. Oh, how cunning you have become, my manling! How I love this constant proof that we are bound in substance stronger than blood!*

Yes, yes, bring them, bring the children, and I shall feast as I have before and you shall fetch me more . . . and more . . . and more. . . .

The knight dropped his shield. The whisper grew to a whirling wind inside his head, a growing wind that swelled his temples with pain until he had to open his mouth and let the dragon's voice bellow from his own throat, "Bring them! Bring the children! I am waiting, my love, my manling, my own; I am waiting for you all!" He pitched forward in blackness.

Chapter XII

RIMMON

In the half-light filtering through the beech leaves of Beltrani, Rimmon sat and carved a creamy stone. The milky surface was soft, ceding easily to the skillfully wielded stylus, its curves revealing multicolored gleams as delicately tinted as wildflowers. A denar dipped into the clearing, shrieking as it dived, its scarlet wings brushing the tip of Rimmon's ear and leaving a mark like rouge. He did not even spare the effort to swat it away.

The denar alighted on a twisted branch and stared down at the elf with its burning, opaque eyes. They looked like roundels of smoky quartz through which you could see an inferno. It gnashed its needle teeth and pondered the situation. It was never truly wise to attack an elf. Men were another matter, but elves—this one could be on his feet, an arrow in his hand, nocked, aimed, and flying through the denar's crinkled body in the moment it took to leap from its perch to strike.

Of course, this elf did not seem to be like the others. His bow and quiver lay on a grassy bank barely out of reach, and his looks were all rapt concentration on the plaything he was working on. The denar knew little of art, but he did know blood. The pleasures of blood were still preserved in this twilight place where a dead world went on in much the same way it had before the coming of the dragon.

The sound of branches breaking and leaves rustling madly broke the denar's sanguine daydreams. The taste of elf-blood would have to wait. Someone else was coming, and no self-respecting denar ever tempted unfavorable odds.

Rimmon reluctantly pulled his eyes away from his work. Whoever was coming came with much assurance and little grace. The forest of Beltrani shook beneath the heavy footfalls. A small army would have to struggle to equal such an uproar; a league of elves could never even hope to do so.

The elf set down his stylus and his stone, a knowing smile on his face. This burst into a broad grin when the last of the underbrush was torn aside and a huge, ferocious-visaged, lumbering bear of a man broke free of the leaves.

He was taller than any elf, much taller than any mortal. He claimed to be a man, yet even his closest companions believed him to be the last of a lost race who had held Khwarema before the coming of the elves and long before the birth of man. His thick black hair hung in four braids, the ends banded with bronze, and a band of iron encircled his brows. He could stand against his enemy barehanded in the middle of a plain and still find something to turn into a killing weapon. Master of sword and spear, lord of the arrow's flight, commander of the King's hosts: Conchobar.

Even now he was well-armed. A spiked mace hung from his belt beside a sword no other could wield. The jeweled butt of a hunting dagger winked out of the top of his boot. Beyond these conventional weapons, he could turn any article of his dress into something deadly within seconds. And still he had fallen with the rest before the dragon.

"Good hunting and high wandering to you," growled Conchobar. "It's been a long time, Rippon."

"Rimmon," the elf corrected him indifferently. Conchobar was always like that, in spite of the fact that they and all with them had passed so long together that it was nearly impossible to forget each other's names.

"Ah?" Conchobar nodded his heavy head. His eyes were placid and large, the luminous eyes of a wild bull left in peace. "Sorry. I thought you were someone else." It was his usual disclaimer. "Well, so what? Good hunting and high wandering to everyone, I say! And above all to you and yours, elf. It's been too long for me away from the camp. I've missed your songs and the tall tales. Made up any new ones?"

"About you?" teased Rimmon. Everyone knew that Conchobar was a great lover of the arts when the arts praised Conchobar.

"Oh, maybe about me, or someone else," the giant shrugged, pretending not to care. "I like a good song. And I like news."

"For the songs," said Rimmon, "you'll have to go into the camp. I mangle harp strings, Conchobar, but a bowstring's another matter."

"Do say!" marveled Conchobar. "I thought all you elves were born singing; learned to play the harp at your mothers' breast. Must be hard to play there!" He guffawed. Rimmon failed to see the humor. Conchobar's idea of the comic was strictly limited to his own taste.

"Persiles came," said the elf. He looked well-pleased when this simple bit of news lopped off Conchobar's gruff laughter. He stared at Rimmon, kneeling down to meet the elf's eye.

"When?" he demanded. "When?"

"You've been gone long, Conchobar. He came once before, to see the Lady—"

"I was there then! He brought blue pearls for her throat; blue pearls! I don't forget wonders that easily."

Rimmon knitted his brows. "Yes, then you were here the last time he came. This time he brought others with him. He has a new squire and—" Rimmon hesitated. He didn't like to speak of Sandy. The shard of white stone grew warm in his open palm, the opalescent lights in it twinkling.

"I don't care who was with him, elf!" snarled Conchobar. "What does that matter? The *call!* Did he give the call?"

Rimmon gazed directly into Conchobar's tense, eager face. In life he had been chief archer and huntsman to one of the premier lords of Elfin. He would not lower his eyes, not even for Conchobar. Not even for the anger he knew would come when he said, "He will never give the call. The horn shall stay as lost as the sword."

To Rimmon's surprise, Conchobar did not explode into a whirlwind of rage. There were treeless plains where forests had once stood until Conchobar lost his temper. Instead, the titan collapsed onto his rump with a clash of weapons and a loud *woof* of astonishment.

"Lost the sword," Conchobar marveled. "Went and lost the sword."

"Robbed of it," clarified Rimmon. "He's using his new companions to locate it again, but from what I've heard, the world he now walks is thick with hiding places. He sends his thoughts after the sword, and nothing comes back."

"Belgor lost," sighed Conchobar, still overwhelmed by the idea. "Lost or taken, still means it's gone. Belgor gone. I always said Persiles was more suited to a lute than a sword; I said it from the moment I first met him. But we had to go believe a prophecy instead of our own eyes, elf! There's no good ever came of listening to wizards. Half of them are crazy and the other half are so old they *sound* crazy. And we listened! We're the craziest of the lot."

Conchobar and Rimmon sat in silence for a time. The elf knew better than to contradict Conchobar; it was a waste of time. Nor was he going to agree with him. Instead he resumed work on his carven stone.

"What's that for?" the tall one asked at last. He jabbed a finger thick and strong as an iron bar at the fragile slip of rock. Under Rimmon's delicate blade a pattern of lacy flowers was emerging, each one shimmering with hidden splendor.

"To hold a bloodstone," replied the elf.

"Bloodstone?" Conchobar puzzled. "But that's only given when—" Rimmon's cool glance reduced the big man to stammers. "That is—I thought—I'd heard you had a lady who was—"

"You listen to too many elfin songs, Conchobar," said Rimmon evenly. "We don't all play the harp from birth, and we don't all love faithfully to beyond the grave."

"Is she—your lady—anyone I know?" faltered Conchobar. Elves had always made him nervous. He couldn't understand what made them tick. The littlest thing would mortally insult them for no good reason, yet you could curse them to their faces for an hour and they'd only laugh and offer you a drink. Now Rimmon was giving him one of those queer looks and it made the big man's skin feel too tight. But still he longed to be in on the gossip. "Can I—guess, if you won't speak her name?"

That made Rimmon laugh. "You've aimed too high to hit it," he said. "She's not of Khwarema. When Persiles came with his squire, she came too."

"By Huro!" swore Conchobar. "You mean you've taken Persiles' wench, elfman? He'll kill you for it, and I'll cut him down myself for what he's done to the Lady!"

Rimmon raised one pale, slender hand to calm him. "You will not," he said softly, "call her wench. You will not call me elfman. And you tell no one here about my lady, or the bloodstone, or this." He held out the finished carving.

Conchobar's fingers were blunt, but it takes a certain artistry to handle every sort of weapon ever devised. He had a firm yet gentle touch. He held the carving heedfully, with the same care he would use to cradle a sprig of maidenhope in his calloused palm.

"Magnificent," he breathed. The stone appeared to shift shape slightly as he watched, the edges flowing in the dappled-green light. "But, Rimmon"—a sudden realization struck him—"will Persiles return with her?"

The elf's eyes took on something of the verdant twilight of the woods. Conchobar wondered what it was that elves could see; surely a vision that drifted far beyond the forest of Beltrani and the peace of dead Khwarema.

"I doubt if he will return at all," said Rimmon.

Conchobar's jaw set. "Oh, he'll be back!" he stated firmly. "He's going to have to come back now. Lost Belgor, that's what's done it. You mark my words. He'll have to give the call now, elf; give the call and bring us through, armed for the fight. Either that or let the dragon go, and by Huro, you know what the chances of that are!" Conchobar clenched a fist in excitement. "I could almost be glad he lost the blade. But we'll wash our own swords clean in dragon's blood!"

Rimmon lowered his lids and gave the giant a

mild look. "If the call comes, we must wait for it,"
he said. "But I don't care to wait. I am going to
my lady, Conchobar. I've made her this to hold the
bloodstone pledge I gave her, and I mean to see
her wear it. At my pleasure, not Persiles' whim. I
am going to her." He unfolded his long limbs and
dropped the finished carving into his quiver, its
leather sides made bright with a cunning inlay of
kingfisher feathers. He gazed at the openmouthed
giant and added, "You can join me, if you like."

Huro's help! groaned Conchobar inwardly. Ves
take me if I ever understand elves!

Aloud he said, "You're crazy, Rimmon! Go to
her? *How?*"

Rimmon leaned casually against the trunk of an
aged beech. "Have you never thought," he asked,
"whether there was only one road leading from
Khwarema? The call, and no other way? I think
there is another road, Conchobar. Maybe not a fit
road for a living man like Persiles to take, but a
road of shadows. And we are shadows, Conchobar.
Now we are nothing more than shadows." He stood
up and gestured off into the primeval silence of
the woods. "Are you coming?" He did not wait for
the giant's answer. He melted away into the leafy
darkness.

It took Conchobar only a moment to decide.
Then he was on his feet and crashing hotfoot
through the branches after the elf. The denar
chittered its disappointment and swooped away
by another route through the hush of immortal
trees.

Chapter XIII

THE WIZARD

Come to me, said the dragon, and the wizard came.

His rainbow crest was down, his wings were folded and concealed. The curve of his green-gold back resembled one of the grassy hills, but at a moment's notice he could swell to his full size and blot out the stars. His talons reflected the moon.

Few people frequented the park at that hour. Fewer passed the starlit bronze of the Alice statue where the dragon curled himself comfortably around the icy metal mushroom and sent out his summons. There was a chill in the air, a feeling of uncertain dread about the place that sent the people marching briskly back the way they had come, victims and hunters both made afraid in the clammy stillness. The stars themselves took on the cold, repulsive glitter of scales.

Come to me.

The dragon's golden eyes held a reflection of water nearby, and the water held the moon, full and clear. Traces of blood entwined the silver circle, gradually molding it into a third eye. The surface of the water rippled and the wizard rose from the face of the moon.

He was built along broad lines, his wide shoul-

151

ders bent from books or burdens. His limbs were twig-thin beneath the clinging gray of his robes, fine and soft as the fanning weeds that grow under the waves where sunlight never comes. His beard was short, only beginning to grow back to its full impressive length after the brutal necessity of being shorn for battle. An amethyst glowed on his right hand and a jacinth shone from its silver setting atop his rod of blackthorn.

Come.

He swept the waters away to either side with a flourish of his cloak and walked out of the lake. The dragon noted with satisfaction the blot of red that still marred the wizard's translucent, wrinkled skin precisely over the left temple. There were some things best never to forget.

"I am here," said the wizard. "Why have you summoned me?" His voice was bitter, crackly as nutshells underfoot.

Because it is my pleasure, replied the dragon.

"That again," sneered the wizard. "You're no wiser than you ever were."

I was wise enough to slay you, returned the dragon.

"Strong enough, you mean!" the wizard shouted. "Sly and strong, like all your kind, and I was careless. You flatter yourself as to your powers."

I have power enough to summon you, said the dragon, somewhat irritably. Slyness alone—since you think me so sly—is not enough to call up the dead, Mage. The strength of my wings alone is not enough to take me from world to world. But I go.

"What sort of world have you brought me to now?" asked the dead wizard. He looked around him, but could make out little by the lamplight except the statue of Alice.

A rich world. A good world. A world ripe for my

touch. A world that suits me. See how well! The dragon raised his crest and extended his wings. They clapped together above his mighty haunches and the report reverberated from the lake and the trees and the buildings.

The wizard was duly admiring. "You were a stripling when you slew me. You've come to full growth now. In all my life I never saw a worm to match you." The jacinth bubbled with light as he spoke. There were wise men who set jacinth into the side of their drinking cups, for the stone would change in the presence of poison, and poison is only a face of treachery.

Is that so? asked the dragon, smiling complacently. And so you admit that I am rather more than the beast of burden you made of me all those years.

"I saved your life!" protested the magician. "What would have been easier than giving my blessing to the kill and leaving you dead on a hero's sword? But I spared you; I made them spare you."

To feed your own vanity, Mage, said the dragon without rancor. To have the yokels gape at the great wizard who rides on dragonback. I was more merciful to you. The dragon closed his golden eyes. A sulfurous flame trickled down the moon.

Did you love me, Mage? asked the dragon.

The wizard drew back, bewildered by the abruptness of the question. "Love you?" he echoed dumbly.

You must tell me if you did, the worm went on, a thread of gilded light seeping out from beneath his lids. Tell me. Why did you really save me? Was I a pretty thing to hold and admire? Was I something young to force into your image of my future? Was I too precious to part with, you who had watched my lair and thrown the spells that bound me helpless for the hero's sword?

The wizard looked past the dragon's wavering wings to where the moon shone like a wafer of silver paper on a velvet sky. "None of those are love," he said. His eyes filled with regret. "I have never loved, worm. Not even you, and you were beautiful. You should have discovered my mirror of enchantment before you touched my book. That would have held you forever. The young strength of your wings! The perfect lines, the painfully perfect lines of your body, the glory I saw in you—! No man alive can hope to equal the splendor or the raw beauty of a dragon. We deceive ourselves, we call you monsters, and all monsters must be ugly, but envy blinds us. You are beautiful. There is nothing in all the worlds more beautiful than you."

The dragon sighed. A little wisp of steam escaped from his nostrils. A warm breeze puffed it toward the wizard where it wreathed his head like a misty halo.

Forgive me, thought the wizard. A cavalcade of unicorns trailed across his memory, a flight of griffins with iridescent wings, a gleam of small, dark eyes among the moist fronds of a lost forest. Forgive me for a lie, but the dead fight with the weapons they have.

So I am beautiful, mused the dragon. It's always easier to love the beautiful, isn't it? Then why, Mage, why do they betray? If beauty is so easily loved, why is it so easily abandoned? Is it just the contrary nature of a mortal heart?

The dragon squirmed like a puppy. The bronze mushroom base of the statue groaned as his tail twisted tighter around it, the green scales cutting into the verdigris of the stem.

Or is it love to leave me?

The wizard frowned. "You are thinking of the boy again."

The dragon laughed. Boy no longer! A full-grown man, and one who would like nothing better than to sink a sword into my flesh. My enemy. We should always think of our enemies.

"Whatever form he wears now, he will always be that boy to you," the wizard sagely maintained. "You know it and I know it. But you did not summon me here to discuss him, did you?"

Perish the thought! mocked the dragon. I have called you here to ask your wise counsel, Mage. I feel that this world is rotten-ripe. I have spent time enough marshaling my powers. I am strong enough to take what will be mine. Invisibility is a bothersome thing. I don't need to fear the creatures who dwell here.

"And what of your enemy?" asked the wizard. "Does he still follow? The last time you commanded me—"

We will not speak of the last time! roared the dragon. His tail made a chirring noise where it scraped against the pavement. The wizard went on nonetheless, unafraid. Death had some consolations.

"The last time he almost had you."

But he never will. His power is scattered far from him. Do you know, I was even able to strike him down at a distance? The dragon chuckled. To strike him down as if he were some superstitious bumpkin whose fear of dragons did my task for me!

"I see," said the wizard. "Well, then . . . if he is truly powerless, nothing exists to stop you. Nothing. You can take what you like. This world will have to be yours."

I thought you might see it that way, smirked the

dragon. Voluptuously he uncoiled himself from around the Alice statue. A pile of creamy bones clattered free under the moon. They were very small bones.

I have already begun, said the dragon. The wizard groaned and flung his arms over his face to hide the grisly sight. For a moment he stood there like a twisted gray seashell, then dispersed like smoke on the wind. The dragon filled the empty midnight of the park with hideous laughter.

The moon seemed to grow fat and swollen as a great white grape about to burst with juice. It tilted down the sky as dawn came on. The dragon stretched his limbs and began to walk out of the park by one of the many breaks in the low stone wall running along the Fifth Avenue side. He passed the children's zoo on his right, the endless row of block after block of towering, expensive, slick-faced apartment buildings on his left. The reek of him sent the donkeys, the goats, even the ducks and geese into a noisy panic. Across the avenue a drowsy doorman saw him go by and fled into the safety of the lobby. Only a dream, only a dream, you dozed off for a moment and you had a bad dream, he told himself again and again, wiping off the cold sweat with his shaking hands.

By full daylight he was not the only man in New York with the same bad dream.

The dragon strolled as leisurely as if he were leading off a parade. The false château front of the Plaza Hotel reared up in the dawn from across the fountain square. The lady of the fountain watched the dragon pass, her gray eyes eternal, immune. He paused and looked up at her in pretended salutation, then filled his flaring nostrils with the warm aroma of horse manure that faintly tinged the air.

By day the fountain plaza was the terminal stop for the hansom cabs that gave tourists and native New Yorkers alike a fast go around the park or down the avenue; a brief opportunity to close your eyes, feel the breeze on your face, and dream of more elegant days.

This time there was nothing sarcastic in the reverence the dragon made to the empty square.

You have been here, he murmured. You will come again. Without you the boy is nothing, because it has been ordained to happen in one way and no other from the time I came out of the egg. I can only die in one way, and you are part of it. Therefore, you must die. You will recognize me when my creature has done my will, but not until too late. A pity. I will always remember you in the open field, the free charge of battle. You were fit to be mounted by a god. You were the wind-god's child in your glory. I do what I must. Regrettable. Honor to you, enemy.

He left the plaza behind him and continued down Fifth Avenue, his heavy belly dragging the ground. A street sweeper saw him coming and didn't wait to check the evidence; he ran. A window washer looked down from his aerie and lost his balance, his safety belt the only thing saving him from a fall. His cry made the dragon look up. Almost indifferently he spread his wings and rose to a level with the trembling man, his jaws hanging slack with impulsive hunger. They snapped together over man, scream, safety belt and all. Then the dragon settled earthward with the silence of a maple wing.

At Tiffany's the dragon paused. He scented gold, jewels, the precious makings of a worthy bed. But not just yet. He licked his lips and went on. All around him he sensed vast warehouses of riches, things precious, things fragile, things fit only for men, things fit for his use alone. Velvets, satins shot with metallic threads, leaf-thin porcelain vases painted like a spring morning, sparkling confections of glass, artful combinations of perfumes and colors, all, all for his pleasure. He peered into the window of Valentino's and contemplated the delicious dresses on the mannequins. He imagined Diane made ready in one of them, scent in her hair, jewels flashing on the honeyed skin, painted according to ritual—if this world had any rituals—and left to serve him in the way he desired.

He dreamed awhile, and while he dreamed he was unaware of the growing attention he attracted. Cars coming down Fifth Avenue saw him and swerved wildly, missing collisions by inches. Pedestrians paused in the uncertain hours of a cloudy day, thinking that perhaps here was another inconvenient construction job to block the sidewalk, until they were close enough to see what he really was. They ran like mice, too frightened to scream.

Riley came whistling as he ambled carelessly from Lexington and East Fifty-ninth Street. His uniform looked especially smart, the way navy blue alone can look when spotless and lintless. His badge caught a wayward shaft of sunlight. He was feeling prime. He had made a collar the other day, a shoplifter at the Godiva chocolate shop caught with a five-pound *ballotin* crammed into an Alexander's shopping bag. The shopgirls had made an inordinate fuss over him; God knows how bloody exorbitant those chocolates were! They had offered him a small box as a thanks-gift, and when he refused it they had pressed individual candies to his lips. All in all, a good day.

Fifty-ninth Street intersected Fifth Avenue and Riley thought he'd mosey uptown first, toward the park. It always calmed him, seeing those banks of green treetops in the middle of the city. even though he knew the things that went on in their shade. But then the unwonted sound of loud commotion made him stop his uptown ramble and turn, reluctantly, to do his duty as one of New York's Finest. Even the most dedicated policeman dislikes abandoning his daydreams.

And suddenly, the commonplace morning switched into the crowd scene from a 1950's Japanese horror flick. People were running, screaming, trampling each other, elbowing women into the gutters where cars raced against the One Way signs and disappeared down side streets faster than he'd ever seen Manhattan crosstown traffic go. The sounds of the inevitable crashes, brake squeals, and horn blasts came muted by the intervening buildings.

Riley drew his nightstick and used it to part the surging crowd like Moses parting a human Red Sea. It was pure reflex, and it saved his life, as did his uniform. Even in the midst of total panic, the blue beacon and the badge had their effect on the average New Yorker, and the brandished nightstick worked like a charm. They gave Riley a wide berth until a myopic soul, all nose and eyeglasses, ran under the nightstick and smack into Riley.

"Here now!" cried Riley, steadying the wispy man while the crowd still came running by them. The jolt had snapped Riley back into his best nononsense policeman mode and the first order of business was to discover what the hell was going on. "What's the matter here?"

The little man cowered and moaned, plucking at Riley's bright uniform buttons in a most disconcerting way. The cop pulled him over to the side, into the shelter of a storefront. Whatever had caused this madness, Riley thought, at least it's got them too scared to try stopping and looting. "Now you're safe," he told his catch. "Why were you running?"

"Look, I'm not crazy, OK?" whimpered the little man. "I mean, if I am, they are too. There's this— this *thing!* Jesus Christ, this big green thing like I never saw, and it's walking down Fifth Avenue like it owned the place."

A big green *thing?* wondered Riley. He ran through a mental list of big green things, from tanks to the Incredible Hulk, and unfortunate memories of Tokugawa Studio's lost classic, *The Broccoli of Doom*.

"Hey, I didn't do nothing, OK?" whined Riley's informant. He seemed to shrink inside his clothes. "I just saw it and ran. I mean, how about letting me go? In case it maybe decides it's tired of St. Patrick's, you know?"

"St. Patrick's?" echoed Riley.

"That's where I saw it," the little man affirmed. "Ran all the way from St. Patrick's to here, and I'm not stopping until I'm safe home in Astoria again. Look, Officer, I'll give you my name and address and everything. You call me any time you want to ask me a question. I'm not crazy; I got a good job doing mail orders for Sak's, you know? So I'm not just Joe Shmu—uh—Shmoe. But I saw what I saw and I never want to see it again!" With that he bolted from the storefront and was lost in the crowd.

Riley wedged his way through the stampeding multitude to the nearest police call box. His call for help was brief, and he didn't mention anything about big green things. If the Broccoli of Doom was on the loose, let some rookie get it on his permanent file. He'd had enough grief over the white horse in Harlem. Big disturbance on Fifth Avenue, point of origin alleged to be St. Patrick's

Cathedral, send backup units to rendezvous with assigned patrolman there. He hung up and began the arduous fight through the crowd toward the cathedral.

It would take the patrol cars a damn long time to get there. Manhattan midtown side streets, impassable in the best of times, were now a choked mass of vehicles pointed in every direction, including straight across the road like barricades. The symphony of horns and curses was now very audible.

The crowd was thinning out. Everyone who might have run away was already blocks past the cathedral. The only stragglers Riley encountered were folks who had come, all unsuspecting, out of the cross streets from the east and west of the avenue. The sun was burning off the clouds, picking up flecks of gold from the statue reclining above the Rockefeller Center rink, and shining down on the impossible: a weekday on Fifth Avenue and not a soul in sight.

Riley leaned against the windows of Roberta di Camerino and studied the cathedral across the street. Nothing. The towering gray facade looked as cool and out of place as always, a pleasant refuge, a gracious bastion against the city. The great bronze doors were ajar. Riley caught a whiff of old incense, dry and bittersweet, as he cautiously mounted the steps and peered into the shady recesses.

The banks of votive candles were all out. Threads of smoke like scratches in the dark were all that marked them. There was nothing of the soft, golden light that Riley recalled so well from previous visits, both for prayer and to admire the artistry invested in the place. Far off in the shadows a single golden lantern seemed to burn with a cold yellow light. Riley paused. It was impossible to see a thing, big and green or otherwise. The smart thing to do would be to wait for the backups, go outside and wait. He turned to go.

Small, smooth hands clutched at his sleeve. He raised his nightstick defensively and yanked his flashlight from his belt, shining it with blinding intensity into his assailant's face.

Assailant? Her hands fluttered and crossed themselves to shield her eyes from the light, like a pair of silver butterflies. Her face was exquisite, radiant with a transparent beauty made even more appealing by her air of helplessness. She cried out like a child and hid her head.

"Miss, I—what is it, miss?" faltered Riley. His breath was still half-stolen by the sudden lovely apparition he held in his service flashlight's beam. "You can tell me, miss; don't be afraid. I'm a policemen, and there are more—"

She whirled and ran, dashing into the blackness surrounding the high altar. Riley followed without thinking, his light picking out a clear path between the rows of pews. The light rested on gold and silver, a small mountain of churchly paraphernalia heaped in a tangle of riches at the foot of the altar itself. Riley stopped in his tracks and let the beam illuminate that strange, precious conglomeration. Censers, crucifixes, thuribles, even a monstrance blinked back at him, and just beyond the far edge of the pile he glimpsed the feet of the woman.

Welcome.

A second yellow light flared and suddenly the entire cathedral was suffused in a greenish-golden aura chill as an arctic breath. The dragon folded his forepaws more comfortably on the high altar and gave Riley a lewd smile. The woman curled up like a kitten in a bend of the dragon's tail.

Oh God, thought Riley, but a dank hopelessness seeped into his soul from the dragon's presence and laughed down his every prayer contemptuously.

So this is the house of your god? asked the dragon, and Riley realized that something had slipped into his brain and knew what was there and had left by the same route it had come. He felt naked, contaminated, weak.

How appropriate, the worm continued, that I should choose this for my dwelling. It suits me well, manling. For the present it suits me very well. Now hear me!

The sharp command exploded like a thunderclap inside Riley's head. He groaned and tottered under the impact. His nightstick and flashlight clattered to the floor as his knees gave way.

Rise up, the dragon intoned. Rise up and give thanks to your fate, manling. The chosen voice, the chosen one to bring my desires to your people, the chosen keeper of my will, all these!

The voice inside him changed its tone and became wheedling, warm, confidential. You are very young and strong, manling. You will have many years to serve me, to bring this world to serve me. Think of the power you will command! Think of it, you who only dare approach power in timid dreams.

Riley was past responding. The woman, obeying an order he could not hear, got up from her huddled place and moved gracefully away, out of sight behind the dragon. She returned momentarily, accompanied by a smaller woman whose head was as dark as hers was fair. She had an infant slung in front of her, but her hands were free. Between them they carried heavy folds of cloth that shone like a beaten-copper basin just beginning to go green. It was a robe. Gently they helped Riley to his feet and draped it across his shoulders, covering his uniform. Dimly he heard a screech of tires and the slamming of many car doors outside. The distant whup-whup-whup of a police helicopter sounded like a mosquito's song in the vast vaults of the shrine. Footsteps, men carefully entering, seeing him in his new splendor, not knowing him, coming closer, drawn by a force more powerful than any human compulsion or instinct for survival. The dragon's eyes were whirlpools of gold around them. Training. They were well trained. Before they could decide whether they believed what they were seeing, they drew their service revolvers.

"Be careful! There's a baby—" Riley stretched out his hands in a gesture meant to make them hold their fire. One of the men recognized his voice.

"Riley?" he marveled, lowering his gun. He never had an answer.

Ice-blue brilliance like a virgin sword streamed from Riley's outthrust palms. Blue tinged with green, it leaped across the eerily lighted cathedral and smashed down upon the policemen like a tidal wave. In fountain sprays of might it danced in and out, freed, delighted, reveling in its mission while the men shrieked and their weapons exploded into fireballs in their hands.

They looked as if they had been trapped in a burning building. Their eyes were gone, and their skin crisped and peeled into small flakes of black ashes. Riley stared at the bodies, then at his hands, and he felt the sour taste rising in his throat. He fell to his knees on the stones and retched. The dragon frowned.

You will learn, he said severely. You will learn to serve me better than this. I have not vested you as my priest wrongly. That is impossible. But you will have few warnings. Serve me well henceforth, priest, and serve me utterly.

Riley tried to shut out his words. Tears were streaming down his face, choking him. The little woman with the baby was already mopping up the traces of his sickness. The tall, lovely one brought a basin of water and laved his sweating, beslimed face. Her touch was expert, professional, detached, and yet Riley thought he could see something in her eyes that called to him desperately, although it had no voice.

All, said the dragon smugly, shall serve me.

Chapter XIV

CROSSINGS

Mrs. Horowitz knew nothing of dragons and cared less. She came to the Plaza from the West Side and ignored the scream of sirens from farther downtown, shrugging her fashionably adorned shoulders and dismissing all the brouhaha as no doubt the work of "a bunch of crazy kids." This covered nearly every situation, social or political or even fashionable, in New York. The sole exception to the rule, as she frequently pointed out to her skeptical neighbor, Mrs. Feeley, was her own daughter, her Sandra, the princess. Mrs. Feeley listened and shrugged her not-so-fashionably adorned shoulders. Mrs. Horowitz, she reasoned, could talk all she liked; one day she'd learn. Mrs. Feeley had learned. Her princess, Irene, had gone to Radcliffe with a full scholarship and come home with a full belly. Something about higher education for women being against the Lord's will, thought Mrs. Feeley.

Mrs. Horowitz hated to admit it, but the neighborhood Cassandra's predictions were starting to ring true. Perhaps it was best to expect the worst. Who would have imagined her pearl, her angel-child, involved with some pervert and dropping out of school? At least Mrs. Feeley's daughter had been put "in the family way" by a Harvard man. Who even knew if Sandy's flame could read a beer-can label? It was lately all the rage to take up with the less-educated orders, the "real" people. As if you had to have a tattoo and drive a tank truck before they admitted you to reality! Weren't professional men just as real? Was being street-wise the only route to the authentic?

All in all it was pretty high-flown stuff crowding Mrs. Horowitz's potent brain as she plunked her-self down at a table for two in the Palm Court and ordered tea. She had majored in Philosophy at Vassar. It wasn't the sort of thing one got over easily.

As for the wayward princess herself, she breezed through the potted palm-fronds approximately five minutes later and stifled a groan. Mommy was there first. God alone knew how long she'd been there, but that could be determined by taking the cube root of however long she claimed to have been kept waiting, then subtracting forty-five minutes.

"Well," Mrs. Horowitz said through tightly drawn lips as highly polished as her kitchen floor. "So it's finally you."

Sandy looked self-righteously at her watch. "You said you'd be here at noon and it's only ten to now."

"Is it," stated Mrs. Horowitz. "What a nice watch you have there, darling. Was it a gift from *him?*" Her eyebrows went up like two frightened gulls.

"Mother, you know very well that you and Daddy gave me this watch."

"Oh?" Again the flight of gulls. "What's the mat-ter? Can't your young man afford to buy you some-thing better than your father's and my poor gift?"

Sandy sighed. She had been through too much

in one day and it wasn't half-over yet. On her way to the Plaza from Sanchi's old house she had seen a disproportionate number of people heading uptown, too far uptown for the way they were dressed. Something must be going on downtown, she reasoned, something no one was in a rush to witness. A bomb plant? A demonstration for or against anything from life to Lithuania? Or had the Moonies and the Moral Majority finally met in a blazing-dogma showdown to make Armageddon look like Disneyland?

The end of the world can't come soon enough for me, thought Sandy, and she got off the bus without giving it another thought. She had her hands full. After George's unexplained collapse, she and Sanchi had agreed on one thing—they could no longer afford to stay in that apartment. It was known and they were known and the one man capable of protecting them was now no longer capable of protecting himself.

"We'll have to strip him," Sandy had said, eyeing the sprawled knight. "We can't drag him out of here dressed like that."

"We sure as hell can't risk losing his armor again, man," protested Sanchi. "And we're gonna need both of us to carry him out of here. How we gonna do that and lug a shopping bag full of iron too?"

"It doesn't look like iron," Sandy opined. "It's lighter. I've picked up the cuirass and—"

"You ever picked it *all* up?" sneered Sanchi. "At once? And how about the swords? They're steel for sure!"

"Damn, we don't even know where we can take him and we're worrying about getting him there!" exclaimed Sandy, at the end of her rope. To top matters off, the room was still a mess of decapitated serpents and clinging smoke. "Maybe we should just get him into a Times Square movie house or something. They'd never notice him there."

Sanchi decided the girl had lost her mind. He knew exactly what to do. He was at the phone in a minute and punching out a merry ditty on the touch-tone system.

"What are you doing?" demanded Sandy. "Sending out for pizza?"

Sanchi made a friendly obscene gesture. "Sending out for help, man," he smiled. "The Seventh Cavalry. Better than nine-one-one and a lot faster getting here. You wait."

He was right. Papi was pounding at the apartment door in record time. He embraced Sanchi, he embraced Sandy, and he whisked them and the knight back to the sheltering haven of his home, where the black cat had just had another litter and one of the three stray mutts had eaten Elena's diary. Sanchi had explained things over the phone, and Papi had commandeered Mr.-Ortega-downstairs' pickup truck for the mission. Knight, squire, shield-maiden, and a full set of armor plus surplus swords rode uptown in Byzantine splendor.

So that settled that. Settling Sandy's mother was going to take more than Papi and Mr.-Ortega-downstairs, however. Sandy recalled the pyrotechnics that had gone on when she suggested taking a year off after high school, taking a real job before going back to college. Mrs. Horowitz deserved either an Oscar or Thorazine for her set of hysterics. Even being in the Palm Court of the Plaza Hotel might not dissuade her from a minor tantrum. Especially if Sandy told her the truth.

Which she did. She was simply too damned tired to come up with a rational excuse for George, for Sanchi, or for herself. The dragon, the knight, the sword, the wizard, everything smack in the im-

maculate dead center of Mrs. Horowitz's Sanfor-
ized lap.

"Really," said Mrs. Horowitz.

"Is that it? *'Really'?*" demanded her child when
the divine Mrs. H. did not offer to add any further observations, comments, or condemnations.
" *'Really'?*"

"My dear, what do you want me to say?" replied
Sandy's mom with yet another Homeric shrug.
"The first thing I thought of saying was that you've
obviously gone crazy. The second thing I wanted
to say was that you must be on drugs. However,"
she cocked her head to one side and regarded her
bedraggled chick critically, "I really doubt you've
gone insane and I really don't see any physical
evidence of drugs—your eyes are lovely like that,
dear; don't ever abuse mascara—so what else could
I say? Just really."

A crash of cutlery and china shook the serene
atmosphere of the Plaza. One of the hotel chefs, his
goatee pointed toward True North, came bowling
out of the kitchen like a juggernaut, crushing a tea
cart and a busboy in his flight. He was followed by
two uniformed waiters and a sous chef. Their way
was blocked by the obviously irritated maître d',
lips pursed, eyes narrowed, arms akimbo. Whatever the reason for the breakdown of Plaza disci-
pline, it had better be something pretty damn
good—like Judgment Day, for instance.

"It's the end of the world!" shrieked the chef.

"Not yet, Raoul, but you're pushing for it," replied the maître d'.

"But it is! It is! I just heard it on the radio!"
yowled one of the waiters, chalky white. "So we
turned on the TV, and we *saw* it! It's in St. Pat's,
honest it is. We *saw!*"

"The end of the world in St. Patrick's Cathedral,'' repeated the maître d'. "Well, unless it's a catered affair, you can get right back to your posts. I will not—"

"*Geraldo Rivera* saw it, man!'' shrieked the sous chef, and before the maître d' could react, they had sent him the way of the tea cart and the busboy.

"Oh, dear," sighed Mrs. Horowitz. "You used to be able to *depend* on the Plaza.''

"Where are we?'' asked Conchobar. The mists swirled up around his massive thighs like phantom shackles. They had been traveling in a world of half-darkness for—how long? Impossible to say. There were no clear markings to separate day from night, and anyway, what did time mean to the dead?

"I'm a stranger here myself,'' answered Rimmon, leading the way. His white-fletched arrows gave off a queer green radiance, a bobbing ghost-light that Conchobar followed. It had grown foggier and darker the farther they'd gone. At each step he took, Rimmon felt as if he were pushing aside an infinite fall of heavy gray-velvet curtains.

"Wait,'' called Conchobar. The elf stopped in his footsteps. The green glow over his left shoulder looked milkier, almost absorbed into the cottony haze. Conchobar's eyes were still good enough to realize they were going farther into the thick stuff, and neither he nor Rimmon had any idea whether it would get better, take them somewhere, or even allow them to return the way they had come. How do you blaze a trail through mist? Conchobar had never feared the spirits of the dead while he lived, but in this place it was possible to tremble.

"Are you still there, Rimmon?'' he called.

"Still here and waiting,'' answered the elf, his

words muffled by the rising vapors of the earth. Conchobar tasted salt on his lips and realized he had been sweating. Fear-sweat.

"I was just—wondering if we could—that is, in case it turns out that this trail's cold or a dead end and we want to go back to Khwarema and start over . . . can we?"

Rimmon was silent. The milky-green glow grew yellower and fainter as new waves of fog drifted in. At last he said, "I don't know. We've left Khwarema, that's for sure, and we're the first I know to have done so. We may have gone so far we can't turn back. Or perhaps, once you leave, some barricade falls to keep you out forever."

"Is that all you can say?" roared Conchobar. "Plague and fire take you, elfman, I thought your people had some scrap of magic a master wizard'd give his beard for! Can't you conjure up a guide? Or an answer besides 'I don't know'?"

"Conchobar," said Rimmon, and his voice seemed to ebb away like the tide when the moon calls it. "Not all magic dies with the body, but most fades away. Living flesh and blood forms a strong bowl to hold wonders, but if a skeleton cups his hands to hold water, most of it trickles away. I'm sorry."

Conchobar could not even make out the yellowing light now. "But haven't you anything left?" he protested, his hands closing automatically on his sword hilt. "Anything?"

"I have my eyes," Rimmon replied, sounding almost cheerful. "And my arrows. And perhaps—no harm trying. . . ." He raised his hand.

Clear light, fresh and clean as a spring streamlet, flowed out in ripples from the tall elfin archer. The mists threw themselves against the wall of bright air like breakers smashing themselves to nothing on a rocky shore. The light withstood them and grew, gently grew until it found Conchobar and locked him with Rimmon in its embrace of luminous protection.

Conchobar looked at Rimmon. "I called you elfman again, when I was upset. I'm sorry," he mumbled.

"We'll forget all slights from here on in," grinned Rimmon, slapping the huge warrior on the back. Then he stared at his hand. "I didn't think I could do it," he whispered. "I was just as surprised as you. Perhaps we'll have a few more surprises waiting for us on the other side."

If we ever get there, thought Conchobar, but he said nothing. He was getting a familiar feeling, a well-remembered tingling in the small of his back that ran down his legs like a squirrel, then climbed his spine on burning feet. Battle-feel. Someone coming up on you, coming closer, and something inside you saying that it's not a friend. A coldness in the hands, a blaze in the brain, a breathless waiting. And here they stood, the only clearly visible target for miles around. Conchobar knew he was dead, but that didn't matter. You could do worse things to the dead than kill them.

Spirits.

"What was that?" snapped Conchobar, sword out, flashing cold blue in the shadows.

Hear me, O spirits.

The voice came high and wavering, a thread of sound in a world of smoke. Rimmon grinned. He made no move to draw his bow. Conchobar looked uneasy.

Spirits, I conjure you, in the name of the terrestrial powers, answer me. One rap means yes, two raps mean no.

The mist was parting like cheap muslin, leaving threads of vapor between the wanderers and the small, darkened room where three black candles burned and seven people sat hunched over a round, green-baize-covered table, fingers touching. A woman swathed in layers of scarves and tiers of parti-colored satin skirts was ululating, her eyes rolling free in her head, her lank black hair, streaked with gray, streaming down her fat back.

"We seek the spirit of Edwin Armstrong!" she moaned. A thin, blue-haired lady, all in black, sniffled and rubbed her nose on her shoulder, not daring to break contact with the mystic circle. A curdy-faced young man with a weasel's glare sat beside her, looking bored.

"Hear me, O spirits, and obey!" called the fat woman.

Rimmon stepped through the gateway.

Later he remarked to Conchobar that perhaps the giant should not have made such a bellicose entrance. The curdy-faced young man was still slumped in the corner, his eyes glazed, muttering nonsense. There was serious doubt about his continued mental health.

"And while I'm no wizard," added the elf, "I'd say that the fat woman in those beggar gauds is an even worse case." As if in answer there came a string of muffled shrieks and spells in garbled Romany from the coat closet where the fat woman had locked herself in against the invasion from the "other side."

"Dragon take all of them," snorted Conchobar, tearing down the heavy draperies from the windows and sizing up the terrain outside. The sun was shining brilliantly. Children played rough games in the narrow street below. Teenage boys and young men lounged on the brownstone stoop. A game of pitching pennies was under way down the block. The street smells rose with the heat and made Conchobar shake his head to clear it.

"Worse than dragon might have taken us," Rimmon pointed out, "if we'd wandered back and forth aimlessly in that nowhere region for long. We owe these people gratitude. Their spells of calling guided us through."

"Through to where?" snapped Conchobar testily. "How do we know we're on the right world? Persiles galloped through half a hundred lives before he found Khwarema. He passed through half a hundred more before he came to the one he's on now. Why should we happen to light on the right world just like that, eh?"

Rimmon only smiled and held out his hand. Nestled in his palm, the carved white stone took on a delicately rosy hue, a tender blush like the petal of an apple blossom.

"Because she is here" said Rimmon, "and she still wears the stone I gave her. Stone draws stone with certain spells on it."

"Well," Conchobar grumbled, "at least that makes sense. For a while there I was afraid you'd give me some slop about your heart following your true love to her own world, just like a bloody boarhound on the scent."

"We elves," returned Rimmon pleasantly, "have a bad reputation for being sentimental, haven't we?" But to himself he admitted that he would have known Sandra's world anywhere, and the pull of the enchanted bloodstone was the pull of his heart.

"Come on, Conchobar," he added. "We've found the right world, but finding Persiles may be something else again."

"Use magic," suggested the giant.

Rimmon studied his hands. "No," he said. "I

doubt I could summon up much. This world seems hostile to enchantments, all but the truest and strongest. We'll have to use our wits."

"Our wits," said Conchobar, seeming rather put out. But he followed Rimmon out of the apartment and down the stairs. The young men on the stoop looked at the pair quizzically, but the heat made them too indolent to offer comment. Rimmon sniffed the air and headed west. There was greenery there, and greenery was rare on this bit of the alien world. He would find the woods and the woods would guide him to his lady if the stone could not.

"Jeez-*us*. Halloween came early this year," said the candy-store man.

"New York," shrugged his wife. "Go figure." She went back to counting packs of Juicy Fruit gum.

Lionel cradled the enamel box in his hand and cast a cursory glance over the rank of horse-drawn hansoms lined up in front of the Plaza. A refreshing breeze blew up out of nowhere, carrying with it the confused mutters and shouts of the crowd that had gathered behind the police barricade. Fifth Avenue was cordoned off from Forty-second Street to Fifty-seventh. Of all the crowd, Lionel Walters was probably the only human being who didn't have to ask why.

The media were making hay out of the situation, but even the indefatigable anchormen had to realize that this was no ordinary natural-disaster picnic, no water shortage, garbage strike, job action or attempted terrorist act. This was—and how they blushed to report it!—a dragon.

The mayor could not be reached for comment.

None of this mattered to Lionel. He was intent on other matters. The sugar cube glistened white inside the enamel box, just as white as the horse he was looking for, the horse he would feed, and then. . . . Better not think of *and then*. It was only an animal, after all. What difference would it make if he poisoned it? The knight—if there was any knight—could find another horse. All that stuff about needing a special steed, a special shield, an enchanted sword, that was probably just legend. Bunk. He could pick up another horse anywhere. He could pick up this filthy beast, the one pulling an open carriage with a bunch of pussy willows in the side vase, and ride against the dragon just as well. A horse was only a horse, but if Lionel didn't do as he'd been told, three innocent people would pay for it. And maybe the dragon would decide to come after him again, too. Better get on with it.

Come to think of it, the smeary horse pulling the pussy-willow chariot wasn't your ordinary cut of animal. Lionel gave the beast a hard stare, reached for his pocket handkerchief and spat copiously into it, then began to rub it on the steed's beautifully arched neck. A layer of brown grime came off. Whiteness gleamed beneath like a phantom cloud.

"It's you," said Lionel in a small voice. The horse returned his gaze out of large golden eyes, eyes hiding pride and fire such as Lionel had seldom seen in the people he met each day. The horse whickered softly at him and nudged him with its muzzle. Lionel wetted the handkerchief again and scrubbed the horse's face. The driver of the cab was nowhere in sight, most likely down at the police barricades to see what was going on. The horse allowed himself this undignified, unorthodox washing. He stood several hands higher than the other horses in the rank, and he held himself as if it were no strange thing for humans to scurry back and forth doing things for his comfort. He was white to the end of his muzzle, darkening to cream only where the softness of the lips began.

"You're the one," said Lionel. The enamel box felt hot and heavy in his hand. He stroked the creature's nose. It took a step forward and stamped its hoof.

I have awaited you.

The horse spoke with his eyes. There was no small voice in Lionel's head, nor did the beast itself utter human syllables. And still Lionel knew exactly what this magnificent animal wished to say.

You have come to take me to him. You have come to take me to my master.

"Good horse," muttered Lionel, fumbling to open the enamel box. "Good boy. Got something for you. Nice horse." The sugar cube tumbled into his palm.

You are good. You will reunite me with my beloved master. You are a good man. I trust you. A man of honor.

Lionel dropped his eyes. He could no longer bear to look at the creature. The golden eyes flashed with barely suppressed battle hunger. The great stallion fidgeted his hooves, prancing and curvetting in place. He tossed his majestic head and whinnied shrilly, and at the sound, the traces binding him to the carriage dropped of their own accord. Lionel heard them fall.

"Nice horse," he croaked idiotically. He raised the lump of sugar in the flat of his palm. The horse sniffed at it, curling back his lip and snorting pleasantly. Lionel felt the warm breath on his hand. The horse was lipping the sugar, getting ready to take it entirely, getting ready to—

"Oh!" The girl stumbled into Lionel hard and

the sugar cube went flying. It lay in the gutter, miraculously whole, winking in the sunlight. Lionel staggered under her impact and leaned against the white horse's neck to steady himself. "Oh, dear, I'm sorry," said the girl hastily, reaching out to offer him a hand under the elbow. "I wasn't looking where I was going. I was in a hurry and kind of upset. In fact—"

She stopped speaking. Lionel felt himself go hot and red in the face. Why was she staring at him like that? If she could read the crime he'd already committed in his mind, he wouldn't be at all surprised. The red stone on a silver cord shone like a drop of blood against her pale skin.

"It's him," she said, and Lionel realized she wasn't staring at him after all, but past him, full into the golden eyes of the horse. Golden eyes, he thought irrationally. The dragon has golden eyes too. Maybe this is the dragon himself, taking a different shape to trap me.

But would the dragon allow this strange young woman to stroke his muzzle so familiarly? Would he go so docilely with her as she led him out of the traces and, as calmly as you please, began to guide him away from the Plaza, heading north up Fifth Avenue? Would he—?

"Sandra Horowitz, what do you think you're doing?" Mrs. Horowitz demanded, in fine voice. Her little talk with her darling daughter had ended on a most unsatisfactory note. The hubbub in the Plaza kitchens had spread rapidly, abetted by hordes of guests—whose breeding should have made them know better—intent on swarming downtown to view the alleged dragon . . . from a safe distance, of course. Sandra had taken advantage of all the to-do to announce that she hadn't a moment to lose. Something about a sword or a quest or something. . . . Well, that didn't matter, but to catch her child in the act of stealing a horse—well!

"You put that right back where you found it," directed Mrs. Horowitz. "It isn't yours."

Sandy sighed and looked exasperated. "I know it's not mine, Mother," she said, holding tight to the horse's bridle. "It's his."

She meant the knight; her mother took her to mean Lionel, still standing there in awe of Mrs. Horowitz, terrible in her wrath.

"Is this true?" she countered, fixing Lionel with the look that had often flushed the truth out of her wayward girl.

"Yes," peeped Lionel automatically.

"It is?" Mrs. Horowitz was more than suspicious. "You mean that this is *your horse?*"

Sandy opened her mouth to clear up the matter, then thought better of it. Dragon or no dragon, her mother wasn't one to swallow too many wonders at a time. Claiming this nag to be the long-lost charger of an armed knight might undo everything. So instead, Sandy gave Lionel a pleading look and waited.

Lionel swallowed hard. Mrs. Horowitz was possessed of a gimlet eye fit to rival the dragon's. "It's mine," he replied in something almost his normal voice, and waited for the blow to fall. Either Mrs. Horowitz or the dragon would pounce, and he was betting on Mrs. H. but hoping for the dragon. A quick, clean death.

"So," said Mrs. Horowitz, and frost formed on the air. "We finally meet. I was wondering if Sandra would do the right thing. Apparently she exerts enough influence to get you *outside* the Plaza, but could not persuade you to come in and meet me, as any well-bred young person should."

"*Mother—!*"

"Quiet, Sandra," said Mrs. Horowitz with imperial disdain. "If this is the only way I'll get to acquaint myself with your young man, I'd best make the most of it. I do have responsibilities as your mother. I *am* still your mother, am I not?" Her voice crept perilously up the scale and her eyebrows followed. "Perhaps we might start with your name?" she inquired sweetly.

Lionel gave it. The horse rested its head on his shoulder and blew furry puffs of air into his ear. Mrs. Horowitz had an ill-omened look about her. She reminded Lionel of the hunting hounds in the Unicorn Tapestry series, especially at the moment they fix their teeth into the unicorn's flank.

"Lionel Walters," repeated Mrs. Horowitz. "I went to school with a Francine Walters from Dubuque. Are you one of *her* people?" The tone implied that the Dubuque Walters had sent their child to Vassar on the profits of white slavery. Lionel denied all knowledge of Francine and Dubuque.

"Well then, perhaps you wouldn't mind telling me just who *your* people are," said Mrs. H., and folded her arms, awaiting the awful revelations of alcoholism, idiocy, and inbreeding.

Instead she got a roll call of lawyers, educators, doctors, Episcopal clergymen, and veterans of the War of 1812. Beyond that lay England and a smattering of Hon.'s and Bart.'s.

"Is that so," said Mrs. Horowitz. "How nice for you. And what do you do for a living, Mr. Walters?" It was her last bolt.

"I'm a professor of medieval studies at Columbia, madam."

"Tenured?"

"Tenured."

"Oh." Mrs. Horowitz, the wind out her sails, was becalmed.

Now Sandra made her move. It wasn't every day her mother had nothing to say, and Nature abhors a vacuum. "Lionel couldn't come in to meet you, Mother, because he had to stay out here with his horse. If you don't exercise thoroughbreds every day at the same time they get spavined." She didn't have the faintest idea what *spavined* meant beyond the fact that she had seen the word in books about equines.

"But, Mr. Walters," said Sandy's mother, "if you've been exercising this—uh—lovely animal, where is his saddle?"

"Oh, I never use one," said Lionel hastily. "No *real* horseman does. Only for show, a saddle." The horse gave a whicker that sounded a lot like a laugh.

Mrs. Horowitz stroked the stallion's nose and her whole look softened. She had always been fond of horses and cursed the fate that made her have to give them up. Human beings might be compelled to inhabit the Greater New York area, but there was no reason to subject horses to it. Horses were sensitive.

"What's his name?" she asked tenderly.

"Beauregard," said Sandy.

"Whitey," said Lionel simultaneously. Mrs. Horowitz whirled on them, the hawk once more. *"What?"*

Sandra took a deep breath. "Lord Mayor Beauregard Whitefoot of Heatherdown Sunnyvale's Pride," she recited. "But we have our own little nicknames for him."

"An infinite variety, it seems," said Mrs. H. slowly, her eyes going from one too-innocent face to the other and back again. The horse was the only honest soul present, but she had no time to thrash matters out. She was meeting her cousin

Sherry for a late lunch, and the antics of Sherry's daughter Allyson would prove a welcome respite from her bitter reflections about Sandy. Allyson was living with a tuba player.

"Well, Mr. Walters, this has certainly been a pleasure. I do hope we shall meet again. And if I might appeal to you as an educated man, would you *please* try to influence Sandra to return to her studies? We both know the value of a degree, do we not?" She left in a flutter of fingers.

"Ah!" sighed Sandy, slumping with relief against Lionel. With her on one shoulder and the horse's head on the other he felt like the ham between the slabs of rye. Sandy recovered herself and added, "Whoever you are, sir, I can't thank you enough. You have just saved me from a fate worse than death, and you don't get many chances for that kind of chivalry these days. Do you really teach medieval studies at Columbia?"

Lionel allowed that he did. "But I lied about the tenure."

"Well, you ought to get it," said Sandy firmly. "For this alone. I'm an art major, but I'll take every last living course you ever teach when I go back to school."

Lionel laughed. "I wonder if we'll either of us get back to school now," he said. The shriek of an ambulance siren rose in trails of sound between the buildings. Farther downtown the doors of St. Patrick's Cathedral were swinging ponderously wide. The smell of burning flesh wafted out, mixed with incense, sending a few less-toughened policemen reeling back. A shadow was in the archway, robed in the full regalia of a high priest. There was a glint of silver between his hands.

Sandy and Lionel drew closer together, each holding the horse's bridle. The ambulance siren ceased its wail. The sun still shone, but a wing of darkness seemed to cast a chill over them where they stood, a breath of starless cold that other passersby could not feel. The silver between Riley's hands was a delicately chased salver, and on it rested bones.

"I'd better be going now," murmured Sandy, staring into the stallion's eyes. "He'll be waiting."

"I suppose *he* refers to whomever your mother took me to be."

"That's right. She thinks I'm living with some guy and screwing up my life. She'd never guess—" Sandy stopped herself.

"Go on," coaxed Lionel. "What wouldn't she guess?" Sandy shook her head and tried to lead the horse away. Lionel's grip on the bridle tightened. They could not move. "You owe me a little explanation," he said. "I just slew the dragon, remember?"

He was speaking figuratively, and once the words were out he realized too late that an ordinary young lady might not like hearing her mother referred to as a dragon. But he was entirely unprepared for Sandy's reaction.

"Oh, thank God!" she exclaimed, and threw herself passionately into his arms. They both dropped the bridle in the fury of her grateful assault, but the horse made no move to escape, bemused by these bizarre creatures. "I didn't think anyone but he could do it," she added between kisses. "Where did you find the sword? When did you do it? Did he hurt you? How big was he? Was—?"

Thunder sounded, and a shuddering cry from the deeply packed ranks behind the police barricades. Wings unfurled, rainbow crest glittered with deadly beauty in the sunlight, golden eyes reviewed the madly scrambling police with bottomless scorn.

Idly the dragon raised one gigantic paw and sent a patrol car flying end over end through the air, like a falling leaf. It soared above the barricade and crushed screams from a knot of onlookers. The endless wings spread across the face of the cathedral and blocked the sun's sparkle on the stained glass.

Ages away, by the dry fountain near the Plaza Hotel, Sandy and Lionel exchanged their stories before making their first clumsy attempts to mount the white stallion and head him uptown. In the end they had to make him stand next to the fountain itself and get on his back from the stone rim.

"Hup," said Lionel. The horse looked at him drolly and tossed his head. He headed up Fifth Avenue at a smooth canter, a gait so fluid that his riders felt only the exhilarating sensation of earthbound flight. Then, abruptly, Lionel tugged on the reins.

"What in the world are you—?" But Lionel was already off the horse's back and jogging back toward the Plaza. Sandy turned the animal and followed until she found Lionel behaving like a madman, jumping up and down in the gutter between two hansom cabs whose horses had the same bewildered look as Sandy.

Panting, Lionel grinned up at her and said, "Get him over by the fountain again, would you? I'm no Roy Rogers."

Sandy complied, and once he was back in the saddleless saddle again she asked, "Mind telling me what all that was?"

"In the reign of Richard the Second of England," said Lionel, "there happened a strange thing. The clods of the earth rebelled against their natural masters. No one was more surprised than those selfsame masters, because the very souls they always thought too puny to be fully human were actually *winning*. In the end, the only reason that the Peasant's Revolt failed was because of antiquated and misplaced trust in the King's good faith."

"And so?" demanded Sandy.

"And so I have struck the first blow in a Peasant's Revolt of my own, no quarter asked or given. And no trust placed in anyone. Or anything. Not until we've slain him."

The battered blue-enamel box lay among the particles of pulverized sugar cube in the gutter until the next rain.

Chapter XV

FILM AT ELEVEN

On the whole, the media handled it well. The *Daily News* limited itself to *HORROR SEIZES CITY*. The *Post*, coming out in the afternoon, had more time to ruminate over the matter of a living, breathing dragon in St. Patrick's; *DRAGON!* was all they cared to say on their front page. The *Times* remained circumspect as always: *Mythical Beast Alleged Inhabiting Landmark*, followed by cogent interviews with the chief of police, the head curator of the Museum of Natural History, and Dick Cavett.

But the clincher came on Sunday, the day after the dragon first made the headlines. In a frenzy equaled only by certain sects of dervishes, the entire crew of *60 Minutes* came pouring into New York with drawn minicams and mikes to camp on the cathedral steps and play paper-scissors-stone over who would venture to step inside for a picture of the beast and a hard-hitting personal interview.

Not that anyone disbelieved the beast's existence. The dragon had been sighted over and over again, soaring through the air above his island, sunlight brilliant on his glittering wings. In an excess of generosity he had commanded his handmaidens and his priest to bring out the charred bodies of the slain policemen and lay them on the steps for all to see. The prowl car he had personally demolished lay in a crumpled heap across the street. Aside from tilting it slightly to remove the bodies of the living and dead pinned beneath, no one dared move the hulk more. Maybe the dragon wanted it left where it was. Maybe he liked to look out of the great cathedral doors and view clear and present evidence of his power. Suddenly the people of New York had become very conscious of what the dragon might and might not like. Suddenly it became very important to please him, at least until the government could intervene.

The dragon reclined on a pile of church treasures and had the first decent sleep he'd enjoyed in ages. He knew nothing of the thoughts clustering in the minds of the people outside the cathedral. He could not have cared less. Their thoughts were as insignificant as themselves. He could obliterate them, but first they might provide a little entertainment. Any halfway competent adept could wipe out a world. Even these puny creatures had the ability to destroy. Somehow that cheapened it for the dragon.

I will not condescend to annihilate them, he mused sleepily. I will not bring myself down to their level thereby. Let them live. They may be useful. And I have an odd desire to add to the paltry number of my priests.

The dragon dreamed true. The airwaves over the city were thick that sunny Sunday morning with news bulletins and the collective wailing, prayers, and imprecations of the network evangelists. Never in the course of history had the people been treated to so many different sermons all preached on the Book of Revelation. The Beast had come. The Dragon had come. The end of the world was near.

The churches were jammed. One devout **Park Avenue** matron did public penance, barefoot **and** wearing nothing more than a cloth coat. Busy executives tied up the phone lines in a panic **to** return the calls of various charities. Privately **they** had sworn not to give another penny until doomsday. Now it looked as if that meant Wednesday **at** the latest.

But there were others, many others in the **great** city who greeted the news of a dragon in **their** midst with emotions other than terror or **hasty** repentance. Subway graffiti, once the province of CHICO-3 and LITTLE ANNIE #19, vanished under coats of concealing latex over which appeared countless lines in praise of the dragon as savior, the dragon who would take his followers to **the** pinnacles they had envied for so long, the dragon who would amply reward the faithful in this world and leave fools to seek comfort in the next.

Sunday passed. At sundown a bizarre procession came winding down Fifth Avenue with lighted candles, transforming the line of march into the semblance of a writhing, glowing, flaming worm seeking its master. The marchers all wore black—not Gothically correct black monks' cowls, but black-satin shirts, black stretch pants, black-polyester blouses, black designer jeans, black-silk dresses slit to the thigh, black leather. The *60 Minutes* people got plenty of good footage and seriously discussed the possibility of doing their feature on the weird goings-on around the dragon rather than risk an in-depth interview with the monster himself. The dragon might be camera shy. It would not pay to annoy him.

The black procession came in twos all the way up to the police barricades. There they stopped, but they kept on singing. It was hard to understand the words. The tune itself was a wild, nerve-twisting ululation that grated on the ear and set fists clenching, teeth on edge. When the chant stopped, you could hear the grateful sighs. They had come with their candles and their weird music and now it looked as if they would go. The double column began to part. They were splitting up to go their separate ways.

Down the center of the aisle they had formed, the living barricade against any interference, a black-clad giant came running with a small, white bundle in his arms. Before the police could protest, before they even understood what was happening, the giant smashed through their barricades, racing up the cathedral steps and in. The bundle gave a thin, wavering cry. When the giant emerged a moment later, he was smiling. His arms were empty. He raised them toward the massed and somber congregation in grim triumph.

The door behind him opened a crack and a golden-haired girl no more than four years old came toddling out on unsteady feet. Her nose was running and she scrubbed tears from her eyes, wiping her hands on her filmy white gown. The dark worshipers gasped with horror.

Their gasp was swallowed up in a shriek of terror as a livid tongue of blue-white splendor licked out to wrap the giant in screaming agony. The little girl, still drying her eyes, did not see it. She stumbled down the steps into the waiting arms of a policeman. The black-clad giant crumbled into a heap of glowing ashes and spindly blackened bones.

They scattered then, trampling their colleagues, clawing at anything in their way. Night came, its darkness hiding their own. The cathedral doors opened wide in the glare of spotlights.

In an unearthly mix of vestments, Riley stepped

into the light and raised his hands for silence. A gunshot was heard, and then a scream, but they didn't find the rookie's body until morning. It looked as if he had turned his service revolver on himself, but there were no powder burns, and the angle of the bullet was impossible. The coroner shrugged and called it suicide, even though a motive was lacking and the evidence was so strange. His buddy swore he had been aiming at the dragon's priest, not himself. No one cared. They'd sort it out later, if later came.

Riley looked haggard. He was as bent as an old man. If they hadn't known who he was, none of his old comrades behind the barricades would have recognized him. The *60 Minutes* gang, joined by the local media night shift, immortalized his image and his words.

"Uh—he said he didn't want her," stammered Riley. He knew he should deliver the dragon's message more impressively, but he couldn't help himself. Some madman had barged into the cathedral with a child sacrifice, and the monster had clearly shown his displeasure. The sacrifice went free, the supplicant was dead.

"He says—he says not to bother him. No more sacrifices. He says he'll let you know what he wants when he wants it. And when he does . . . I guess you'd better do it." He gave a small gesture of despair and vanished into the cathedral again.

The mayor resigned.

The President heard the news from New York and watched the film of the dragon's flight with undivided attention. He did not say it was all a hoax. He had no reason to, although he dearly wished he had. But the truth was evident. A routine reconnaissance flight dispatched to check on the situation in New York had been intercepted and destroyed. No heat-seeking missile did it, no surface-to-air warhead, no hostile plane. The pilot's last words were, "Hey, you're not going to believe this, but—"

But the President believed. The plane was equipped with cameras, and these faithfully transmitted everything the pilot saw and quite a bit he didn't see. One frame of the film was enlarged and mounted on the President's desk. There was no other name for what it showed but dragon. No explosion, no flaming wreck of a flighter plummeting into the Hudson, no fallout of any kind. The plane had ceased to be. The President remembered the old rule that matter could be neither created nor destroyed, but now it looked as if all rules were subject to revision.

The President reached for a Swedish-crystal bowl that was always kept filled and handy. Sometimes it held peanuts, frequently tobacco, this time Raisinets. The President's teeth were in bad shape, but New York was in worse. He swallowed a handful of the chocolate-covered raisins and called for his advisers. He hadn't one damned idea what to do, and they probably didn't either, but calling them in was better than nothing. Always look like you're busy, he thought.

The President's press secretary informed reporters that all possible federal resources were being aimed at New York. The press took notes, shot film, and hid their skepticism poorly. It was, after all, an election year.

"What are we going to do?" Robert Collins asked plaintively. Tamara Bowyer looked startled. Was he actually talking to her? It was the first miracle she was ever able to believe in. But then again, it wasn't so hard to believe. They were the only two people who had showed up for work at City Hall this portentous Tuesday morning.

Tamara thought nothing of the reports of a dragon in St. Patrick's. She had spent the entire Three Mile Island crisis wondering whether a meltdown would mean an end to her *Cosmopolitan* subscription. She celebrated the end of it by getting violet-tinted contact lenses, but they didn't help. Robert, who looked heartbreakingly like Luke on *General Hospital*, still regarded Tamara as a typewriter with legs. You don't get to be the Mayor's hottest young aide by recognizing secretaries as human life-forms.

"What are we going to do?" Robert repeated, the note of desperation rising. "What are we going to *do?*"

Tamara hadn't a clue. She supposed it had something to do with the dragon, but dealing with dragons wasn't her department. What would she do about a dragon, if it came down to it? Weren't there people out there who knew as much about dragons as she knew about Gregg? She often wrote to her mother that you could find anything you wanted in New York, and quite a bit you didn't want, and more than a few things you didn't really want but the department-store displays convinced you you needed. Certainly a city of so many resources could come up with a person capable of disposing of one lousy dragon. Weren't there stories about people like that? Knights. Knights were always slaying dragons. They seemed to make a habit of it. Wasn't there at least one man in all New York who could pass for a knight? It wasn't as if they were dealing with Chicago. Sure, just pop him into one of those suits of armor they had on display at the Metropolitan Museum of Art and presto, instant chivalry!

"Advertise," said Tamara.

"Huh?" said Robert.

"For a knight, you know? To kill the dragon. I bet everyone comes back to work if you get that dragon killed."

"Aha," said Robert, then extended it to, "Ahaha-hahahaha—" until Tamara did the unthinkable; she smacked his face.

"You needed that," she supplied. Judging from the look he was giving her, he thought she was nuts, and she doubted that *Cosmo* ranked insanity as one of its top ten turn-ons. "I didn't mean a real knight," she clarified. "I know there's no real knights left. I just thought that if this is a real dragon, maybe he knows about how knights slay dragons. So we advertise for some guy to dress up like a knight and scare the dragon away. You know, like in the stories. The knight always wins, you know? So what smart dragon's going to stick around to see if he can beat that kind of odds?"

"Do you think it'll work?"

Tamara shrugged. "If it does, it does. If it doesn't, we're not any worse off."

"No," admitted Robert. "Only the guy we hire to play the knight. He'd be dead."

"So advertise in the *Village Voice*," offered Tamara.

"It just might work," said Robert, and gave the overjoyed young secretary an Argentine Back-breaker kiss that would have made the cover of *Cosmopolitan*.

"And now over to you, Jim, for an analysis."

"Thank you, Sonya. The eyes of the world turn today, as so often in the past, to the small island that is New York City, Manhattan, the heart of countless cultural, ethnic, and political kingdoms. New York itself is a kingdom, but now it looks as if there is a dragon at the gates. Yes, in this day and age, a dragon. We don't know where he came from or why, nor do we know what lured him to New York. His power is indisputable, his potential menace tremendous, and one of the greatest cities on the face of the earth finds itself as paralyzed as the tiniest medieval backwater ever was by this creature's ancestors.

"That is, if the dragon is an earthly creature. Theories are as numerous as ideas for dealing with the monster are few. Scientists have offered everything from suggestions of extraterrestrial invasion to hints that our dragon is nothing more than a second cousin once removed to the Loch Ness monster. Nessie, however, is a shrinking violet compared to the creature currently terrorizing New York. The whole affair is reminiscent of those late, great 1950's horror movies. You can almost imagine the young Steve McQueen on the steps of St. Patrick's—the dragon's current lair—imploring the massed townsfolk to listen to him if they want to destroy the monster.

"Steve McQueen is dead, but self-proclaimed savants abound, each with his own line on dealing with dragons. Will we slay the beast, or will we ourselves be vanquished? And if we triumph, will it be a hollow victory? Already there are many voices raised in defense of the dragon's right to live, and our right to learn from it. But in spite of the fear, the conflict, and the tension, life goes on."

(Cut to videotape of kid hawking dragon T-shirts. Music.)

Wednesday. The day that the world would end. The sandwich-board man who usually paraded opposite St. Patrick's Cathedral wearing a placard for Husband Liberation was gone, replaced by a scraggly-bearded, middle-aged stereotypical sidewalk crazy, a prophet in coarse robes whose sign read *THE DRAGON HAS COME. THE WORLD WILL END.* Not one passerby laughed at him. Not one.

Precious few ordinary mortals walked the streets that day. The people in black had returned, their faces hungry, stark white, bloodless as wandering ghosts, red-lipped as sated vampires. They had lost one leader to the dragon's wrath, but their society was hydra-headed, and their supreme lord was not human at all. Soon he would emerge from his lair and recognize their faith in him and grant them their reward.

A second group also gathered. The police had long since given up trying to get the opposing mobs to disperse. They would obey, only to drift back together again. It was like riding herd on an amoeba. The second group wore no uniform color, but you could tell they belonged together; they prayed. On their feet or on their knees, they prayed. Some held rosaries, some stood with their arms spread-eagled in a cross, some carried velvet-wrapped scrolls, some spun prayer wheels and danced, and some tried to stir up the others to attack the black-clad enemy if they could not attack the dragon himself.

Between the two groups stood the media. They were sleepy and more irritable than normal. Here, they realized, was one potential interviewee who would not like any sly questions or barbed innuendo. Courtesy became their new watchword, and they were feeling the strain.

A hush. Riley had come outside so quietly that suddenly he was simply standing there. The dragon had made him take off the vestments. He was tired of the game, and Riley looked ridiculous in them. Riley was back in full policeman's uniform, with only a gold-embroidered, heavily jeweled miter to indicate his rank as the dragon's hierophant.

"He's coming," said Riley in a squeak, and flitted inside.

Cameras, questions, and getaway cars warmed up simultaneously. The bronze doors swung back on their hinges; the dragon's majesty poured out onto the steps in a cascade of green and gold. The sheen of his furled wings was dim, but his scales shone and flashed like multicolored mirrors. Diane and Cruz—her baby wrapped in Riley's old vestments and dreaming peacefully in a pew—flanked him, their presence serving no purpose but dramatic effect. The dragon loved such things. They knelt and prostrated themselves at his silent command. The people who prayed, prayed louder; the people in black prostrated themselves in reverent imitation and waited.

"Mortals," the dragon said aloud, and there was more contempt in that word than anyone except the dragon could know. "Mortals. Know your master."

A hoarse cheer went up from the black-garbed congregation, but not one among them raised his head. The dragon's words slithered through the airwaves, his might transmitted as certainly as his voice. People watching the broadcast on TV suddenly lost the safe sensation of witnessing disaster from a distance.

"Your world is mine," the beast went on. "I have chosen it for mine, and my will shall rule it. Choice is at an end; serve me or perish. Serve me, or the world shall perish!"

Everyone—even the ones in black, even the distant watchers—let out an animal moan of fear. For the dragon sent mounting visions of the worlds he had destroyed, visions that burned the brain and assaulted the ears with the dying screams of whole races, the useless mercy-pleas of vanished worlds. Palaces tumbled into churning seas, forests blazed, mountains seethed and melted into floods of white-hot destruction, and the people perished. The dragon smiled. It was only the smallest of sendings.

"Will you serve me?" he asked softly.

They swarmed forward, screaming oaths of loyalty, promises of abject, total obedience. Not all who groveled before him wore black. The ranks of prayer broke into mass defection, and there was more than one dark-blue policeman's uniform among them. The dragon was pleased. He raised his paw and they scurried back, silent, humbly patient to hear his words.

"Proof," the dragon said, and he sent again. Hundreds of minds held the sudden image. Thousands perceived it flowing impossibly beyond the limits of their television screens. It was the face of a man, a man in armor. Find him. Bind him. Bring him helpless to their lord.

"You have no excuses," said the dragon. He sent a detailed vision of an unpretentious apartment building far uptown. They could read the address clearly. They could almost touch the elevator controls as the dragon guided them up. Then they were taken down a hall to a certain green door and inside where José María and his family sat calmly around a formica-topped kitchen table.

"No excuses," repeated the beast. "You know his shape and where he is and who shelters him! Bring him to me. Tomorrow at dawn, for then there will be blood. His blood . . . and another's." The heavy head turned languidly to rest on Diane's bare shoulder, a shoulder abruptly bare. Her clothes had vanished at the dragon's touch, her long blond hair all that was left to veil her nakedness. Silver bound her wrists. She was the picture of a maiden about to be sacrificed to a dragon.

"Attend me!" commanded the worm. "With tomorrow's dawn you shall learn the proper manner for all future sacrifice to me. Heed well; I give no second lessons. And bring the manling I seek, bring him to seal my sovereignty! Or else I swear by the strength of my teeth and claws, by the power of my wings, by worlds already dead, yours shall be next, and with a very painful dying!"

He swept back into the cool darkness of the cathedral, hastily followed by Cruz, leaving Diane to face the whirring cameras until Riley recovered his senses enough to lead the trembling woman inside.

They streamed away, some shouting, some singing, some wearing the death-angel's robe of silence. They surged uptown, and their numbers swelled with each doorway they passed, swelled by those who had watched it all on television and had thought themselves safe. No one was safe. You were either the dragon's minion, or you were dead. With one will they marched north, to José María's home.

Chapter XVI

MEETINGS

"**S**o what's the newest?" asked Roberto, looking up from his homework.

Manuel was only too glad to abandon the ins and outs of mathematics to answer his brother. "Sealed off the city," he said. "I heard it from some kid who brought his box to class. Teacher didn't even make him turn it off when the news came on. Everyone wants to know if they found that guy yet."

Mike giggled. "Now's our big chance, huh? We got him right here. We could sell him to the highest bidder, and throw the horse in for free. Say, where did Papi stow the horse?"

Roberto ignored the question. "Sell him?" he marveled. "Sell him, is that what you said? Hey, man, if Papi heard you talking that way—"

"Aw, come on!" protested Mike. "Can't you take a joke either? Although," he mused, "although . . . wouldn't it be something to see what the dragon's gonna give whoever brings him the knight tomorrow?" He looked Roberto straight in the eyes and added, "He's the one, Berto. He's got the city. He's got the power. He can do anything he wants. He could make us all rich, man. We could be princes.

Straight out of a book, princes! There's no price we couldn't ask him."

"Mike's right," Manuel chimed in. "We better face it, too. I saw that dragon. He's real, man! I saw him on the news and I saw him once with my own eyes, flying over. He wants the *loco*? I say give him what he wants before he comes up here and helps himself? And if Papi says anything about it—"

A hand, still young, but stronger than ever from long days of bearing his master's armor, fell heavily on Manuel's shoulder. Sanchi stared at his foster brother, his eyes unforgiving, his mouth a tight, narrow line. Manuel froze like a deer caught in the glare of oncoming headlights.

"If Papi says anything about it," said Sanchi slowly, *"what?"*

"None of your business!' Manuel snapped nervously, jerking out of Sanchi's grip. "Leave me alone. I got work to—"

Sanchi siezed Manuel's shoulder again, giving it a hard squeeze just this side of painful. Manuel fought down a shudder. He couldn't look Sanchi in the eye. They weren't Sanchi's eyes anymore, the old Sanchi. The Sanchi Manuel remembered was a kid, a boy, little more than a baby, beneath notice. It was unnerving to face Sanchi the man, and Manuel didn't like it.

"Your work will wait. I want to hear what you're saying. I heard you talk about selling someone. Who, Manuel?"

"Hey, I didn't start talk like that!" protested Manuel. "You want to go one-on-one with someone, you go on Mike. He said we should sell the *loco*, not me!"

"Yeah, all you did was agree with him. You're innocent as hell, Mani. Innocent as hell."

"Save it!" Manuel lashed out.

"Yeah." said Mike, coming to his brother's aid. "Lay off him, Sanchi. It's a free country. He can say what he wants."

"Not about Papi." Sanchi was cold as ice. "And not against George. Not around me." The brothers retreated behind their textbooks with mumbled curses, but they made no further comments about surrendering Sanchi's weird friend. George, huh? Funny name for a *loco*.

"How's he doing, Sanchi?" Roberto asked kindly. Sanchi did not answer immediately. He nodded his head slightly, beckoning Roberto to step out of Mike's earshot. Roberto followed him into the closet that was once his room.

"So?" said Roberto, sitting on the bed. The bed was Sanchi's again, but for the first few days after he and Sandy and the knight had come, this had been George's sickroom. George wasn't bedridden any more, not by a long shot, but instead—well, that was why he didn't want to talk about George in front of Mike and Manuel.

"He's up on the roof again," said Sanchi.

"Yeah?" Berto smiled. "Then he must be OK. Isn't he?"

Sanchi shook his head helplessly. "I wish I could tell, Berto. I wish I could just say hey, sure, he's OK. But he's not. It's like—like whatever got into him made him hollow inside. He's not the same. He knows where the dragon is—hey, remember when we used to make fun of him, him and his dragon-killing sword stories?"

"No one's laughing now."

"No one is. So he knows where it is, waiting for him to hunt it down in the cathedral, waiting for someone to hunt George down for it, but he's not doing anything about it, Berto! It's like he's waiting to be found. Like he's waiting to die!" Silent tears trickled down Sanchi's cheek. Roberto gently wiped them away and pretended he hadn't seen them.

"Hold on, *hermanito*. If he really wants to die, would he be up on our roof every day, practicing with the sword and shield? He's just in training. They get crazy in training, you know?" He lowered his voice and added knowledgeably, "No women."

José María opened the door and announced, "Come out, *muchachos!* Time for the news!" No one missed the news in his house. Papi insisted on that. He hated ignorance, and book-ignorance was only one kind. A kid had to know that the world wasn't nothing but half-hour time slots where everyone gets rich and happy between the commercials.

It was too early in the afternoon for the normal news programs, but normal was out with a dragon in the city. Any channel you wanted had hourly bulletins on the beast, and NBC had full-time coverage. José María turned on the set.

The last they'd seen had been a feature on the beast itself. The cameras never left its eternally grinning face. What was hotter news than hearing the dragon speak? José María had heard it all. He knew the dragon was after the man from nowhere that he was sheltering for the second time. It didn't frighten him and he wasn't going to kick the man out, not for a dozen dragons.

But now the screen showed the marchers. They were massed and moving, and José María thought he recognized the neighborhood they strode through. Five, maybe six blocks south of his house, that's where they were. He recognized the Chinese restaurant on the corner. Some symbol-happy cameraman zoomed in to focus on the name of the place, the Red Dragon. Five blocks away they were, and there were a hell of a lot of them.

"*Jesús,*" murmured José María.

"Papi," said Roberto quietly, "they're coming here after all, aren't they?"

Sandy and Lionel came in. They had just returned from feeding the horse. José María had talked a neighbor into giving the animal space in his garage. No one goes to the upper levels but the owner and his employees, right? So who will know, my friend, whether there is a horse or a Honda in #409? But now José María's resourcefulness had vanished. Mamacita was weeping softly. The mob was coming straight for them, ruthless, mindless, driven. She read the end in those bloodless, set, determined faces.

Sandra slipped away and sped to the roof of the building. An empty pigeon coop was there, a few beer cans, other refuse. For a moment she could not find Persiles. Had he wandered off? Was he already in the street, wandering straight into the heart of the mob that hunted him? For a moment she feared he had jumped. Then she saw him hunched over apparently asleep in a corner, his head resting on his knees.

"Oh, thank God!" she cried. He stirred and smiled at her.

"Did you think I was dead?" he asked.

"Well, I didn't see you, and you haven't been yourself the past few days. When I couldn't see you right off—"

"You thought I had taken my own life." He lurched to his feet and enveloped her in a brotherly hug. "Dear Sandra. So true. So loyal. No knight was ever so well-served as I by you. And Sanchi, of course." There was a strange serenity in his face, a fathomless calm that sent a sick feeling to the pit of Sandy's stomach. She hardly heard him say, "There are worlds where females attain knighthood, did you know that? I wish I could take you to one. You are worthy to wield a sword and shield. Your spirit knows no limits." A wisp of pain misted his eyes and he released her. Leaning on the parapet, he surveyed the city streets below. The first heralding shouts of the mob wafted faintly to Sandy's ears.

"Oh, look," he said dully. "Look at all the people. I wonder what the parade is all about."

"Parade?" she echoed. He was smiling again. She had never seen him truly solemn for more than two minutes together, not since he first recovered his senses after the dragon's attack. "Parade? Persiles, you think—? They're his people! He's sent them for you. The dragon's done it, declared war, and there are plenty of people stupid or scared enough to believe they'll save themselves by serving him."

"They won't, you know," said the knight, still staring out over the rooftops. "He's had servitors before, on other worlds. They are the first he slays when he tires of their antics."

"Persiles," Sandy insisted, "they're coming now! Coming here! They know he wants you and where to find you, and they won't let anyone or anything stop them. What can we do? What about José María's family? He—they—they'll feel honor-bound to defend you. They'll die defending you, Persiles!"

He said nothing. His head moved slightly to follow the flight of a pigeon. The sounds from the street grew louder. Sandra seized the knight and whirled him around to face her as easily as if she had been the hardened warrior and he the barely grown young woman.

"What's the matter with you?" she demanded. "He'll have them all killed, do you understand? He'll make his slaves kill them, and then he'll have them kill you!"

The knight shrugged. "That is always the way. Always the way it has been, always the way it will be until one of us is dead. I am tired, Sandra. Why must the death be his? Perhaps he was meant to triumph from the beginning. I have lost the one sword meant to slay him. Maybe the shape of the universe was always meant to hold a dragon. Maybe all the worlds we dream of lie inside a dragon's egg."

His voice grew soft as he spoke, soft and softer, almost womanish. His eyes were a dreamer's, a prophet's. With a cold shock, Sandra realized there was nothing left of Persiles but a shell to hold the final sigh of his soul. The real Persiles was gone, banished by the supreme force of the dragon's sorcerous power. She was as good as alone on the litter-strewn rooftop.

She gave him one final, hopeless shake and released him. He fell lke a rag doll and curled up into a ball, eyes closed, silently trying to burrow his way back into dreams. She ran down the stairs as if they flamed behind her and pounded on José María's door. "Lionel! Lionel!"

"I'm here! What is it? What does he want us to do?"

"The horse! Get it! Come on, move!" To Sanchi she shouted, "Bring me his robes and armor! Ready the shield! The lance, too, and the one-handed sword!"

"He's gonna fight the dragon!" crowed Sanchi, then turned to his trembling foster family. "You hear that? Everything's gonna be great! He's gonna kill that son-of-a-bitchin' lizard!"

"Not if you don't bring me his sword, damn it!" snapped Sandy. Sanchi hurried to obey. The armor had been unceremoniously piled into one of Mamacita's heavier shopping bags, and the robes worn beneath it were finely woven enough to fit into the same humble carrier. The sword required special handling, the shield and lance required Sanchi to make a second trip. Sandy snatched the sword and bag from his hands and commanded, "Take the shield and lance downstairs. Watch for Lionel, he's bringing the steed. Fix them to the saddle and hold the bridle ready." She was halfway up the stairs to the roof when she heard Sanchi calling her.

"Hey! I'm his page, remember? I've gotta help him arm. He trained me for it enough."

"No," said Sandra tersely. "We're not playing knights and pageboys now. Do as you're told." His eyes hardened and she gentled her tone. "Please, Sanchi. We don't have time for explanations. Please."

Sanchi looked away from her, back to the television set where the dragon's face leered, spilling promises. It was a rerun of the moment when the beast had demanded Persiles brought to it by tomorrow's dawn. It lolled on the steps, two women flanking it. Sanchi stared. He had not yet seen the actual broadcast, only heard of it. Again Diane stood naked and bound, again the dragon hissed sacrifice, again the mob surged north to serve their master, but Sanchi never noticed. His eyes were only for the small, dark-haired woman lost in the dragon's shadow. José María also watched, and made the sign of the cross.

Sanchi sought his foster father's eyes and there read that he had seen true, seen the woman, not some dragon-born shadow wrenched out of the hidden paths of his mind.

"Mi madre," he whispered hoarsely. José María could only nod. He left his chair and tried to touch Sanchi, but the boy backed away, head down like an alley dog. "No," he said slowly, shaking his head. "Not now. No." He whirled and bolted from the room. José María would have followed, but Mamacita was crying again. They were showing the mob's progress on the screen. They were closer, and there were more of them. Her prayers became confused with sobs. José María could not leave her.

Sanchi's eyes were flaming; he thought they would burn right through his head. And no tears. He had imagined how he would act if he ever saw his mother again, he had imagined all the vile names he would call her, but he had also imagined himself in her arms, himself as her baby again, crying for her, and she with her soft hands and butterfly-kiss of a voice soothing away the tears.

There were no tears. He thrust his arm through the straps of the shield and hefted the long battle lance with his other hand. The fire spread from his eyes, devoured his face, sent a roaring sound into his ears, half-blinded him. He took the stairs recklessly, leaping down half a flight in a stride, feeling the butt end of the lance jar when he landed, nearly pitching him off-balance. He didn't care. A broken neck at the foot of the stairs suddenly seemed like a damn good idea.

In the street, Lionel was waiting with the horse. It had thrived under José María's care, and its coat held the glory of a daybreak of pearl and silver. Its great eyes shone like liquid gold, the perfectly formed hollows of the mighty neck held snow-blue shadows, the delicate velvety nostrils blushed against the white like roses. The great steed did not prance or paw the ground, but waited as sedately as a prince who awaits the coming of a king. Beside him, Lionel looked like a servant.

Sanchi did not answer Lionel's greeting. He hung the shield carefully on the saddle bracket designed to bear it, then raised the lance like a mast to catch the wind. From its tip fluttered a yellow silken banner embroidered with a captive unicorn. It flapped bravely in the breeze.

"I said, 'Is he coming?' " repeated Lionel, tapping Sanchi's shoulder. He gazed southward. There was no further need of television coverage to see where the mob was; they were visible little more than a block away. Lionel saw a few of them jogging into the van, but he relaxed when he saw that none of them held any weapons.

"This might not be so bad," he remarked. "They're unarmed."

"Yeah," sneered Sanchi. "You count how many of them? You don't need a knife if you got enough people. They could tear us apart, man, and they look like they'd really dig doing it."

Lionel swallowed hard. His sedentary intellectual's life had been limited on the physical side. A thrice-weekly workout at a neighborhood health spa, an occasional weekend game of racquetball, and that was it. Hand-to-hand combat with a crazed mob? Sorry, that space on Lionel's résumé would have to remain blank. In fact, he doubted how well he would be able to do even if they surged against him while he sat behind the trigger of a machine gun.

"I'm no coward," he mumbled. Sanchi looked at him.

"No one said you were, man. This isn't the place

to find that out. I'm scared too. I bet even George is gonna be scared when he gets his first look at these dudes. I bet—hey! Here he comes!"

Lionel's hand tightened on the bridle. Automatically he stroked the horse's nose, deriving comfort from the indescribably soft feel of it. Sunlight glinted on armor. Sanchi knelt and offered his hands, linked together, to boost his master to the saddle. The horse skittered under the weight and yanked the bridle out of Lionel's hand before he could pass it to the mounted knight. The great white head swiveled back over one shoulder and the stallion drew a deep breath of the rider's scent, then whuffed it out and seemed somewhat satisfied. He permitted Lionel to take the reins again and turn them over to the knight.

Sanchi handed up the lance. It took the knight obvious effort to find the proper balance of the things, but then, Sanchi reasoned, George hadn't been well, and he'd never done much practice with the lance before. Maybe you could forget how to handle such things.

"George," said Sanchi, rapping on the brilliant metal sheathing one thigh. The visored head bobbed lower, acknowledging the boy's presence. "George, I got a favor to ask. You're going to kill the dragon. I know you can do it, man. But listen, he's got people with him. Maybe they're with him 'cause they want to, maybe not. Find out before you kill them, too, huh? Just try to find out." Sanchi's voice dropped, then came back with surprising ferocity. "But if they went with him because they wanted, you kill them! You don't ask them anything, man, you just kill them! Kill them!"

Lionel gaped at Sanchi, but the knight did no more than nod once and gently put spurs to the horse's flank. Sanchi and Lionel watched, waiting for the point where the lone rider would meet the churning frenzy of the dragon's servants.

How the hell did I get myself into this mess? Sandy wondered as she peered through the slits of the visor. Sandra Horowitz, you've done some stupid things before, but this transcends everything. This is stupidity on a heroic scale!

The view through the unfamiliar visor made her squint. She was almost on top of the first comers, the heralds of the swarm. The horse would not let anything turn him. He knew that the one he carried was not his master, but still was his friend. He would fight for the two of them.

A man in black screamed as the horse's ironshod hooves trampled him. Sandy was unaware of what was happening, too intent on keeping her seat, balancing the lance, and all the hundred concerns of a mounted knight at full gallop on a blooded destrier. With this difference: Sandra Horowitz had not been on a horse since a distant summer at Camp Wermagaskett, and that time she had fallen off into a pile of manure.

The stallion charged through the mass of people, cutting through them like a ship through stormy waves. He lashed out with hooves and monstrous teeth, and Sandy's lance managed to sweep a few of the mob out of their way. The people roared on all sides, some clawing at her, some trying to pull her from her seat. She reacted without thinking, swinging the lance. She watched with horror and disbelief as chance allowed her to pierce the body of a man who stood before her. The impetus of the white stallion's charge did the deed, no deliberate thrust from Sandy's hand, but still she felt the momentary resistance of human flesh against the steel-tipped lance, the thick, muffled sound of lance passing through snapping bone and yielding blood.

Mechanically she shook the lance to dislodge the body.

Then they were through. They had sliced the crowd apart and broken through the ranks of the last stragglers. Fifth Avenue, by some trick of perspective, shimmered before Sandy's eyes like the curved purple peak of a distant island. She pulled on the horse's reins. He wanted to turn and cut a new path of destruction through the mob, but she fought him. She only wanted to lure them after and, if she could, get away.

The stallion tossed his head, but obeyed. Behind them, the crush of people set up a din of triumph. The quarry was afraid! He was running from them! Their master would give them the victory, and his blessings when the knight was in his grasp. They stopped counting their dead and wounded, leaving the breathing bodies to lie with the silent ones. They pursued the hunt.

In José María's house the television screen exploded in a flurry of images as the white stallion plowed through the people as if they were wheat. Blood spattered the spotless white of the destrier's flanks, blood dripped from the point of the knight's lance. Elena gave a little cry of dismay and rushed out to hide where she always did, on the rooftop.

"Let her go, Papi," counseled Roberto mildly. "She'll be all right."

"*Ay! Válgame Dios!*" squealed Manuel, pointing wildly at the screen. "What's happening with this city, man? *Hay dos!*"

And so there were two. Sandy thought she was going mad from the jouncing gallop inside the silvery armor, her brains rattled loose perhaps by the occasional rough step the stallion took. Because madness was the only way to explain the vision in armor that now came trotting placidly up the avenue toward her.

Inside his own suit of armor, Jonathan Gutmann was wondering the same thing. Was he finally hitting the sharp edge he'd skirted for so long? He hadn't been told about this part of the deal when he showed up for that interview with old whodo-youcallum—that bozo from the Mayor's office and his dippy secretary. Holy Christ, what a pair! But Jon had needed the bucks, and it seemed like a smooth way to get them. Payment in advance, of course, because he could see he was the only guy in New York crazy enough to answer that weirded-out mimeographed ad some turkey had stuck up on every lightpost in the Village.

No big deal, they told him. Dress up like a knight and ride down Fifth Avenue, give the dragon one good look, then watch him run for Jersey. Dragons are afraid of knights, any fool knows that. Easy money, and Jon needed easy money. He had sold every negotiable commodity and service his body could provide just to make some easy money. Playing Sir Galahad was cream compared to some of the things he'd had to do to earn his keep.

So they took him up to the Metropolitan Museum of Art and bullied one of the curators into unhitching this really wild suit of armor off the back of the model horse. They stripped the fake horse's armor too, and slung it onto the back of the sorrel gelding they'd scrounged while the curator and his assistants crammed Jon into his tin can. It was a tight fit; people were shorter in those days. Not enough junk food, thought Jon, and the thought combined with a rush from his latest hit to send him off in a muzzy cloud of giggles. The laughter echoed weirdly inside the bull-horned helm he wore.

They hoisted him onto the horse, and the horse nearly folded until it got used to the weight. Jon waved one mailed hand and dug his spurs into his steed. Someone on the museum steps yelled, "Godspeed!" It made Jon giggle some more.

God nothing; speed was more like it. He didn't have the slightest notion of carrying out his part of the bargain. If the suckers paid him in advance, that was their lookout. He wasn't going to play tag with a dragon. What if this worm was the one dragon you never heard of, the one who wasn't afraid of knights? Jon would bet his life that it was; bet it from a safe distance. He cut down a side street and doubled back, coming onto Fifth again and urging his nag to try for a trot. The sooner he was safe the better, and he had pals uptown. They'd really celebrate this score. Hell, maybe they could help him fence the horse and armor. All this iron crap must be worth something. People collect the damnedest things and call it a hobby.

Hobby? Jon had only one. Sometimes it did strange things to his eyes. Like now. Like seeing this mirror-image knight come charging right at him, lance couched for the impact, and behind him a bellowing mob of crazies. No, not a mirror image after all. The horse was white, unarmored, the knight's helm sprouted no horns. And he had a lance. Jon didn't have anything like that. They hadn't thought the dragon would wait around to check out his equipment. All he had was a sword and shield. He wrenched them out and cowered behind the steel rim.

The white stallion never slackened pace. He saw the stranger knight, he recognized naked steel and he knew what that meant. Challenge. His master had never refused honorable challenge. For a moment he forgot that it was not his master he carried. His hooves struck sparks from the asphalt, and rained the green fire that was the steed's own sorcery, the power with which he was born. He thundered toward the enemy in a shower of hellish brilliance.

Sandy's whole right side ached with the impact of the lance striking the shield. The lance itself shattered when it hit, splintering like kindling wood. She discarded it and rode on. To her right she recognized the museum, and she realized that they had been racing alongside Central Park for a good while. The park, the huge park, with more than enough places to hide until the mob gave up and dispersed. She pulled on the bridle and made her mount dive into the sheltering green.

Behind her, the crowd had caught up with Jonathan Gutmann. He lay stunned, weighted down with the ancient armor, as helpless as an upended sea turtle, but he could see their white faces looming over him, their eyes no more than black smudges, lightless caverns, their lips very red. They were kneeling. They were slipping cold hands under his armor. He began to gibber and sweat ice at their touch. They were smiling. Some of them were arguing that no, this wasn't the one, that the one they sought had galloped into the park, but most of them were smiling. Their master wanted a knight, and they would bring him one. They let the dissenters go chase phantoms in the park.

Jon felt himself lifted and slung over his horse. He knew where they were taking him. He could imagine what the dragon would do, especially when it learned it had been cheated. He knew he would not be spared.

Mindless laughter glided up like smoke from the bull-horned helmet. It rose and fell and rose again to a squeak of insane glee, then was silenced. The captive knight made no further sound after that, and when his captors took him down from the horse's back he was unnaturally still.

Some of them fled when they saw he was dead. Their master had wanted him helpless but alive. Those who remained shrugged and replaced the helmet to cover Jon's blank and glassy eyes. Let their master think his enemy had died of fright, died out of sheer dread in the dragon's presence. They bound the dead man hand and foot as if he might try to escape any moment and led his horse to the steps of the public library to wait for dawn.

Elena came downstairs just as her family finished watching the short, sharp joust and the fate of the loser. She led the knight gently by the hand. "I found him on the roof," she said.

"Holy Virgin! *Three* of them?" howled Manuel. Sanchi smacked him across the face, making him quiet. He shoved Elena aside and confronted his master.

"What happened? Come on, man, talk! Who's got your armor? Who's that riding your horse? This more magic? You can be two places at once?"

The knight shook his head. "Only a few can do that," he replied humbly. "I have not the skill."

"Then who the hell does?" Sanchi yelled, shaking him, trying to get that queer, bloodless, milk-fed look off Persiles' face. "Who the hell—"

"Where's Sandy?" asked Lionel. No one knew until someone guessed right.

Under an arch of oak leaves, Sandy was asking herself the same question. She had given her steed his head once they entered the park, and he had taken it joyously. Her hands were no longer encumbered with the lance, and she was grateful for that. She needed both hands free to grasp the saddle and keep her seat. The shield rattled against her left leg and branches scraped across her helm with bony fingers. The sun had gone down, and still the great horse ran. There seemed no end to his strength or endurance, but Sandy was almost at the end of hers. When at last he stopped, she slid wearily from the saddle and collapsed in a jangle of metal on the ground.

When she came to, she glimpsed the horse cropping grass beside her in the the moist darkness, his pale coat glimmering like a cloud holding the moon. She saw him entire, not just the tight vision granted by the visor slit, yet she could not recall ever having removed her helm. Her hands fluttered up and confirmed that she was bareheaded. She groped around her in the dark and could not find the silvery casque.

"It's safe," said a gruff voice, and Sandy threw herself flat on her stomach. Persiles' armor was as light as it was strong, tempered from an alloy known only to one lost wizard, and the dragon had slain him. A child could have worn it comfortably. Now, timorous as a child, Sandy raised her eyes from the dewy grass.

She had never seen a man like him before. His shoulders seemed to press against the vault of the night sky, his eyes to glow like dark amber lighted from within. His arms were bare, brushed with four trailing black braids, and on his forehead an iron band gave back a death-dulled gleam of moonlight. He sat a spear's toss away from her; a spear's toss as Sandy would toss it, not he.

"I am Conchobar," rumbled the giant. "No one's made off with your helmet, my girl, not with me minding it. But what a wench is doing all gauded out in man's armor—"

"You will not," said a sweet, deep voice, "call

her wench again, Conchobar. My final warning."
Sandy's hands touched her throat where the bloodstone had begun to pulse with a sure, slow warmth
the moment she heard that beloved voice. From
behind the stallion's left flank came Rimmon.

She could not throw herself into his arms; the
armor interfered. But they could kiss and embrace
after a fashion, while Conchobar looked on and
shook his head and the horse went on grazing.

With an effort, Rimmon was the one to break
away. He held her at arm's length and seemed to
study the contours of her face so earnestly that
Sandra felt afraid. Small winged insects like float-
ing jewels danced and bobbed in the dark air,
lured by the elfin archer's pale brightness, and
with a flicker of his eye he caused a coronet of
these to settle in a living wreath on Sandra's tou-
sled hair.

"My princess," he murmured. She thought he
was going to say more, to send Conchobar away,
to touch the armor casing her and make it slide
away from her body like spring-freed sheets of
mountain ice. Instead he looked down and fum-
bled with a small leather pouch that hung from
his belt. He opened his hand to show her something small and pearly, intricately carved.

"For you," he said. "To hold the bloodstone."
She made no move to accept it, so he removed the
necklace she wore and set the luminous stone se-
curely in its radiant bed of whiteness, then refas-
tened the chain on her neck. Bloodstone and
whitestone shimmered, looking as right together
as if the earth had formed the two stones together
in an indisoluable embrace.

Rimmon smiled and touched Sandy's cheek
lightly. "A true bond," he said. Conchobar tossed

his head like a horse and snorted. Without taking his eyes from Sandra, Rimmon said, "Conchobar! Did you hear me? A true bond, by Sel! You'd better be warned, old friend. Call her wench now, and I'll cover you with more shafts than quills on a porcupine."

Conchobar guffawed. "Elf's not born can do that," he replied, "but I'll respect the w—the lady—for our friendship's sake."

"Stuff it in your ear, you condescending bastard!" barked Sandy. Rimmon gaped, but Conchobar only redoubled his laughter.

"Spirit in her, too! Rimmon, you've won a prize, no mistake. Who else would find a lady so gracious of tongue and dress?"

Sandy was furious. She stalked up to the giant and tried to stare him down, an impossible feat given his height. "I can trade compliments as well as insults when I'm dealing with human beings. And as for the way I'm dressed, I don't like it any more than you do, but I—I had to do something! He wasn't going to do a thing but grin and nod and say how tired he was of all the fighting. The dragon was sending a mob of people up to get him, so I had to dress up in his armor and lure them away. They would've killed anyone in their path. They would've killed the whole family that's taking care of him!"

"Uh?" grunted Conchobar, well-confused. But Rimmon's wits were somewhat quicker.

"You speak of Persiles," he said. "This is his armor; I should have recognized it. What ails him, Sandra? Where is he?"

"Oh, he's safe enough," said Sandy contemptuously. "The great knight, ready to slay the dragon and slay the world! He hasn't the backbone of a newborn kitten! I've never fainted in my life," she lied, "but him? He collapsed for—for no reason, and since then—since then, nothing. He's given up. He's chased that goddamned lizard here, and now it's up to us to finish the job for him!"

Rimmon tried to calm her, tried to stroke her hair, dislodging the circlet of living lights and sending them off in a flutter of confusion into the velvet night. She jerked away from him, too frightened to give up the shield of anger. If she forgot her rage at Persiles for abandoning them that way, she knew she would cry.

"You?" Conchobar could barely contain his hilarity. *"You* finish off that—that *lizard*, as you call it?" His laughter reverberated like thunder under the trees. "Why, listen, woman! There's only one man to defeat the dragon, and that's Persiles! Only the man armed with the sword and the shield, riding the chosen steed, has the slimmest *hope* of ending the monster! Not the certainty, just the *hope!"*

"Oh, yeah?" Sandy countered, with a rough feistiness no elf or giant could hope to understand, not knowing New York. "Well, I've *got* the horse, and I've *got* the shield, and I've *got* the sword, so there! So who says I don't have the same hope Persiles had? At least I'm willing to fight."

Conchobar scooped her up as easily as if she were a doll and kissed her. The wet smack echoed the length of the park. "Spirit! I like that. I'll swear by every weapon I've ever held that this woman *could* slay the dragon. She'd frighten him to death! And with us beside her to help—uh—what did you say, Rimmon?"

"I said," replied the elfin archer, gliding toward them from where he had been examining the white stallion and the weapons he bore, "that she hasn't got the sword. She's got a sword, but not the one meant to do it. I'm sorry, my lady," he gazed at her tenderly, "but you would be the loser."

Sandy started to protest that a sword was a sword, but she did not. She had seen too much not to realize that there are some worlds where a sword is not a sword, and where the power of magic breathes fate into a blade. "What can we do, then?" she murmured. "The dragon wants his first sacrifice at dawn. He knows where Persiles is, and if his creatures don't bring him the man he wants, he'll go after Persiles himself."

"Or Persiles," corrected Rimmon quietly, "will go after him. My lady, keep safe and hidden. Come, Conchobar! You and I have a job of healing work to do!"

Sandra stumbled and sprawled in her effort to dart after elf and giant warrior. The titan had obeyed Rimmon's command instantly, and they were flickering through the trees almost before the last syllable left Rimmon's lips. "Wait! Wait! Where are you going?"

Rimmon paused. "We go to save Persiles, my love. There's still time, and the hope that he'll find the sword, once he's himself again."

"But you have to wait for me! You don't know where he—"

"My lady," Rimmon's voice breathed warmly in her ear although she could see his body drifting ever farther and farther away in the shadows. "My lady, we are one. No thought of yours is unknown to me. Keep safe. We will come for you." Then he and Conchobar vanished, blown to scraps of mist by a sudden wind.

Sandra stared hopelessly into the trees. She groped for the stallion's strong neck and leaned against him, breathing deeply of the pungent, good, horsey smell. It brought her back down to earth and steadied her. How hard to recall that her lover was no more than a phantom from a perished world, a lover who could be real enough to stir a mortal woman, ghost enough to walk paths closed to her. Heavily she swung up into the saddle and tugged at the reins, making the steed take her back uptown, where her beloved might even now be.

They had emerged from the woods to the hard pave of a path before Sandy realized she had forgotten the helmet, still safe at the roots of the oak. She pulled her mount around and headed back to retrieve it. The stallion seemed to understand.

She thought she remembered where that patch of trees had been, but she did not want to find it by the stallion's method, plunging into the thicket of branches again. She compelled him to mind her and keep to a parallel route over open ground, a blacktopped road that took them past the lake where the moon winked and waned and cast dull-umber shadows over the features of Alice and her court. The stallion began to shy inexplicably. Sandra tightened her legs around his barrel and gave him a small touch of the spurs. In response he plunged and reared wildly. The moon's reflection shimmered.

Outrage, said the dragon. The wizard's shade hovered in the lee of its folded wings. It stretched out one paw and struck the ground with a force that shattered the pavement and rived a crack through the Alice statue.

Sandra gaped into golden eyes that poured back a flood tide of cold hatred and jealousy. The dragon raised himself up out of the darkness and spread his wings in a snap of flame. The wizard's phantom trembled and vanished. You dishonor him, intoned the beast. Unworthy to wear his armor, you wear it. You lessen me by lessening him! You shall pay for all debts to both of us. At dawn, you and the other. You and, if I choose, your world. All worlds that dare to hold him, to keep him from me! Death. Death to you all, bloodless, fireless, petty loves of his heart. I claim it, I alone claim it! Living or dead, I will have it. I will have him!

The dragon swooped a claw down out of the night as swiftly as the killing rush of a hawk. It was meant to kill Sandra where she sat, meant perhaps to slay the stallion as well. But the stallion was not held slave to the dragon's eyes. His great eyes flamed into golden fire in the face of his old, old foe, and just as the dragon struck he leaped for the creature's throat, teeth gnashing, hooves flailing in a burning evergreen fire storm.

The stallion's attack was so unlooked-for that the dragon sprang back out of range of the maddened spirit-horse. The stallion, just as unexpectedly, wheeled and galloped headlong away, Sandra clinging to the pommel in a daze. Behind them she heard the dragon roar his rage.

He can't catch us, she thought numbly. He'll never catch us. This horse is wind, nothing swifter, nothing more—

She thought she felt a second rider clinging to her waist, perching postilion, and her skin seemed to cry out that it was Rimmon, Rimmon come back for her, to save her. A gentle hand caressed her face, and she loosed one hand to reach for it, to gain strength from knowing he was there, her love, her only love.

The searching hand caught in the branches of a low-hanging maple, and the shock wrenched her from the saddle. As she rolled over and over in the grass she glimpsed the stallion racing on. There was no other rider. The bloodstone was chill against her throat. Rimmon had never been there at all.

Too late, much too late, she knew the dragon's mastering power of dreams, his sovereignty of illusion. She came to rest on her back, gazing up at the moon. Under her she felt the earth shake with the heavy tread that came for her.

Chapter XVII

SACRIFICE

Who had slept that night?

Not the silent watchers. They stood waiting in their ranks of blue and black and scarlet on the library steps under the sightless eyes of the stone lions. There were streaks of cloud visible in short strokes across the wedge of sky glimpsed between the tall buildings running up Fifth Avenue to the north. Their master would come out of the north, and so they stood, guarding the dead body of a knight in armor, and waited.

Who had slept that night?

Not the family, gathered to witness a circle of healing. They stood like timorous children, peeping in through the open door of the bedroom where the stranger lay, the one they had taken in. Things out of legend moved in that room, garnering added strangeness merely from comparison with the mundaneness of their surroundings. Conchobar stood guard, a sword in his hand curving out of the darkness like the horns of the moon. The elfin archer knelt beside the bed, his bow and quiver tossed into the same corner where José María's tackle box stood gathering dust and waiting for spring. A fine thread of sound sang in the still air, a song of healing. Persiles, eyes veiled doubly, felt the elf's will pierce his own with the force of a snow-fletched arrow tipped with fire.

Who could sleep that night?

Not the old and young comrades in arms. They had gone from the warm sureness of the family, impelled by a great fear and a great love. There had been little need for them to tell each other of their intentions when they left the small apartment. She was gone, and they would find her. She was their third self, her soul and fate bonded to theirs, her courage shining brighter than the armor she had put on, her face shining brighter still, for Lionel's eyes alone. They would go to her, they would save her.

Save her? For all they knew, she might yet save them. But however it would be, they knew they needed weapons. They realized this too late, when they were well downtown, far from José María's home where the rest of the swords Sanchi had gathered for his master lay unused, a strange pile of discarded beauty.

"Come with me," said Lionel. "We won't go unarmed." Sanchi followed him, and the professor took the boy down a prim side street and into the lobby of the building where he lived. A pile of circulars and periodicals, all with Lionel's name on them, littered the cherry-wood sideboard beneath the row of brassy mailboxes. The mailbox with Lionel's name was stuffed thick. It had been too long since he had come home.

Everything was as he had left it. Dust had only settled lightly. The Thuringian triptych glowed like a golden star in the murky light, the unscrolled map of uncharted seas with the isle of Prester John marked scarlet still lay untouched on the leather-topped desk, the unknown regions of the deep wreathed by a twist of dragons and the legend, "Here Be Demons." The sword still rested in its tarnished scabbard across the arms of the leather-covered chair.

Lionel took up the sword and hung it at his belt. He looked ridiculous, a bizarre, bearded apparition playing the hero. But Sanchi did not laugh. His face mirrored Lionel's, grim-eyed, holding in the fears of imagination, each step closer to battle an irrevocable one.

"At least now we have a fighting chance," said Lionel, trying to smile.

"He's had it," Sanchi agreed with a brittle grin. "We've got him now. He better hope nothing's happened to Sandy, that's all."

"Nothing has happened to Sandy," repeated Lionel. He said it to gain courage, to make it so by saying it was so, but his heart shivered with the emptiness of not knowing anything, anything at all. He gave Sanchi a small Persian dagger to wear. Little use against monsters, but sometimes a gesture was more necessary than sword and shield and full armor and a silken banner. They walked with echoes slowly to dawn.

Who had slept that night? Not the woman in armor. She sat with her wrists bound loosely to her ankles and looked across the cold expanse of cathedral floor to where a naked woman draped with her own golden hair stared off into space. Another woman, smaller, darker, nursed her infant and put him down to sleep in one of the pews, cushioned with soft vestments formed into a nest where the baby cooed and kicked and wet himself as casually as if he were in a crib that was a crate, on linens that were faded and worn.

I am going to die tomorrow, she thought. I'm not afraid of it. I don't think I believe it's going to happen. But I know it will. That woman there, she looks more the part of the dragon's sacrifice, the golden princess. I wonder if she is a princess? If anyone comes tomorrow to stop the sacrifice, they won't be coming to save me. I am expendable, like the extras they used to have on every episode of *Star Trek*. If there was a monster, they always showed it destroying someone nonessential, just to make it all that much greater when Captain Kirk and his regular crew finally killed it. I am the expendable extra in this little fairy tale. I am all the maidens the dragon devoured before St. George deigned to show up and rescue the king's daughter. I am every peasant girl slain by the sea beast before Perseus came to deliver the royal Andromeda. You won't hear much about me when this is over, but Persiles and that woman—Good God, she's crying again, the nitwit!—they'll live happily ever after in the castle on top of the hill. Only this is New York. Maybe she's got a townhouse for her palace, or a co-op, or even a penthouse. And she is very pretty. That much I'll have to give her. If she died, it would matter.

Maybe I'm not afraid because I'm dreaming that I'll wake up in another fairy tale, with another princess and another knight. Maybe another dragon? No. One of these is quite enough for anyone's reality.

Sandy sighed and closed her eyes.

Who had slept that night?

Not the dragon. He dropped the second skin over his glaring golden eyes, but he did not sleep. A phantom, small and brown and naked, scampered on sandaled feet across his inner eye. A little naked boy played among the heaps of gold, the hoarded jewels of the centuries of unchallenged power.

There had been others. They had served him, amused him, felt his commands in their heads and obeyed, and when they grew too old or too ugly or too clumsy, he killed them. This one he loved. Why?

The dragon shuddered, and the tremor arced across the floor and woke the drowsing baby. The dragon switched his tail, annoyed. The naked boy capered through his mind and touched all the old, dreaming aches to full wakefulness again. He had loved him. Of all the children given to his power, he had loved one alone, and the one had betrayed him.

A rainy day, gray and chill. A hunt—or was it a clean, happy killing? A would-be hero dead, his head cradled in the crumbling leaves that dwindled into mold along the woodland paths. The dragon exultant, never more sure of his strength, returning to his lair and finding it . . . empty. Calling, softly at first, with just a thin probing into darkness for the boy's mind, then louder, more insistent, calling for him aloud, in roars that shook gently blooming fungus flowers from the cave walls. He had not roared in centuries. The child was gone.

He had stopped searching for reasons behind the desertion. He had destroyed the sage who had sheltered his boy, who had instructed him, who had sent him on his way armed with the knowledge capable of bringing the dragon down. And yet what rankled in him like a poisoned wound was not so much the boy's power of death over him, but that his own one, his beloved, would give him his death willingly. That he did not love as he was beloved. That he could love another, and not him.

That second loving had not come right away. First there had been the hard years, the years when sheer force of heartbreak drove the dragon to flee from the one he had loved, the one who

could not love him in return. Through worlds and
worlds they had run, and the boy had become a
stripling, the stripling a youth, the youth a man
who never lost the pure light of a long-dead boy's
innocence in his eyes.

There had been women. The dragon knew the
moment when his dearling had first gone in to a
woman. Initiation was short and joyless, and although he knew that the knight went on in spite of
the flat bitterness of those encounters with tavern
wench and priestess and peasant girl and princess,
he also knew that it would not be so forever. The
worlds were finite. Love waited to be discovered
on Khwarema.

Rage. Rage and jealousy and a hatred so all-
consuming that the heralds of his coming were
enough to lay waste a third of that unfortunate
world. She, the stealer, was among the first who
died. It was the metallic taste of disappointment
that the dragon held in his scarlet mouth when he
learned that she was safely dead. He had meant
other deaths for her, fitting for the creature who
dared to rival him. His destruction of her would
have melted her ghost to steam.

*I have been cheated so deeply that no holocaust
of worlds will ever be enough to make up for what
she stole from me,* the dragon thought, and his
claws grooved complaining furrows on the icy floor.
*But I will still slay this world, because that is all
he understands me as, a monster of destruction.
Let it be so. And if he wished, he might have saved
every world I ever obliterated. He had only to
return to me. There were few killings when he
shared my heart.*

The dragon gazed in a flaming slit beneath scaly
lids and drew a long, hissing breath of disgust for
the crumpled bits of this world's human populace

now sharing his roof. The one he would have made his priest was pathetic, the yellow-haired woman a bundle of sobs and twitches, the dark woman all softness set on edge each time he so much as glanced at her baby, the baby already showing the full promise of mediocrity. Only the one in armor held a worthy soul, but she had suborned it to unworthy deeds. The armor was his, his beloved's. She had dared. There were always prices.

Tomorrow, if they did not bring his beloved before him, he would add another world to his roll of obliterations. And if they did, he would slay only the humans already pent within the circle of his paws. The dragon narrowed his glance still more, focusing on the sleeping baby. The baby first, he thought. I shall have the baby first.

Who had slept that night? Not the city. Not with a dragon dreaming visions of death so casually in the heart of the island. The island itself became the world-heart, throbbing sullenly, begrudged each further moment of life by the endless creature sprawled leisurely across their days. If the heart stopped, the world would stop. All deaths would be equal. But even the few close believers in an empty afterlife feared to die.

Who had been able to surprise sleep? Babies and the old, equally indifferent to the end of worlds.

It is dawn, said the dragon.

It was very cold. The cross streets funneled up a wet breeze from the East River, heavy with the hint of mizzling gray rain. Wedges of light angled sharply in between the buildings, crimson, scarlet, and gold between clouds the color of new swords. The dragon stepped out of the incense-laden cathedral close and took a deep, joyful breath of cool, moist air. Come, he commanded.

What a travesty of an Easter-morning parade, although last Easter was long gone and no one could say when they might be privileged to see another. The dragon called forth his captives and compelled them to march before him down the dawn-empty streets to the dingy white steps of the library where the lions waited and the body of a knight in armor lay fenced in a circle of watchful worshipers. First Riley walked, each step unsure, holding back as if hoping that soon a voice would come out of a cloud and tell him it was all right, it was over, he would wake up soon in Bellevue the victim of a madness that had begun on the night he saw a knight's white stallion race through Harlem. The pressures of a policeman's job, after all.

The women had no similar fantasies to give them comfort. Cruz, holding her baby, walked between Sandy and Diane, free where they wore silver shackles. There had been a chief of the Taino Indians who once reigned over the island she and her kin had come from, a chief who admired the pretty silver bracelets the Spaniards showed him. He had asked for them to show him how they worked. The rest is easy to divine, and the pretty silver bracelets glimmered out of the legend to bind pale wrists this time, but Cruz held her baby close to her breast and knew that the dragon had bound her with chains that were stronger, if unseen.

Someone began to sing. The chant was solemn, nearly atonal, harsh and wild in places, random in its rise and fall. The television people were there to record it, and the radio people to transmit it, and the entire city and the entire world, now apprised of the strange dark thing that held the world-heart, waited and listened.

No, said the dragon.

Men screamed like rabbits. Whiteness flared out

of the lenses of minicams and Minoltas, all glass
writhed and changed into blinding swaths of pure
brilliance, burning cold as the polar star, trickling
down across unsuspecting human flesh and sear-
ing it on the bone. Skin bubbled and cracked where
the dragon-touched glass made contact. Wires
twisted like snakes, tangling and binding without
pattern. The only light left was the coming sun,
the only whir the dragon's wings, unfurled, holding colors from beyond the sunrise. When all was
calm again, the dragon spoke.

Where is he?

They brought the body of the knight toward
him, the dead feet made to stagger with the semblance of a living man drugged with fear. Two of
the black-garbed ones carried him between them
like friends carrying home a drunkard. They lowered the body at the dragon's feet and grinned.
The helmeted head lolled forward on the armored
chest.

He changed their bones to fires. They flamed up
from the inside, taken too quickly with the surprise of inburning pain to open their mouths. He
sent ice into the shaking cells of their flesh, ice to
meet the fire of their bones and melt away bone
and flesh and blood and skin into twin pillars of
steam the color of roses. The others saw, and tried
to run. They ran into walls of solid air raised up in
a flicker of the dragon's sorcery. They clawed at
nothingness, held in a cage without doors. They
whimpered for help from powers they had abandoned long ago and cursed forces whose existence
they doubted.

The dragon gripped the stone under his feet and
a chasm opened, deep and wide, riving the black-
top of the avenue. Some tumbled into it, wailing
in a fall to last forever. The canyon stretched to

the measured limit, then snapped shut with a clap
of thunder.

You have failed me, said the dragon. I am
disappointed.

Someone somewhere giggled nervously. The silence was otherwise absolute, the dragon's thoughts
breathing cold fear into every mind.

The dragon took an idle swipe at the inert figure
in armor. It soared through the air, steel-cased
limbs jangling, and crashed through the window
of the steak place across the street. The crowd
drew back, away from the dragon, their eyes daz-
zled by the daylight reflecting from his wings.

Later, promised the beast, I will deal with you.
Obey me, and perhaps it will not be as harsh as I
am thinking of making it now. Prepare the sacrifice.

His thoughts trickled down to their hands. Four
of the strongest among them, male and female,
trudged up the steps and seized Sandy and Diane.
Diane did not fight them. Her limp, white, nude
body pressed thigh to thigh against the men who
carried her to the left-hand pedestaled lion and
slung her across its cold paws, face to the sky.

Sandy fought. She struggled against the two
women in black who came to arrange her as the
dragon wanted. Sandy was not about to be ar-
ranged. She still wore Persiles' armor, and even
with bound hands she was a formidable opponent.
The woman groping for the shackle chain received
Sandy's bunched and tied fists full in the stomach,
knocking the breath out of her. The other gaped,
and in the unguarded moment Sandy's foot lashed
out and caught her just under the right-hand-side
ribs. She turned and ran up the library steps before two more dark minions could separate themselves from the crowd and wrestle her to the lion
altar. The steps were worn into gentle dips in the

places where patrons had most often climbed; they made her slip. But no one was following her. No one seemed to care. Not even the dragon. She scrabbled to the top of the steps and stared down at the monster's rippling back, the wings rising and falling like the swell of the sea. He did not even turn to see if she had escaped or not, and that indifference was more terrifying than the hottest of pursuits could be.

He was that sure of her death. One way or the other, he would have it. If not as his first sacrifice, then as part of a subsequent one, but there was no need to trouble himself about her now. He would take a substitute life at his pleasure. He sent the command.

Cruz, kneeling on the rough stones, saw them coming toward her. Riley, standing helplessly nearby, saw them too, and understood. Cruz screamed and clutched her child. She too understood. Even Diane, so silently waiting for her death, knew of the dragon's second choice. One child at least who would not grow up to betray the one that loved him. A child's death to numb the pain of what another child had done.

They wrenched the baby from Cruz's arms and laid it with obscene delicacy between the paws of the lion. The air grew storm-heavy, pulsing slowly with the dragon's anticipation. The crowds that had come to stare in horror or witness with awful joy stood massed to either side of the monster, a human Red Sea. The dragon curled its tail close around its body, its glorious eyes cold and golden, fixed greedily on the tableau before it: Diane draped across the paws of one lion, the baby squirming uncomfortably in the chill stone embrace of the other.

"Oh!" One of the women lunged forward. The

baby had wriggled out from between the lion's paws and tottered on the edge of the plinth, about to fall. She caught the child and replaced him. The dragon's laughter blew her halfway up the library steps.

What's the matter? Afraid something will happen to him? the dragon chuckled.

Then he reared himself up, wings fanned, the tips beginning to glow scarlet. The twin crowds fell back, those in the front ranks whimpering, shielding their faces from the burning mountain of scales, the wings of all-consuming fire. The dragon's claws caught the sunlight and froze it into ten arctic moons.

Now I will begin it.

"Dragon!"

The city stopped. There was no gasp from the crowd, no cry of fear or wonder. They were all long past amazement. They were leaves dead on the branch, and the naked man walked among them cutting his path as easily as a sword.

His body was hard with muscle, brown with sun, scarred with battle. Jeweled sandals were on his feet; he wore nothing else. He carried an unsheathed sword. The thick eyelids of the worm blinked slowly. The dragon's golden eyes struggled to interpret clearly what they saw.

Is it you? Is it truly you?

"This is the last battleground, killer," said Persiles. "You won't eat another world after this day's fight."

Your armor—

"I need nothing more than I have. I never needed anything else to slay you. I should have realized that long ago." He glanced down at his own nakedness and laughed. "Does this remind you of the past? You had my brother first, if I recall. It was a very long time ago. How many years, dragon? How many worlds? We've gone beyond spells and sorceries, you and I. The old wizard's words were meaningless, nothing but trappings. What does it matter what sword, shield, or horse? It's my hand alone that's meant to end you, and I don't need any special magic for that."

The dragon sank down, wrapping its bulk tighter and tighter in against itself. A nervous murmur went up from the people. The dragon was afraid. The dragon was actually afraid. Someone ventured a prayer. Cruz stole up quietly, unperceived, and took back her child. She would have run, but the dragon's servants still stood guard. They would not let her pass.

From her perch, Sandy watched all that happened as numbly as if it were all a nightmare of her own making. Only when a loved voice behind her spoke suddenly—"My lady"—did she spin around and fall shaking into Rimmon's arms.

"You're here! Oh, thank God! And Persiles—why is he—? Couldn't you find him something to wear?" The question sounded stupid, but she had to ask it. Her dry lips trembled. She tasted salt on them.

Rimmon forced her to step back. Conchobar's looming shadow fell across her silver shackles. The giant's gnarled hand closed on the chain and twisted it to an easily snapped thread of metal. Huge fingers gave each cuff a practiced flick and they fell to the pavement with a sound like bells.

"He would wear nothing," said the elf. "I have no way of knowing what paths his soul wandered while he lay sick of the dragon's sending. I thought I had healed him. Healed or not, he means to fight. And there will be no magic in this battle." His eyes looked grim.

Sandy's fists knotted. "He'll win," she stated,

looking down. The crowds were drawing away, moving faster than a riptide in spite of their numbers. They were clearing a space for the combat. The dragon was a mound of darkness, all the beauty of his scales, his crest, his wings strangely extinguished. Persiles, naked and with drawn sword, shone like a spear of light against the darkness.

"He's gotta win," said Sanchi. He and Lionel had crept up on the library from the back, coming through the park where winos dozed and junkies sought brief refuge. It had been deserted. Even the pigeons had found other roosts.

Lionel passed a free hand wearily across his forehead. "Of course," he mumbled. "He has to." But inside him all the reasons why Persiles could not possibly win began to call to one another, and over all came the bitter memory of the dragon's mocking laughter when he had served the beast in captivity.

"Hey." Sanchi was tugging at his arm. "Hey, look who's over there." Slowly Lionel followed Sanchi's eagerly pointing finger across the portico of the library.

"Sandy," he said low. "But who are those people with her?" He strained his myopic eyes.

"It's them, Persiles' friends. Man, look at the giant! What's he waiting for? I bet he could slice that snake to pieces if he tried halfway. What's he waiting for?" Sanchi snarled, then shouted, "Sandy! Hey, Sandy!"

"Quiet, damn it," Lionel snapped. He looked quickly to see if Sanchi's unthinking shout had made Persiles look up, break the terrible concentration as the naked knight wove in ever closer to the waiting dragon. His fears were hollow. Knight and dragon both were held fast in their own world, a slow circling dance of death. Only death itself could break the ring they made.

Sandy's head jerked at the call. Happily Sanchi scrambled toward her, threw himself into her arms in a way he would never have done if he'd thought about it. "Jesus, am I glad to see you!"

"Me, too," she beamed. Her eyes found Lionel, walking to their side of the library steps as softly as if he were afraid of waking sleepers. He took her hand and squeezed it, feeling words rise in his throat, then die on his lips when he glanced at the elfin archer. Rimmon laid a tapering hand on Sandy's shoulder. Conchobar, like the ghost of a cave bear, loomed up behind them.

"Your part in this is over," said the elf. "So is our own. It is where it was fated to be from the first. Persiles and the dragon."

"But what—" Lionel's protest was cut off by a hoarse cry. It was Sanchi, fighting fiercely in Sandy's grasp. They had stepped aside, woman and boy, and while Lionel and Rimmon measured each other, they had happened to gaze back down the steps to where Diane still lay bound across the lion's paws. That was when Sanchi had yelled.

"They still got her! Goddamn bastards, they still got her! You let me go, man! They're gonna kill her! Win or lose, they'll kill her!" He lunged for the steps. Sandy seized his arm and restrained him. Now they were fighting.

Below, surrounded by the dark guards, Cruz looked up and saw the armored woman struggling with the thin-limbed boy. The infant in her arms kicked and began to wail, but she was past noticing it. For the first time in her life, she ignored its cries. She was drinking in a face, dark, with troubled eyes; a familiar face that had been lost for too long. It wasn't possible, her mind told her. At the gate of death you saw a lot of ghosts. This one couldn't be real.

"*Mamita! Déjenla, hidepútas! Déjenla! Suelten! Que les voy a matar, cochinos!*"

"Sanchi!" It burst from her in a scream. She clutched the baby tighter and hurled herself against the wall of dark ones. "Sanchi!" They shoved her back. She tottered into the lion's plinth and felt her head make dull contact. Lights flashed inside, and she was only vaguely aware of someone taking the baby from her.

"*Mamita!*" His voice was hoarse with anguish when he saw her go down, saw the man in priest's robes snatch the baby away from her. He drew the short dagger, ready to fling it even if he hadn't the faintest idea of how to throw a knife. Again Sandy's hand seized his, prevented him. The tears began to streak his face as he sobbed for her.

Lionel came to Sandy's relief. The boy pummeled him hopelessly. "Let me go, you bastard! That's my mother they hurt. I gotta help her. Let me loose!"

"Your mother?" Lionel repeated dumbly. Rimmon and Conchobar had come to join them. The elf's hand stretched out tentatively, then withdrew without touching the boy. While Lionel held Sanchi, now crumpled into a ball of grief against him, Rimmon whispered something inaudible in Sandy's ear.

"What?" she asked.

"I said, I find this strange, my lady. I read hate in him before this. When I walked into his thoughts, hate burned there, hate for her." He nodded to where Riley stood, shielding Cruz, cradling her child. He regarded Sanchi again. "Maybe I've known the dragon's shadow too long. Can your kind slay hate so easily?"

Sandra did not answer. Once again her eyes were on the weaving dance playing itself out at the foot of the stairs. A cold wind sliced up sharply through the streets and the bleak sunlight faded to gray. It was incredible, but she had to make an effort to see the dragon now. He had melted in on himself, lost light and power with every circling step Persiles took. Sunlight glinted from the bare blade. When its reflection struck him, the dragon cringed.

"He's afraid," Sandy breathed, folding her hands on her armored chest. "He'll kill him, and he knows it."

"Sel guide his sword," came Rimmon's reply, "and not make him too sure of victory until he has it. The old prophecies are broken if he succeeds. And if he fails—"

"He won't!" Sandy threw back at him. "Look, Rimmon, look! This is it, the end of the monster! He's not even trying to fight back. He knows he's as good as dead. Fear's eating him alive!"

Aaaahhh!

The sound of it spread over them all like the firebloom of a mushroom cloud. It seemed to come from everywhere, from every mouth, the long indrawing of breath, the gasp that could have been marvel, fulfillment, final cry of victory. The sword swung high as Persiles leaped forward to strike the cowering shape of the dragon. His whole body was a second sword, beautifully curved and deadly. The blade fell in a silver hiss.

Air.

The sword cleaved air and darkness. The shadow Persiles had stalked crumbled to dusty ghosts that flew away through the crowd, chittering and clawing. The people screamed to feel phantom claws rake their faces.

Then he was there.

Earth or air, no one could tell from where he came. He was huger and more horrible than ever before, the sight of him enough to wipe out a man's mind, fill it only with emptiness. His beauty was untellable, and the evil of it seared the soul. It left no room for any thought of flight or fight. He was all. His power was an ending to all endings. His claws swept down.

They heard Persiles gasp, too shocked by his own death to scream. His nakedness disappeared beneath a cloak of blood. The sword fell before the second blow from the dragon's claws. The knight was nothing, a mark of scarlet on the abysmally black and lonely street.

The dragon smiled.

The death beyond death, he said, leering down at the pitiful remains. Forever alone in the darkness, and far from her. Never to find her. Never! You should have served only me.

The dragon dipped his head and began to feed.

The horse burst through the crowds like a star, his nostrils flaming. The people covered their ears against the maddened shrieks, a sound no horse had ever made before. The stallion's hooves cut shallow gashes along the monster's flank, his teeth snapped wildly against the gorgeous scales. The dragon raised his head lazily, and his paw swung casually back. He would send the horse to follow the rider.

Pain struck him. The white-fletched arrow protruded from his paw, and another flew to lodge a handbreadth from his right eye. He shook them loose, but the pain stayed. More arrows came whistling to their marks, and a battle cry rode on their shafts.

They were coming.

Sandy was the first, leaping down the steps bare-handed to snatch Persiles' sword from under the dragon's nose while Rimmon's arrows hummed distraction all around the monstrous head. Sanchi ran after her, brandishing the dagger, and Conchobar lumbered along behind, his battle-ax thrumming as he whirled it overhead. Rimmon crouched at the flank of the left-hand lion, his shafts true, if not inexhaustible.

The dragon snarled and swished his tail like a scythe. Sandy dodged in close and slashed at the gaping mouth. Blood dripped hot on her blade. She leaped away, out of his reach, then closed with him again. Conchobar's ax fell and rose and fell again, carving pain.

Slowly, a man in a dream, Lionel descended the steps, his sword still sheathed at his side. His right hand groped for it, found the pommel, but stopped there.

You . . . *dare?*

The dragon's rage was palpable, a hot breath that swept them all from their feet. Even Rimmon, crouched by the lion, tottered backward. Conchobar sprawled drunkenly on the pavement. Sandy and Sanchi toppled into one another, a human tumbleweed that rolled away to knock down Lionel. The three of them were a tangle of arms and legs, a bizarre many-limbed insect beneath the hard silver carapace of Sandy's armor. The dragon curved like a cobra against the sky.

The white stallion lay beside his master, blood and snow.

Dead! the dragon gloated, his claws marking the air. Horse and rider, now less than shadows. The magic cannot touch me. I am beyond magic. I will wipe it from the worlds, and the worlds themselves from existence. I am all! I am—!

Armor sparkled in a sudden ray of sunlight. A whirlwind of arms flailed out, three blades shining. They stood together, a wedge, an arrowhead whose point was the sword Lionel now finally drew from its scabbard. Sandy made her stand on his left, inexpertly guarding his flank. Sanchi crouched below the swing of Lionel's sword, ready to follow up any blow with the sting of his dagger. The dragon met something in their eyes that struck him hard and cold, near the heart.

Why . . . the dragon marveled.

They were Rimmon's last arrow. Together they flew against him, and his fear made him rear up in unfamiliar panic. The great pale belly was a ghostly moon before them. He braced with his tail, ready to heave himself on top of them, crush them. And he knew as he planned it that he had made a grave mistake. Centuries without one, and now . . .

The dragon's death-shriek shook the island to its bedrock. The people cowered, covering their heads, shielding their faces against the shower of shattered glass now falling in a rain of knives from the buildings around them. Fragments drew blood from bare arms and bowed necks. The quake sent Diane rolling from the lion's paws, her wrists still shackled, her long limbs tangled in her hair. The lions rocked and groaned on their pedestals, threatening to rive themselves apart in an agony of stone.

Sandy, Sanchi, and Lionel scattered the moment the sword pierced the dragon's skin. Empty-handed, Lionel was just another face in the crowd, gazing up with his breath frozen in his chest to watch the mortally wounded beast sway drunkenly back and forth on shuddering haunches before the final fall. For a moment the golden eyes drank in the sun, then the milky lids fell over them forever. The dragon toppled, the massive head smashing down at the foot of the library steps, the great tail thrashing out one last time as the wings crumpled into a flame-colored shroud.

Something broke, the iron thread holding the crowd together. Slowly at first, then faster, like ice breaking up in the spring, they began to edge away in groups of two or three, then seven, then ten, then solid streams of people fleeing up and down the avenue. They ducked into crosstown streets, sheltered in storefronts, looked at their watches as if what had just happened were something amusing to fill the lunch hour—like sidewalk mimes or musicians—but now they had to be getting back to *real* business. The dark ones who had served the dragon were less circumspect in their departure. They scuttled away quickly.

"Roaches," mumbled Sanchi, watching them. The dagger in his hand dripped blood so red it looked almost purple. He dropped it and bolted up the library steps to his mother's side. "Mamita?"

She was awake and Riley had given the baby back to her. The policeman took off his dark-blue uniform jacket and draped it around Diane's pale body. Automatically his hand went to his breast-pocket first and took out his pad, ready to write down her statement.

"Sanchi!" The baby nestled in the crook of her left elbow, but her free arm reached out hungrily for him. *"Hijito."*

The thin, endless mewing of a siren slid through the air. "First the cops, then the reporters," sighed Lionel, staring at the sword hilt protruding from the dragon's chest. " 'And tell our viewers, sir, how did it feel to kill a dragon?' I can hardly wait to make the cover of *People.*"

"I think," said Sandy, her eyes on Rimmon and Conchobar, "that a dragon slayer may have to wait one issue. How often do they get elves and giants in New York?''

Conchobar was in a world of his own, a world bounded by the strangely worked pommel of the ancient sword. "Looks like it. But it's been a long time. Can you read these, Rimmon?'' The elf clambered up the giant's limbs as if he were an oak. Keen eyes studied the winding runes.

"Belgor,'' he said at last. "It is the sword.'' He took the hilt in both hands and pulled it free.

New York and every person in it blinked out. They were alone—Sandra and Lionel, Rimmon and Conchobar, dead Persiles and his steed—beside the body of the dragon. It glowed with a chill light, a pyre of ice, the only brilliance in a night filled with swirling mists. Belgor too shone.

Then the mists parted. A distant jingling sound came nearer, the formless music of a cavalcade. They turned their faces toward the sound, but it lost direction, seeming to come from every side at once. Silvery tinklings of harness trappings blended with the softer sounds of fine rustling silks, the bolder notes of a single lute-song.

In the darkness, waiting for something she could not see, Sandy found herself edging closer to Lionel, Rimmon's presence almost entirely forgotten. "Look,'' she whispered. Her borrowed armor held a ghastly blue phosphorescence. By its light, she and Lionel were the ghosts, Rimmon and Conchobar the living. Only the dead did not change.

The mists parted and the riders came. They sat steeds unlike the horses of earth. Their manes rippled and tore across the darkness like lightning-filled storm clouds, and their haunches were the power of great waves. Riding the foremost horse was a lady, a woman whose face Sandy knew.

"The Queen of Elfland," Lionel said softly, his hands tightening on Sandy's shoulders.

"Oh, no," answered Sandy, her fingers lightly touching his. "Not Elfland. It was a place almost as beautiful, though. Persiles called it Khwarema."

The lady dismounted and approached them. Her face was bright. She seemed unaware of the dead horse and rider not two yards from her feet. "So we have been freed," she said. Her hair fell in a silken veil about her face as she curtsied before them. "In the name of all the worlds he once held, I thank you. The gates have been broken. They are all free now."

"They?" Sandy echoed. The lady nodded, smiling.

"Look at the dragon," she said.

They looked to where the massive body lay, still burning. As they watched, they felt new fear, for it looked as if the beast were coming back to life. The huge wings stirred and rose, the scaly flanks began to pulse dully.

Then the shimmering, the blurring began. The golden ice-light melted and ran into wraiths, ghosts, apparitions. Each scale of the dead monster was a death-moan, and then a phantom. From every part of the dragon's body, a victim's ghost was set free. The coldness of the shining light grew warm as many faces—human and past human—regained their shapes and their souls. Their last cries of sorrow turned to cries of gladness, and everywhere the word hushed and whispered and swelled to a sudden shout:

"*Free!*"

Chapter XVIII

THE LAST ROAD

The dragon was gone, bled away bit by bit into all the souls he had held. These circled the dwindling body, watching the end of their old foe without hate, with nothing but acceptance. The great wings spread themselves high on the wind and fluttered down, the robes of a long-dead wizard.

"Fulfilled," he rasped. His beard crackled frostily. "But not as I saw it fulfilled."

"What does it matter?" asked Persiles' lady.

"It doesn't matter," said a familiar voice, and Persiles was there at her side. He embraced her gently, then offered his arms to Sandy and Lionel.

"I want to thank you," he said, "but it seems inadequate. In all the worlds I've traveled, there never was a way to show this much gratitude." His eyes strayed to the sword, still in Rimmon's hand. "Where did you find it?"

"Hard to remember." Lionel shrugged. "I collect lots of things like that. I couldn't classify it when I first bought it—maybe in a pawnshop—but I kept it."

Rimmon handed the blade to Persiles. He accepted it, but not eagerly. "A little too late for me to participate in the prophecy, isn't it? I went against him without shield, sword, or steed. I should have known I'd fail."

"The worm is dead, my love," his lady soothed. "That is enough."

"For whom?" he snapped. "Gods, what a waste I have made! Following him, hunting him, always full of the pride of thinking that if I didn't slay him, no one could! For all I know, I drove him to greater evils because I hunted him. If I'd left well enough alone, who's to say he mightn't have met his death on his own first world, and left the others alone?"

"Persiles—" Sandy ventured. He shook himself free of them and stumbled away, toward some unseen borderland of the surrounding dark. A sudden wall of flame turned him, and the wizard's eyes burned down.

"Knight, you are a man of swords and steel," the mage's voice filled the void with thunder. "Magic and prophecy take more forms than you will ever know. A sword did slay the worm—not yours, though Belgor was the blade he used. A shield was there, impervious to the dragon's power, hardened in a flame never fired. See how she still burns, your shield!" His withered hands swept an arc of brilliance around Sandy. "And the steed was young, untried, but he would have ridden with them, sword and shield, to the end of all the worlds. These were the weapons, Sir Knight, and you were the only one fit to draw them together, to make them the instruments of the dragon's death."

The wizard faded. The ring of ghosts began to pale. The phantom horses snorted and pawed at nothingness, impatient to be gone. Persiles' lady took his hand once more, leading him to where his old loyal stallion waited for him to mount.

Rimmon was at Sandy's side. He spoke to her, but she leaned away from the coldness of his breath. His words were faint, and before she could ask him what he had said, a second elfin voice sang clear above the rustle of departing spirits. A tall elfwoman, her hair a cascade of sun down her back, stepped from between the ranks of the fidgeting horses.

"Jelana!" He cried her name with joy and flew like one of his own arrows to her.

"I am free now, Rimmon," she said. "We are all free." Again the ghosts took up the glad cry, and it echoed and reechoed in Sandy's ears until it was the only thing real. Her head began to spin, and the mists roiled and swirled around her. She felt suddenly cold, and looking down she saw that the knight's armor had melted from her. She sobbed and grabbed for something solid to hang onto, and she found Lionel's equally desperate grasping hand.

"Where have they gone?" he gasped. Their feet were moving, taking them forward through the mists.

"I don't know. And where are we going?"

"Ask me another," said Lionel. "But it feels good to be moving. I think I see something ahead."

"Light at the end of the tunnel," mused Sandy. "Do you think we'll find anything changed when we get home again?"

"What makes you think we'll get home?" he asked, trying to make the question sound like a joke. Then he added, "You know New York. If they remember it ever happened at all, they'll get it all wrong in the telling. And I'm not going to bother setting anyone straight. I kind of hope it's been forgotten; wiped out, the way I'd do if I were any kind of sorcerer. Hey! Hey, you weren't kidding! That *is* light!"

Someone bumped into Sandy in the dark and growled a curse at her. "Dumb bitch, watch it, huh?" There was sunlight ahead, and green, and the music of a wheezy carousel calliope. They emerged from the shade of one of the many under-passes in the park and for a moment they could only stand there, gaping at the calm day, the stroll-ers, the lovers, and the children.

"Normal," said Lionel at last. "Shall we find out if—?"

"No." Sandy's touch stopped him. "Not yet. Let's just walk for now. Let's go over to Fifth and up to the Metropolitan Museum. There's supposed to be a good exhibit on masterpieces of the Middle Ages. I've really got to crack down on my studies when I get back to school . . . if it turns out I've been gone at all."

He offered her his arm with mock gallantry and they left the carousel whirling behind them. A young mother looked up from her Regency ro-mance and smiled to see them, but her reverie was quickly broken by the strident shout of her little boy.

"Ma! Ma!" He was like a puppy, unable to stop against his own momentum. He rammed into her legs, still yelling, "Look at what I found! Look! Look!"

"Billy, I've told you a hundred times— What *is* that thing? It's halfway rusted through. Do want to have to get a shot at the doctor's?"

"Look at it, Ma! Just look!" He raised the bat-tered helmet high, about to put it on. His mother's sharp reflexes interfered. She snatched it from him and pitched it into the bushes behind the bench.

"You leave that alone!" she scolded him while he screwed his face up for a good, loud tantrum. "Playing with junk like that, honestly!" She got to her feet and yanked him off before he could make a scene.

Behind the bench, a gray squirrel sniffed curiously at the discarded helm, then nosed inside it, checking out a possible winter home. Far off, under the shade of an oak, a long lance was being similarly investigated, and somewhere in the wilds of Brooklyn a shield was being considered by a small girl as a maybe-great coaster-saucer for when it snowed.

"Thought I saw something weird in that trash can, man."

"Yeah, like what?"

"I dunno. Looked like a sword."

"Right. And I just spotted a cop riding a unicorn. Come on, stupid."

About the Author

Esther Friesner was born in Brooklyn, NY. She received her B.A. from Vassar and her M.A. and Ph.D. from Yale, where she taught for several years. Now a full-time science fiction and fantasy author, she has published short stories and poems in *Asimov's*, *Amazing*, and *Fantasy Book*, and is the author of four fantasy novels. She currently resides in Connecticut with her husband and two children.